just flirt

Laura Bowers

FARRAR STRAUS GIROUX
New York

Farrar Straus Giroux Books for Young Readers
175 Fifth Avenue, New York 10010

Text copyright © 2012 by Laura Bowers
All rights reserved
Distributed in Canada by D&M Publishers, Inc.
Printed in the United States of America
Designed by Roberta Pressel
First edition, 2012
1 3 5 7 9 10 8 6 4 2

macteenbooks.com

Library of Congress Cataloging-in-Publication Data
Bowers, Laura, 1969–
Just flirt / Laura Bowers. — 1st ed.
p. cm.
Summary: A secret blog brings lies, lawsuits, and love to a
self-proclaimed "Superflirt," a judgmental outcast, and a
boyfriend-stealing bully at a struggling Maryland campground.
ISBN 978-0-374-35515-9 (hardcover)
ISBN 978-1-4299-5507-2 (e-book)
[1. Flirting—Fiction.   2. Interpersonal relations—Fiction.
3. Dating (Social customs)—Fiction.   4. Camping—Fiction.
5. Blogs—Fiction.   6. Maryland—Fiction.]   I. Title.

PZ7.B6766Ju 2012
[Fic]—dc22

2011008419

For my three wonderful guys, Bob, Broc, and Cooper,
for making my life complete

In loving memory of Monica Sue Long
1981–2003
You are forever in our hearts

just flirt

The Superflirt Chronicles
. . . blogs from a teenage flirtologist

Friday, June 11

YES! GOODBYE, SCHOOL. HELLO, SUMMER!
MOOD: Wonderful, blissful, and simply joyful!
MUSIC: "Summer Girl," Jessica Andrews

Ahhhh. Summer, sweet summer.

The sunshine. The smells of freshly mown Maryland grass and chlorine-damp hair. The parents who flood our campground with their loaded RVs, and most important, the flirting with their cute teenage sons! Only one thing could make the last day of school even better: realizing that this is my one-hundredth blog post here at The Superflirt Chronicles!

Ahhhh. Memories, sweet memories.

I so fondly recall the first entry I made here last October. *Trivia Question:* Does anyone remember who it was about? *Answer:* An adorable varsity linebacker I nicknamed Spike, who wore his football uniform to our Halloween haunted hayride.

Original costume? No.

Cute? *Oh, yes.*

Then there was my second post about Check Mate, whose baby blues actually made chess interesting, which—I admit—was a first for me. And how can we forget Bull's Eye, that gorgeous archery champ who showed me how to shoot a compound bow, and the clumsy-yet-adorable Scratch, a terrible pool player who I taught how to bank a combo?

Ahhhh. Scratch, sweet Scratch.

Of course, there have been some duds, like Beater Boy, who wore those thin wife-beater tank tops. He seemed cool at first, but his frequent references to his "beaters" as though he were a future spouse abuser caused me to swear off *all* guys who wear them. But one must take the bad with the good, so in honor of summer, my Ghosts of Flirtcapades Past, and the many new readers here at the Chronicles, allow me to once again post the nine rules of flirting written by me and my partner in all flirting crimes, the fabulous Miss N.

Memorize it, and I promise . . . you'll be mesmerizing!

Superflirt's Nine Rules of Flirting

RULE #1: Smile. Seriously. I cannot stress this enough. Guys don't want to hang around some whiner who complains about parents, school, monster cramps, life's glooms and dooms, wah, wah, wah. *Everyone* has problems, my dears. Even Superflirt has problems, but being miserable won't make them go away. So until they do, smile!

RULE #2: Be confident. Okay, which contestant on a reality show do you think a guy would prefer: A.) the nervous one who's so worried about elimination that she's eliminated, B.) the complainer, C.) the gossip, or D.) the confident girl everyone loves, hmm? Get the picture?

4

RULE #3: Be interested. So simple—so effective. Pay attention to what most people don't notice. Compliment him, in subtle, honest ways with no fake flattery. Ask questions, like what kind of music he's into. Just don't lie and say you love rap unless you want to be dragged to an Eminem concert. And don't try to impress him with any do-or-die debating skills. Playful banter? Good. Ball busting? Bad, very bad.

RULE #4: Make eye contact. Readers often ask how to tell if a guy likes you. Of course, there are the novice observations: the stolen glances he gives you when he thinks you're not looking, the way he "accidentally" bumps into you at different places. But for professional results, do this: Make eye contact. Hold it for three seconds. *One . . . two . . . three.* By the third count, you'll know if he's interested, ladies, you'll know. And then?

Gotcha.

RULE #5: Timing, timing, timing. Do not approach a group of guys and think you'll be able to single one out like a dog herding sheep. Guys get all macho when they're with their friends and will most likely say things such as "Dude, did you see that chick? She wants me, man." So wait until he's away from the testosterone troop before making a move.

RULE #6: Work it. Speak softly; give him a reason to lean in closer. Play with your hair; let him know you're interested without saying a word. Lightly touch his arm, but don't overdo it. And, at opportune moments, lower your gaze . . . wait a second . . . and then look up at him with a soft smile. Killer move. Practice this one in the mirror.

RULE #7: Know when to walk away. Don't let him be the first to end the conversation. Never, never, never. Otherwise, you might appear desperate, and you don't want that. Leave him wanting more by breaking away first.

RULE #8: Know when NOT to flirt. It is *so* not cool to flirt: A.) with someone who's in a relationship, B.) if you're in a relationship, or C.) with hurtful intentions. I also choose not to flirt with guys from school or work (because of the whole *don't poo where you eat* thing), but this I leave to your discretion.

RULE #9: Don't take it seriously! Look, flirting is not about scoring the perfect boyfriend or lifelong mate. Gag. It's about having fun and meeting people.

So here's to a summer of being bold! To being fearless! To Fridays, which bring a fresh crop of campers! Will there be any cute guys among them? Stay tuned to find out . . .

Welcome to the Barton Family Campground's
LIFE'S A BEACH WEEKEND!

Friday, June 11:   7 pm   Surf-dancin' bluegrass
                                  with Butch and the Boys

                        8 pm   Tonight's movie: SURF'S UP

Saturday, June 12:   10 am   Kids' Crafts: Sand candles

                        3 pm   Horseshoe Tournament

                        5 pm   Catch-a-wave Hayride

                        7 pm   Karaoke with DJ Drake

                        8 pm   Tonight's movie:
                                 BLUE CRUSH

                        10 pm   S'mores & cocoa by the
                                 community fire

Sunday, June 13:   9 am   Nondenominational
                                  church service

I ∽ Dee

After spending the afternoon checking in campers, tracking down a lost hiker, and foolishly breaking up a water gun fight while—*duh*—wearing a white T-shirt, I am *more* than ready to celebrate the last day of school by slipping into a most delightful, most decadent poolside nap.

Natalie and her laptop, however, have other plans.

"Rise and shine, sleeping beauty," she says, poking my thigh with her big toe. I open my eyes just enough to see her flashing a wicked grin from underneath the umbrella. "Check out this Web site called *Wedgie-watch.com*, Dee. It's hilarious!"

Wedgies? Okay, that's worth being woken up for, even though surfing the Internet isn't high on my agenda tonight. But Natalie's wild computer addiction does not yield to sun, swimming, or siestas, so I scoot closer to see a display of very graphic, very torturous wedgies that make my *own* cheeks clench in pain.

"Uh, Nat, sweetie, how exactly did you find this?"

"I Googled 'wedgie' and this came up," she says, as though it's totally normal.

"And . . . why did you Google 'wedgie'?"

"Oh, I don't know," Natalie says, picking up her melted cherry snowball. "Why Google anything?"

I grin and lean back in my lounge chair with the warm sun on my face. It is, without a doubt, perfect camping weather. Hot enough to swim, but nippy enough at night to cozy by the fire in a sweatshirt. This is my favorite time of day, when the evening activities kick in and the campground truly comes alive with guests cramming in as much fun as possible before it gets too dark. I love seeing kids zipping by on dusty bikes, determined fishermen casting their lines at the river, volleyball players in a sweaty duel at the sand court, and couples holding hands on their evening stroll.

Natalie groans when the band starts a twangy version of a Beach Boys song. "Ugh, bluegrass. Tell me again why I come here on Friday evenings when it's my night off?"

"To be with your bestest, bestest friend?"

"Eh, not really," she jokes. "You ain't all that."

I drop my jaw in mock protest. "What? Oh, please, without me, you'd be at home hanging out in boring chat rooms or reading all those forums."

She knows I have her on this one. Her latest obsession, besides wedgies, has been a forum dedicated to all things Disney World after her grandmother announced that she's using her tax refund to take Natalie's entire family there in August.

Seriously. Talk about one sweet refund.

Her mom and dad are always swamped at their accounting firm and her older brother is spending the summer in Ocean City with his college buddies, so Natalie has taken it upon herself to plan the ultimate Disney itinerary. She hands me the remains of her snowball—she likes them fresh, I like them melted—and says, "Okay, fine. My name is Natalie and I'm a Webaholic; hello, Natalie. But those forums *did* help me map out where a ton of hidden Mickeys are, so there."

Hidden Mickeys? Yeah, no clue about that one. I've never been to the Magic Kingdom, or on any other real vacation for that matter. There's always too much work to do, and besides, our campground has its own special kind of magic, so why go on vacations when vacations come here? I am curious about the hidden Mickeys, though, but before I can ask, Jake Bollinger strolls in with the chlorine kit, wearing faded Levi's and a SAVE A HORSE, RACE A STOCK CAR T-shirt. Like Nat and me, Jake will be a senior at Riverside High next fall. He mostly hangs with the crowd from his auto mechanics class, so we didn't meet until Mom hired him in April to do odd maintenance chores. She also lets him use one of our empty buildings as a garage for the cute go-kart thingy he races. Just don't call it cute in front of him. Or a thingy.

They're apparently not the manliest of terms.

Natalie's wicked grin returns. She winks at me and says, "Hey, Jake, come check out this dirt bike race on YouTube!"

He hurries over, only to cringe at what must be the mother of all wedgies on the screen. "Dude, that's so wrong! You're sick, Natalie Green. Sick. Both of you are."

Oh, really?

I go into instant flirt mode, dropping my chin and gazing at him through my lashes while seductively running a finger along the side of his arm. "You don't *truly* believe that, now, do you, Jake?" I purr. "Not about little ole me."

A tad over the top, yes, but it's not like I would flirt for real with Jake. Flirting with campground employees is strictly against the rules . . . no matter how cute they happen to be. This goes double for Jake's buddies who hang out at the garage, and I *never* flirt with anyone from school. Flirting is meant to be fresh. Fun. Spontaneous, with someone you don't see on a regular basis. Besides, Jake never takes me seriously.

And after what I did last year, every guy at Riverside thinks I'm a total psychotic flake.

Jake leans forward, his battered cowboy hat almost touching my forehead. He gives me a cocky half smile and says, "You *really* don't expect me to fall for your bullcrap, do ya, Dee-Dee?"

Argh.

I hate being called Dee-Dee. It's Dee. Not Dee-Dee or Didi or Dodo Bird, like this one creep dubbed me in preschool. Just Dee.

It was such a mistake to tell Jake how much it annoyed me when my ex used to call me that. HUGE mistake. But at least I didn't mention the many other things that Blaine Walker did to annoy me when we dated last spring and summer. Like breaking our dates at the last minute. Or always wanting to hang out with his snotty friends instead of mine. And then there was his wandering eye that I tolerated for five months because Lord forbid I dare sound like a jealous cow, and his habit of accusing *me* of flirting with *his* friends if I—Lord forbid—dared to laugh or talk too much.

The most annoying thing? When he dumped me last September with a text message saying how he wanted a "fresh start" for our junior year.

No, that's a lie.

The most annoying thing is the pathetic way I wanted him back . . . and what I did that caused everyone at school to think I am a desperate psycho. But whatever. It's all water under the bridge now. Dirty, nasty, scummy water. So I gaze up at Jake adoringly and say, "I love it when you call me that. Do it again. *Dee-Dee.*"

He rolls his eyes and heads back to the pool. "Aw, come back, Jake!" Natalie calls out with a giggle. "Don't let Dee-Dee scare you away."

"Yeah, Jake, let's talk about your cute race kart thingy!"

"Bite me, sickos," he says over his shoulder.

Whatever comeback Natalie has in mind is cut off when the screen door of the main lodge slams open and the Cutson brothers run out with Sponge Bob temporary tattoos on their foreheads and damp swimsuits hanging on their scrawny bodies. Natalie lets out an annoyed huff. "Lyle! Tanner! Stop banging that door, you little creeps!"

The barefoot twins ignore her, wobbling like ducks on the gravel road and throwing their popsicle wrappers on the ground. "Yeah, and pick up that trash," I add.

Tanner smacks his butt and yells, "Make me!"

Oh, that twerp! Natalie seems tempted to do just that until someone calls out, "Yoo-hoo, girls!" We turn to see Ivy Neville, a retired investment banker and one of our permanent summer guests, walking toward us. She leans her tall frame against the fence and pulls off an outback-style hat that looks like it came straight out of a Cabela's catalog.

"Hey, Miss Ivy. How's everything, you need any more help?"
I ask.

"Oh, no, girls, take your break, I'm all set up." She motions toward a fifth-wheel RV parked by the river at a premier site that's been hers from mid-June to late October for the past three years. When we are closed for the winter, Ivy stays in South Carolina where the warm weather is less harsh on an old woman's body—her words, not mine. "I just wanted to tell you, Natalie," she says, smoothing her silver-gray hair, "how nice it was to meet you earlier today, and how *thrilled* I am to see Dee keeping better company this summer."

Meaning company other than Blaine, who she wasn't exactly a fan of.

"And, Dee, I wanted to tell you that the campground looks just lovely!"

A feeling of pride swells in my chest.

My home *is* lovely. Lovely and charming, with giant oak trees, blooming crepe myrtles, and fifty-five sites woven in among rolling hills, riverbanks, and the flanking mountains I know better than the tops of my favorite flip-flops. Rustic log bathhouses and pavilions surround our eighteenth-century lodge, a row of cozy guest cabins line the trout pond, and on a broad hilltop sits the large cabin my mom and I live in. Everything here is traditional and quaint, unlike Chuck Lambert's pimped-out RV Resort two miles down the road that's more theme park than campground, with its coffee café and spa services by request. But, Chuck's place is always booked solid, and we only reach full capacity on holiday weekends.

Ivy studies me fondly. "And you remind me more of your father every year. Lord, I miss that man. How are things, kiddo, you and your momma getting on okay?"

Just like that, my good mood melts like Natalie's snowball.

You'd think after fifteen months it'd get easier.

You'd think I could hear people talk about Dad without feeling like someone rammed a stick of firewood into my stomach. Instead, each condolence only brings back the unbelievable truth that a man as dynamic and healthy as John Barton could have a heart attack, one that caused him to crash his truck and die instantly.

I still force myself to put on a practiced, polite smile and tell her that we are fine, just fine, because no one likes a drama queen. And no one, not even Ivy, needs to know Mom and I are barely making ends meet. Except for Natalie, of course. She knows everything, because she works here, and, well, I can't imagine *not* telling her everything. She waits until Ivy leaves and asks, "You okay? Want to talk about it?"

No, not really.

And the evening is simply too pretty to be sad.

"Good," Natalie says with a devious glint. "Because *I spy with my naughty little eye* someone who I'll bet one box of oh so delicious Skinny Cow Fudge Bars will put some joy on that pretty face of yours."

This is why I love Natalie—she always says the right thing at just the right time. I personally believe she should be a psychiatrist instead of a journalist, but Natalie has a low tolerance for whiners. And my, my, she's playing the Skinny Cow card? Wow, she's not fooling around. I scan the area and then point to a guy at the putt-putt course who is trying to mess up his father's shot. "Him?"

She pretends to yawn. "Oh, snore, you're boring me, Dee."

Strike one. And I know she isn't talking about Jake, so I shift my attention to the game going on at the basketball court.

"Cold, cold, *very* cold," Natalie teases.

Strike two. In the full-hook-up section, a divorced father is draping a pink bathing suit over a makeshift clothesline that dips like a swayback mare. No cute guys there, just two little girls blowing bubbles and a messy site littered with Barbie bikes, pool noodles, and inner tubes. A few rows over, the Swains' site is sterile in comparison, with their streamlined motor home, posh lounge chairs, and ground mats all in coordinated shades of beige. The awning shakes when the door opens and Roxanne Swain stomps out wearing cargo shorts, a baggy black T-shirt, and a NASCAR cap over her dyed red hair. When her parents checked in for the summer a few days ago, I invited her to go hiking, but she shot me down faster than the Cutsons once emptied the pool by trying to resuscitate a dead fish. When she glances our way, though, I can't stop myself from giving her a small wave.

No reply. Roxanne only glares at me like I'm a whitehead about to pop before flopping down on a lounge chair and putting on her headphones.

"Cold, frigid cold—the girl must pee ice cubes," Natalie says before noticing the concern on my face. "Oh, for the love of Dooney and Bourke Disney bags, stop looking at her with that camp counselor expression. Honestly, Dee, you worry too much. You're not responsible for *everyone's* happiness."

"I know. It's just that she's been here for a few days and hasn't talked with—"

The pool gate opens. All thoughts of Roxanne evaporate as a guy who can only be described as Brad Pitt in his glory, *Thelma and Louise* days strolls in, with shiny chestnut hair, full lips, and board shorts hanging sexily low on his hips.

"Sweet Jesus."

"Told you," Natalie singsongs as he strides past us to an empty chair. He pulls off his shirt to reveal a flat, muscular stomach that causes Natalie to swoon with a deep, contented sigh. "Thank you, thank you, strange guy, whoever you are."

Thank you indeed. I nudge Natalie's arm. "Go on, do the pool trick, Miss N."

"No thanks," she says, nudging me back.

"Why *not?*"

"*Because.* You're better at it."

Argh. If it weren't for her laptop, I'd dunk her in the pool. She's like those cartoon dogs that will speak to their owner, but clam up around anyone else. Not that I own her—God, no, or that she's a dog. Natalie has gorgeous dark hair, killer lips, and a gymnast-lithe build, but even though she's outrageous and bold around me, she chokes when a cute guy is around. She has no problem instigating me, however, as proven by the way she clasps her hands behind her head and says, "Go for it, Super-flirt, I dare you."

"Ooo, a challenge! Fine, then, pool trick it is."

I strike a silly Marilyn Monroe pose and take off my sunglasses, spitting my gum into her outstretched palm before stepping to the deep end. As I curl my toes over the concrete edge, I pull my blond hair out of its ponytail, letting it fall to my waist. Once Natalie gives the signal, I jump, twisting when my feet touch bottom so his face is the first thing I see when I surface. I hold his gaze for one extra beat before swimming to the ladder, *slowly* pulling myself up, and *slooowly* walking back while squeezing water from my hair and—oopsie!—dropping my hair elastic.

"Well, how was that?" I ask Natalie, after stretching out on my chair.

She presses a finger against her cheek. "Hmm, not bad. You could've stayed underwater longer, and—call me fussy—paused for a bikini top adjustment, but that hair toss was legendary. He watched you the entire way back and . . . Oh, wait for it . . . Wait for it . . ."

A deep voice beside me says, "Excuse me, but I think you dropped this."

Ha. Pool trick.

Works every time.

I swiftly move on to FLIRT RULE #1: *Smile*, and make a show of grabbing my now-bare wrist. "Thanks! That's so sweet of you."

He does this cute, boyish shuffle and smiles in return with—adorable!—dimples so deep you could stick your finger in them. "Oh, um, no problem . . ."

RULE #2: *Be confident.* "This is Natalie, and I'm Dee Barton," I tell him, making my name sound intriguing even though I hate it. My father named me after his mother, Madeline Dee Barton, thinking she'd finally approve of his marriage if she had a namesake. Yeah, that didn't exactly work out. My grandmother has hated Mom from day one, and even though I look just like my dad, her feelings apply to me as well.

Especially now that he's gone.

The guy cocks his head to the side and furrows his brow in concentration. "Barton, that sounds familiar. Oh—do your parents own the campground?"

"Yes, my mother does."

Please don't ask about my father.

He doesn't, which is no surprise. Guys don't care about those things. Blaine certainly never did. Whenever I mentioned my dad, he would shrug and say, "Yeah, that sucks." It was a good lesson on what guys want to talk about and what they don't, so I move the conversation along by nodding toward his chair. "So, you're a Boston fan?"

"What?" He seems confused until he remembers his Red Sox beach towel. "Oh, yeah! Awesome, you're a Sox fan as well?"

RULE #3: *Be interested.* "A lot of people are," I coyly say, *except for me, seeing as how my loyalty will always be with the Baltimore Orioles.*

His hypnotic dimples deepen. "Cool, you watching the game tonight?"

Uh, dude, being interested does not mean cheering for the Red Sox. His dimples aren't *that* cute. "Mmm, no, we're going to shoot pool tonight," I say, before hitting him with RULE #4: *Make eye contact* by holding his gaze for three whole seconds.

One . . . two . . . three.

"Mind if I join you?" he asks.

Gotcha.

Sorry, Red Sox, you lose. We make plans to meet in the rec

room later, but before I can skip to RULE #7: *Know when to walk away*, a look of recognition crosses his face. "Wait. Dee Barton. Oh, man, are you the chick who wrote that letter?"

My smile fades.

He's from my school. And he knows about the letter.

A crushing ache swells in my stomach and I suddenly feel like I'm back in class with girls snickering and guys saying, "Take me back, Blaine, I'll do anything, *ANYTHING*." Why did I do it? Why did I send Blaine all those pathetic texts after we broke up? And when they went unanswered, why did I pour all of my heartbreak into a desperate two-page *please don't say it's over* letter? Blaine never even bothered to respond. Instead, on my seventeenth birthday a week later, I saw him kissing Sabrina Owens by his Mercedes after school. On my birthday! And *Sabrina Owens* of all people, one of the nastiest girls in all of Riverside, Maryland, who *did* respond to my letter.

By making copies for nearly everyone.

Devastation. Humiliation. Mortification. There simply aren't enough "ation" words to fully convey my embarrassment. I wanted to die. And to be honest, I might have even briefly considered the option had it not been for Natalie.

Thank God for Natalie.

We first met in ninth grade, after we were the only freshmen to make varsity softball—me because I was the fastest runner and she because her parents are the coach's accountants. Unlike the others on our team, I never held this against her, and she never held it against me when I quit playing after my father died, but we didn't become close until after the letter disaster. She understood what I was going through, seeing as how Sabrina once took a picture of her picking dead skin off her nose that had everyone calling her Nose-Pick Natalie for weeks. She listened to stories about my dad without ever saying "That sucks," like when I talked about his love for Simon & Garfunkel songs and how he'd never pull his truck over to the side of the road if a bad rainstorm came along. Instead, he'd crank up "Bridge over Troubled Water" and say, "Life's full of storms, Dee, so when one hits, just hold the wheel tight and keep driving." It was a policy Natalie and I had decided to adopt, and last Halloween, when she dared me to flirt with an exceptionally cute football player, a new Dee was born.

Her name is Superflirt.

And Superflirt knows how to handle this guy.

I shift to a more flattering position and shoo an imaginary fly from my leg. "Oh, please, you didn't think that letter was real, now, did you?"

It works. Sort of. After staring at my legs, the guy hooks a thumb into the waist of his board shorts and says, "Yeah, I guess no one would be stupid enough to write like that."

Ouch. Despite my efforts to hold the wheel tight, my throat feels as though I inhaled an inner tube. I can't think of anything clever or flirty to say, so I just sit there like a dumb lump until Natalie comes to my rescue. "Dude, some woman is waving at you from the putt-putt course. Is she your mother?"

Thankfully, it is. The guy excuses himself with one of those *catch you later* salutes. Oh, yay, I'm so looking forward to that. Natalie rolls her head toward me once he's gone and says, "Want a Skinny Cow?"

"No, I *need* a Skinny Cow."

We stand, wrapping towels around our waists before heading toward the lodge. The feel of water from my wet hair trickling down my back in the most delightful way instantly lifts my spirits as Natalie links her arm in mine. "Well, that last part was a smidge unexpected, but all in all the pool trick was *very* successful today!"

Someone snorts behind us.

I turn to see Jake frowning at me while digging in his pockets for a set of keys. "Yeah, real slick trick, Dee," he says. "Just like the one you pulled last weekend—and the weekend before that—and what else? Oh, yeah, the weekend before that."

My face flushes with shame as Jake unlocks the storage shed door and steps inside. But seriously, why do I always feel like a total sleaze whenever Jake talks like that? I didn't do anything bad. I mean, what's wrong with flirting? It's harmless. It makes people feel good. And why should I care about his opinion, anyway?

Natalie's right.

I worry too much, over stuff like whether or not I was good enough for Blaine, who brought out the worst in me both during and after our relationship. Over my grandmother, Madeline, who I will *never* be good enough for. Over Chuck Lambert, who'd love to put us out of business. Screw it. It's summer. For the next three months, I'm only going to worry about Mom, the campground, and Natalie. Forget about Madeline. Forget about Blaine, who's better suited to a jerk like Sabrina Owens, anyway, and forget about Roxanne with all her whitehead-popping glares.

As for Jake—

"Hey, let me use your cell," I say to Nat as we step onto the porch that is scratched and worn by an endless stream of guests. She shakes her head at my perpetual habit of forgetting to charge my phone as I scroll through her contacts and hit his name with an angry jab.

"Hello?"

"By the way, Jake? Up yours."

"Took you long enough," he replies before hanging up.

Natalie tosses the phone back in her tote and asks, "Feel better?"

"Getting there."

"Wait here, then." She ducks into the store. I sit on a porch swing and watch two boys sword fighting with tree branches. As the sweet smell of hickory burning in a campfire drifts by on a gentle breeze and one of the boys suffers an agonizing death with a branch tucked under his armpit, Natalie returns and hands me not one, but *two* Skinny Cows.

Yes, now I feel better.

2 ~ Sabrina

Sabrina! *Sabrina!* Have you seen my Spanx?"

Oh my God. I do not understand why that woman finds it so necessary to bellow about her stupid Spanx loud enough for all our neighbors to hear, as though they don't think she's demented enough as it is. I press a hand against my cell and yell back, "Honestly, Mother, I'm on the phone!"

The wood floors echo as Mom pounds out of her bedroom with her hair up in a massive array of hot rollers and a red Chinese silk robe billowing at her knees. "Who are you talking to, that handsome boy Blaine?"

I stare daggers at her. No, as a matter of fact, I am not talking to Blaine.

Not after what he did to me yesterday.

"It's Torrance."

"Oh," Mom says as though she's disappointed. "Well then, tell Miss Torrance I said hello and get off the phone, sweetie, it's six-thirty already! I'm supposed to be at Chuck's in *thirty minutes* and Lord knows I ain't going anywhere without my Spanx!"

She swats my legs off the coffee table and then flings aside the tabloids strewn on the sofa so she can search underneath the faded plaid cushions. I have no choice but to lift a butt cheek as she searches under my cushion, only to find the enormous bra she took off while we watched our Tivo'd soaps last night so her "girls" could breathe. Mom fans her face with it and says, "Mercy, that doggone busted air conditioner is killing me! I'm sweating like a pig in this dump."

"Is that your mother?" Torrance asks, not bothering to hide her amusement over the flamboyant Mona Owens. I ignore her by covering my cell tighter and saying, "Well, we could afford to get it fixed if you didn't buy all that silver jewelry on QVC. And pigs don't sweat, Mother."

Besides, if this house is such a dump, then why did you have your lawyers fight for it?

My father grew up here. He loves it. Mom doesn't. She complains about everything from the split-foyer layout to how our neighbor's huskies always take their daily dumps by our mailbox. But when my parents divorced two years ago, she fought for it purely out of spite, even though Dad offered to buy her out. So because of her, he now lives forty minutes away in Harpers Ferry.

Thanks a ton, Mom.

She presses a hand against her ample hip that refuses to slim due to her ice cream addiction, and says, "I had a moment of weakness, okay? And if you're so clever about pigs and stuff, Miss Smarty Pants, then *you* go find my Spanx." Mom tightens her robe and claps her hands. "Come on, off the phone, chop-chop-chop! And stop calling me Mother!"

"Yes, Mother," I mumble as she whirls back to her bedroom. Knowing there will be no peace until she gets her way, I start to say goodbye to Torrance.

"Oh, no you don't. You're not hanging up until you tell me why you're skipping Prescott's party tomorrow night. And don't give me that *I'm spending the weekend with my father* excuse. You could totally bail if you wanted to."

The sound of scraping hangers tells me Torrance is shopping, probably for yet another forty-dollar designer T-shirt. It's pathetic how she wouldn't be able to survive one day without her parents' credit card. She'd choke on her sugar-free cappuccino if she knew I buy and sell clothes and other items on craigslist and eBay, not that I'm ashamed. It's just none of Torrance's business how tight money has been lately for Mom and me.

I head down to the laundry room in the basement to hunt for my mother's missing Spanx and say, "Dad would be upset if I bailed, Torr. Our last visit was ruined because of my demon stepsister's softball tournament, and besides, Prescott has parties all the time. It's no big deal."

"No big deal, huh?" Torrance asks sarcastically. "Or does it have something to do with Prescott's girlfriend? Vanessa Baker *did* beat you in the election last month after you've been class vice-president for the past three years. No one would blame you for being embarrassed."

I was hardly embarrassed.

And Vanessa did not beat me—I quit before the election. Everyone knew Prescott was a shoo-in for president again, which gave her a huge advantage because of the boyfriend/girlfriend candidacy angle, so why play a game you know you can't win?

Mom's Spanx aren't in the hamper or dryer. I open the washer lid and a musty stench from a load of wet towels she must have forgotten about hits me in the face. *Really, Mother?* I reach for the laundry detergent to rewash them and say, "I could have totally beaten her, but the senior student council is responsible for all our future reunions, remember? So if Prescott and Vanessa want to deal with our loser class for the rest of their lives, they can have it."

"Oh, yeah, good point."

"Besides. This will give me more time to spend with Blaine."

There's an awkward pause before Torrance says, "Uh, sure, if you two are still together."

Pardon me?

What's *that* all about? Yes, maybe I am furious over the way Blaine nearly drooled over that stupid girl at McDonald's yesterday who bent over in front of him with half her rear hanging out. And he did it right in front of Torrance. But that does *not* mean we're breaking up. After all, we *were* the junior prom's King and Queen.

I am not about to give up my crown.

Mom's piercing screech echoes down the steps. "Sabrina, are you still on the phone?"

For once, her timing is perfect. I use her as an excuse to say, "Sorry, Torr, gotta go. Love ya," before hanging up.

Whether or not Torrance replied, I don't care. She's just jealous because Blaine and I have been together for nine months while her relationships never hit the ninety-day mark. I shut the washer lid and start the cycle before walking upstairs to my mother's bedroom, which reeks of her musky cologne. Mom turns from her antique vanity with an eyelash curler clamped down on her lashes and says, "Look in my closet, will ya?" Sure enough, buried under miniskirts that no decent forty-two-year-old woman would be caught dead in are the notorious Spanx. I toss them to her with pinched fingers.

"Thank you, sugar. Now, sit down and talk to me while I finish putting on my face, okay? We haven't spent any time together this week."

Maybe that's because of her two dates with Roger, a fry cook who first impressed her with his knowledge of butterfly-cut steak and the difference between over-medium and over-easy eggs. Yeah, *keeper.* But whatever. Quality mommy/daughter time it is. I flop on her bed and grab a *Soap Opera Digest* from her nightstand.

Mom rips it from my hands. "Ah, ah, ah! We're gonna talk."

I scoot back and rest against the headboard. "*Fine*, Dad's not going to be here for another hour, anyway." It's torture having my car in the shop because of transmission issues. At least Dad offered to pick me up—and pay the auto bill.

Mom dunks her mascara wand into the tube five times and then brushes the excess off the tip. She puts on a heavy layer before saying, "Well, I've been meaning to talk with you 'bout that, sugar. I sort of called your father and said you have to work with me."

Oh, no. She better not have. "What? You made an agreement with Dad that I would spend two weekends with him each month, remember?"

Mom tosses the mascara aside and walks into her overstuffed closet. "But, darling, that was before I started my karaoke business. You know how hard it is—working at Chuck's on Friday nights and Sundays at the VFW. I need your help!"

Not true. She's a big girl. She can handle things just fine, but it's easier with me there to do the dirty work. Had I known this when she dipped into our savings two months ago to buy used karaoke equipment, I wouldn't have been so supportive— just like I've been for most of her endeavors, like when she was determined to earn a pink Cadillac by selling Mary Kay cosmetics but only ended up buying more than she sold. Or when Rex Reynolds, a wealthy land developer, hired her as a receptionist only to have Mom quit one week later because working nine to five wasn't her "thing," despite her love for that old Dolly Parton song she would sing while making her morning coffee.

In return, Mom was supportive when I decided to put my auction skills to good use by selling items for other people on eBay and craigslist—for commission and fees, of course. And she listened, for once, when I begged her not to accept the bartending position Larson Walker recently offered her. Larson as in Blaine's *father*, who bought the Riverside Inn four years ago when they first moved to town. My mother working for my boyfriend's father? That would have been the very definition of tacky. He also offered me a summer job waitressing, but I have no desire to serve finicky, whiny customers. I pick my own hours, thank you. And it's amazing how much business I got after mailing flyers to everyone in our development and posting them at a few senior centers. Still, sometimes I think Mom *wants* her grand plans to fail, so she can badger my father for more alimony. She resents him for cheating on her with a co-worker named Belinda—and then marrying her—so she will do anything to make him pay.

Such as keep me from seeing him.

Mom steps out of her closet, wearing a pair of skintight jeans and a denim vest. She uncurls the hot rollers from her hair and turns to me. "Well, what do you think?"

Where to begin, where to begin. "Your outfit is too tight, too inappropriate, and don't try to change the subject. Why did you tell Dad I had to work?"

Mom ducks back into the closet and peels off her jeans. "Because *I* need you this weekend. Not him. Why you want to be anywhere near that horrible Belinda woman is beyond me. And you *never* get mad when *he* cancels."

She's wrong. I hate being around Belinda, the home wrecker who tore our family apart, and her brat of a daughter, Angela. And yeah, maybe I don't get mad because he's been paying the price for his mistake by having to work eighty-hour weeks to support two families. Mom steps out again, this time wearing a leopard-print wrap shirt and black skirt. "Okay. How does this look?"

"Like you belong in an '80s Mötley Crüe video."

Mom runs her hands down her hips and smiles. "Aw, thanks, darling! That's such a sweet thing to say. Now, be a love and let me borrow your gold hoop earrings and we'll head out to Chuck's, okay?"

"Can't I please go to Dad's?" I ask again, with a catch in my voice.

Her face hardens. "No. You could see your father all the time if he hadn't run off with that woman, now, couldn't you?

So. Grab a sweater, throw some concealer on that teeny pimple on your nose, and let's go. It's showtime!"

"Testing, testing, one—two—three, can y'all hear me?"

Mom stands center stage in front of the campers gathered at Chuck Lambert's pool, although "pool" is an understatement. It's more like an outdoor night club with its streams of Chinese lanterns, rainbow-colored lights sparkling under the water, and a bar with a row of blenders that churn out daiquiris for six bucks a glass. Mom takes a sip of hers—virgin only, drinking on the job is, surprisingly, one of her big no-no's—and repeats into the mike, "I said, can y'all hear me? Who's ready for some singing?"

A cluster of kids shriek and run over to us, placing their wet, chlorine-soaked hands on the table and almost knocking over the MONA'S LOW-KEY KARAOKE sign.

"I wanna sing some Britney Spears!"

"No, me first! Taylor Swift! Taylor Swift!"

"Can—can I sing a Barney song?" a shivering little girl asks.

Ugh. Their chatter gives me an instant headache. That and knowing I'll be listening to the same annoying pop songs all night long. I glare down at the girl and say, "No, sorry, Barney's dead."

Her lower lip begins to quiver.

"Now, now, Sabrina," Mom scolds. She takes the girl's hand and leads her to the mike stand. "Sure, honey, you can sing some Barney and I'll even let you go first if you promise not to cry or tell your momma what mean ole Sabrina said."

After she cues up the music and the girl starts to mumble

the lyrics, Mom sits down with clenched teeth. "Must you, Sabrina? Look at this turnout. Word about my business is getting around, so don't blow it for me."

Me? Blow it for her? Not hardly. The woman is quite capable of her own sabotage, thanks to her short skirts and obnoxious flirting. And although Chuck is a complete slime, *he's* the one having a good turnout, not her. This place is an adolescent fantasyland, with moon bounces and an outdoor movie screen. Chuck told us that next year he's putting in water slides, once he raises more capital. I watch as he licks the rim of his margarita glass while leering at a female camper. Gross. He probably uses this place to target single, lonely mothers. At least Mom has the good sense to stay away from him . . . so far.

"And," she continues, pointing down the river, "my horoscope said this is a good week for new business ventures, so I'm thinking about visiting that Barton place to see if they want to hire me. I was gonna stop in today, but my Sunshine nails needed redoing."

Mom wiggles her fingernails, which are painted bright orange with tiny yellow suns. For as long as I can remember, she has always named her manicures, like her Glory, Glory, Hallelujah nails that had small flags in honor of Memorial Day. She collects a song selection slip from an older man—"The Devil Went Down to Georgia," oh, joy—and says, "Aren't you friends with the owner's daughter? Lee? Bee?"

My mouth goes dry.

Friends? I was *never* friends with Dee Barton—not when she was dating Blaine, not when she was trying to steal him back, and certainly not now.

"Dee!" Mom snaps her fingers. "That's her name, right? Think you can ask her to put in a good word for me?"

I think not. It was enough that I was polite to Dee when Blaine dragged her to our crowd's parties. It was enough that I never flaunted our relationship when we started dating a week after they broke up, even though she bombarded him with texts like a desperate stalker. But when Dee wrote him that letter— trying to break us up just like Belinda did to my family—I did something to make sure everyone knew what kind of person she really is.

Mom notices my scowl and brushes my brown hair back with one of her Sunshine nails. "Why are you cranky, honey, because you and Blaine are fighting?"

I almost drop a Charlie Daniels CD. "How did you know?"

She sips her daiquiri, leaving a giant red lipstick print on the cup's brim. "Oh, I borrowed your cell while you were in the bathroom and stumbled upon a text by accident."

Accident, my rear. And Blaine sent me a text? I grab my phone off the table.

Ur not still angry, r u Sabbie?

Of course I'm angry, not just because of his female scoping, but because of his inability to see *why* it upset me, just like he didn't understand why those photos of Dee he kept in his room hurt my feelings. And I *hate* being called Sabbie.

"Well, what happened?" Mom asks.

"Nothing. Stop reading my messages."

"Come on, tell Momma all about it," she urges, scooting her

chair closer and wrapping an arm around my shoulders. "You'll feel better if you do."

Common sense tells me to keep my mouth shut. Firmly shut. But it would be nice to talk to *somebody*. After all, this isn't a conversation I can have with Torrance or my other best friend, Bridget, so I tell her everything, including all about the tramp stamp tattoo the girl had on her lower back that captured Blaine's attention.

"Oh, honey, is that why you're mad, because he snuck a peekie at another gal?" Mom reaches for my hand. "Darling, he's a *guy*. That's what guys do! You just need to keep him happy so his wandering eye won't stray beyond the borders, if you know what I mean, because—trust me—that boy is a keeper. Don't hurt having a man with money."

And why is that? Because I'm incapable of earning my own? Uh, try again. Just because I have no clue what I want to do in the future—eBay can only get you so far—doesn't mean I won't be successful. Mom is partially right, though. Maybe Blaine's "peekie" didn't mean a thing. And it's not as though girls never check out other guys. We're just less obvious about it.

Besides, if Mom had kept my father happy, then maybe he'd still be around.

Mom nudges me and points at the parking lot. "And see? There's Blaine now, so don't you feel silly?"

My heart leaps when I see Blaine stepping out of his Mercedes looking like a Polo model in his jeans and untucked white shirt. But how did he know I was here? I'm supposed to be in Harpers Ferry with my dad. "Mom, did you call him?"

She plays innocent by laying a hand against her chest, causing her silver bangles to slide down to her elbow with a *clink, clink, clink.* "Of course not, honey! I'd never do that. I only texted him and *pretended* to be you."

Impersonating your daughter is wrong on so many levels, but I am happy to see him. Otherwise, he might have gone to Prescott's party thinking I was angry and if he met someone new, then . . . No, he wouldn't do that to me. Still, as Blaine walks toward the gate I can't help but scan the crowd for any potential competition to worry about. There's a redhead wearing low-cut shorts and a bikini top, but she's packing to leave. So when Blaine strolls into the pool area, I wrap my arms around his neck and kiss him until she's gone.

Give him something to keep him happy.

"Wow," Blaine says. "I take it you're not mad at me anymore."

I pull back and laugh. "Of course not! I know how much you love me, right?"

"Of course. You're my number one girl."

But for once, I wish Blaine would tell me I'm his *only* girl.

"There, isn't this better? Just the two of us?"

Blaine lays a hand on my knee from the driver's seat of his Mercedes, his brown hair draping over one eye and traces of a sunburn from today's golf game on his nose. After listening to thirty minutes of butchered karaoke, he was more than ready to leave when Chuck sauntered over and said, "Now, Sabrina, why is such a good-looking girl working on a Friday night? Get out of here, go have some fun, and I'll help your little sister."

Mom giggled like a preteen when Chuck gave her an exaggerated wink, but to me, his cliché line threw up a huge red flag. I did *not* want to leave her alone with that man in case they hooked up, because once it ended—and yes, it would end—Mom could lose her job. But if I was at Dad's like I'm supposed to be, she'd be on her own anyway. And now that Blaine and I have made up it would be good to spend some time together.

"It sure is better," I reply, trying to sound light and airy. Tonight, we are not going to fight. I am not going to mention the tramp stamp and beat the subject like a dead horse until it is nothing but a pile of hide and hooves. I am going to be the perfect girlfriend.

Blaine puts his blinker on and turns into Riverside Estates, a large development between Chuck's and Dee's campgrounds that Rex Reynolds, Mom's old boss, designed. Talk about McMansions—Rex's model home could put even Torrance's house to shame. Larson and Blaine have a gorgeous Cape Cod right by the river. On the lot beside them, the new owners are having a massive Georgian built, but so far, the house looks like a dismal graveyard with black silt fencing surrounding the rocky yard and stacks of mud-splattered bricks. Blaine waves at Rex, who is talking with a woman wearing a pink suit and a girl standing with arms crossed and a NASCAR cap pulled down low on her forehead. "My new neighbors," he says. "Victoria and Roxanne Swain." Uh, yeah, the mom is total Riverside Estates material, but her daughter? She looks more suited for a trailer park. And seeing her poorly dyed red hair beneath her cap makes me once again think of the bleached blonde at McDonald's with the tramp stamp.

No. Dead subject, dead horse.

But I can't keep my anger from swelling as we walk through the mudroom door. When the security alarm beeps, I stand facing him, refusing to move. "Sabrina, please?" Blaine asks, his fingers lingering above the code box. "I thought you weren't mad anymore."

"I'm not," I lie before reluctantly turning around. "It's just that I . . . I don't understand why Larson doesn't trust me enough to know the alarm code. It's not like I'm going to break in or anything."

The beeping stops. Blaine takes my hand and puts his face inches from mine, the richness of his brown eyes making my heart jump. "Why don't you trust *me*? Don't you know you're the best thing that's happened to me?"

"Better than—"

"Yes, better than Dee Barton," Blaine finishes, kissing me softly. "Better than the girl at McDonald's, better than that redhead at Chuck's, better than *anything*. And come on—if I was going to cheat, don't you think I'd be smart enough not to get caught?"

Well . . . yes, I guess.

"So," Blaine says, with his thousand-watt, knee-weakening smile. He wraps his strong arms around my waist and pulls me close. "Why don't I order a pizza for me and salad for you and we'll watch a movie. Your pick."

I'd rather have pizza than salad, but his offer to let me pick the movie does provide the perfect opportunity to see exactly how willing he is to please me. So I think of the cheesiest, most romantic movie I can. "Fine. How about *Mamma Mia?*"

Blaine starts to protest, but then, to my surprise, he kisses the tip of my nose and says, "Okay. You put it on and I'll be right there."

Well, that's a pleasant change. I walk down the stairs to his suite in the basement, which is decorated with manly chocolate brown walls, leather furniture, and a flat-screen TV. Usually, Blaine convinces me to watch Clint Eastwood or some horrible action movie where nearly everyone ends up as a bloody corpse. Maybe he is trying and I overreacted. After all, his mother did leave to pursue a singing career in Nashville when he was nine, taking Larson's Corvette and the contents of their joint checking account with her. It must have been hard, knowing your own mother wasn't interested in shared custody. So it's no wonder Blaine doesn't know how to act in a relationship. She screwed him over *and* he's been raised by Larson Walker, who's quite the bachelor with an active dating life and who kind of reminds me of Pierce Brosnan in *Mamma Mia* with his rugged good looks and perfectly cut salt-and-pepper hair.

Still, when I notice Blaine's backpack on his desk, a horrible temptation to search every nook and cranny sweeps through me.

No, don't snoop. Only pathetic girls snoop.

But what would've happened if I had never found the letter Dee wrote him hidden in his glove compartment? What if Blaine lied about throwing away all those photos of her? And what if he saved mementos from other relationships, like the serial killers who save their victims' fingers or toes?

I am pathetic.

Because not only did I just compare my boyfriend to a serial killer, I also find absolutely nothing incriminating in his backpack or in his desk drawers, just an old library card and a report card from the school he went to before he moved to Riverside. Pathetic, pathetic, I am pathetic. After all, Blaine said I was better than Dee. Better than the girl at McDonald's and better than the redhead at the campground . . .

Which means even though he was kissing me, he still noticed her.

The Superflirt Chronicles
. . . blogs from a teenage flirtologist

Sunday, June 13

THE WEEKEND FLIRT REPORT!
MOOD: A tad disappointed, but still happy that school's OUT!
MUSIC: "Electric Bird," Sia

It's time, dear readers, for my first summer flirt report!

Oh, how I wish it were full of romance and rapport with a handsome, well-mannered, gentlemanly fellow, but sadly, it's not. Let's all hope it's not a bad omen for the rest of the summer, shall we?

THE DUDE: "Sox," who I thought had such potential!

THE GRADE: Eh . . . C. No, that's mean. I'll give him a C+.

THE BREAKDOWN: Sox definitely has "handsome" down. Great hair. Straight teeth. Abs you could crack an egg on, which would be kind of gross if you think about it. Well-mannered, seeing as how he let me go first when we played pool Friday night, and gentlemanly, seeing as how he didn't gape at my breasts when I made my shots—either that or he was clever enough to get away with it.

So why the C+, a low rating Miss N and I haven't given out since Beater Boy? It's because of his continuous, nonstop, oh so aggravating ramblings about the Boston Red Sox.

Nothing against Boston, so please, no hate mail. It is, after all, admirable to have loyalty to your home team, but, Sox lives in *Maryland*, not New England.

Dude. Dude!

Does the song go *Root, root, root for whatever-team-has-the-best-record*? No, I believe it goes, *Root, root, root for the HOME team.* And his nonstop ragging on *my* home team annoyed me more than skinny models who claim they eat like hogs, so it was adios, Sox the Traitor! Sorry, you're cute, but I no longer tolerate guys who rag, nag, criticize, or hypnotize. I've already been down that road with Mercedes—the KING of rags, nags, criticism, and hypnotism, who was a major lesson on why serious relationships suck.

It's more fun to flirt.

At least Mercedes is now dating a total nightmare of a girl, which does bring me a substantial amount of happiness. And hey, now that I have some time on my hands, how's 'bout I reply to a few comments that readers have posted during the past week? You'll love this one:

Hey, SF, can I ask you something? I'm a college student who works part time at a grocery store. There's this gorgeous guy who sometimes bags for me and I think he likes me from the way he's always checking me out. He has a girlfriend, but he said they're having problems and are breaking up soon, so is it okay for me to flirt with him? —WisconsinWendy

Oh, my dear, dear Wendy. The dude wants to bag more than your groceries, sweetheart—he wants to bag your booty. True,

Superflirt does encourage all kinds of fun, harmless flirting, but with another woman's man? No, no, NO! That's just not cool. So please, immediately point Mr. Booty-Bagger back to his girlfriend, because you, my friend, do not want to be a home wrecker, no matter how wrecked that home already happens to be.

On to the next one, posted by "anonymous," as you'll soon find out why:

So, let me see if I understand this correctly. You drape yourself over a different dude every weekend and then say goodbye without another thought. Wouldn't the correct terminology for someone who behaves in this fashion be a slut? —Anonymous

First off—and I mean this with total love and sisterhood—up yours. Way up. Up, up, up. Second, I'm not doing anything wrong. I am not a tease nor do I sleep with these guys (per MY choice), and third, I'm not hurting anyone. I'm having fun meeting different people, and if there's flirting involved, guess what, sweetheart? It's my right! So go find another Web site to haunt, like www.iamajudgementalbitch.com, okay?

Okay. Time for one more:

Sure, flirting might be fun for the young and pretty, but it's not something a divorced woman in her forties who has two teenage girls, stretch marks, and wrinkles can pull off. I hardly have time to see my friends—what's left of them—let alone date. And what would my kids think? Sorry, but flirting is best left to the young. —Meghan9800

Thank you, Meghan, for bringing up a fascinating topic: When is a woman too old to flirt? To answer that question, here's a little test:

1. Stick out the index and middle fingers on your right hand.
2. Place said fingers gently against the inside of your left wrist.
3. Feel for a pulse.
4. If you find one, then YOU'RE NOT TOO OLD TO FLIRT!

Okay, so you have stretch marks, wrinkles, and things I can't identify with. And yeah, you're divorced with kids. But neither of these facts mean life is over or that you're not entitled to have fun! Meghan, honey, you are my new summer project. First off, I want you to download "Electric Bird" by Sia. Listen to every word. Twice, maybe three times. Then go treat yourself to a total day of beauty, including, but not limited to, a facial, manicure, pedicure, and highlights. Buy yourself a brand-new outfit and then go out to dinner with a girlfriend where you will smile at two different single men. Just not at your waiter, bartender, and for God's sake, not at a Mr. Booty-Bagger.

About your daughters. Look. Any teenage girl would admire a confident, bold mother who lives a life where age is neither an issue nor a hindrance. So in other words, stop using excuses to bury yourself in a hole, my dear.

And I mean that with total love and sisterhood.

Howdy, partners!
Welcome to the Barton Family Campground's
WILD WILD WEST WEEKEND!

Friday, June 18:	7 pm	Two-steppin' with Butch and the Boys
	8 pm	Tonight's movie: CITY SLICKERS
Saturday, June 19:	10 am	Kids' Crafts: Pinecone ornaments
	3 pm	Horseshoe Tournament
	5 pm	Bronco Hayride
	7 pm	Karaoke Hoedown with DJ Drake
	8 pm	Tonight's movie: DAVY CROCKETT, KING OF THE WILD FRONTIER
	10 pm	S'mores & cocoa by the community fire
Sunday, June 20:	9 am	Nondenominational church service

3 ~ Dee

Thank God for quick-brew coffee makers. Seventy dollars for twelve cups in three minutes? Worth every penny, especially at five-thirty on a Saturday morning.

Our cabin's front screen door creaks open. From the kitchen window, I watch Mom stumble out onto the porch, bundled in a quilt with her hair gathered in a sleepy ponytail. She surveys the campground below and then sits in Dad's rocking chair, where he used to watch the sunrise every morning. Back then, Mom was more of a night owl who stayed up late watching *Law & Order* reruns, but one week after his funeral, after the well-wishers had stopped visiting and the flowers had wilted, I was woken by the sound of her rocking slowly in his chair. If she was surprised when I joined her, she didn't show it. "I need to do inventory so we don't run out of anything," she said, maybe to me, maybe to herself. *"I can't run out of anything."*

I didn't know what to say other than "Okay."

"Some of the tent sites need another layer of gravel," she

stammered. "And the hiking paths—your father said something about overgrown briars before he . . ."

Before he died.

Mom stared straight ahead. Her words sounded as wispy as the fog lingering over the fishing pond when she said, "Your grandmother Madeline thinks I won't be able to handle the campground alone, Dee. She thinks I should sell it."

The mere thought made me suck in my breath. "Will you?"

Her jaw tightened. "No. I won't. I *refuse*."

Dad would have been devastated if she did. To John Barton, this place wasn't just a business, it was home and every guest was kin. He grew up here, after his parents, Arthur and Madeline, built the campground in 1972, and to him, it was bad enough when they financed their Florida retirement eight years ago by selling twenty acres to Rex Reynolds, a sleazy land developer. At least my grandparents sold the business to Dad for a price below market value so he could keep the rest in the family and away from Rex. And on that morning with my mother, I vowed to make sure it stayed that way.

"Mom, I'll check the paths . . . but I don't know how to do inventory."

"I don't either," she said in a small voice.

There was a lot we didn't know. Before, our home was my playground rather than a responsibility, and Mom only took care of the social aspects. Dad wanted it that way, to protect his girls from the dirty work. But we eventually did figure out how to do inventory—and fix leaky toilets, repair pool tiles, and pay bills, although we still struggle in that department. I quit softball because sports no longer seemed important, and we set out to prove Madeline wrong—we *can* handle the campground. And we can handle Rex, who came slithering around two weeks ago, now that his swanky development is nearly sold out and we have additional lots he wants to buy.

Yeah, right. Not selling, snake.

Once the coffee is ready, I fill two mugs and step out onto the porch. The smells of dewy earth and a camper's early morning fire welcome me as I hand Mom her coffee. "Mmm, thank you," she says, cupping her mug with both hands and taking a big sip. "Yummy. And can you believe it's already been a week since school ended? You're a *senior* now, Dee!"

Me, a senior. It still hasn't sunk in.

"But it's too early for me to get emotional, so let's talk schedule," Mom says. "How's it looking for today, sweetie?"

I sit down beside her. Flirt-wise? Not good. The only cute guy who's checked in has two strikes against him: he's younger than me *and* he has quite the disgusting spitting habit. Work-wise? Busy. We always go in a thousand different directions on the weekends. "Well, I'm going for a run before my shift in the store starts at seven and then Nat and I are taking the kids hiking to find pinecones for craft hour at ten. After that, we might hang at the river until the horseshoe tournament, unless you need me."

Mom rubs the brim of her mug. "Well, ah, there's that one thing, remember? About training Roxanne how to use the register at eleven?"

The coffee turns to sludge in my stomach. No, I didn't

forget. I just hoped it was only a delusion when Mom told me about her agreement to let Roxanne work on the weekends, because Mrs. Swain is determined to keep her away from video games while their new house is being built. I do *not* want to be anywhere near that girl, but Mom has enough stress to deal with. "Sure, no problem. Anything else?"

"Well, I kind of have to find out if the insurance office is open today," she says, sounding both guilty and embarrassed. "I misfiled our original bill and their overdue notice was buried in paperwork, so I'm late with the payment. Oh, and what about the tractor keys, has anyone found them? I'd hate to cancel the hayride."

"Yeah, Jake did. They were in—" I notice a pile of college brochures on the porch floor. "Um, Mom? What are those for?"

She leans over, almost dripping coffee on her quilt. "Oh, right! A lady from the bank gave them to me. Her daughter is sixteen, but she's been researching colleges and scholarships since she was ten. Ten! I've never done that, Dee!"

I flip through the brochures. Yale, McDaniel, Duke, schools we can't afford and that would never accept me, anyway, unless it's for a janitorial position. "I'm going to Riverside Community College, so who cares?"

She sets her mug down and scoots to the edge of her chair, the worry lines on her forehead deepening. "I care, Dee, you're *graduating* soon! What if I screwed up your future by not giving your education enough importance?"

Okay, now she's getting ridiculous. "Mom, stop. You didn't screw anything up. I *want* to go to Riverside just like I *want*

47

to always help run the campground. What's the big deal? It's a great school. *You* went there."

Mom lets out a sarcastic grunt. "Yeah, for one semester until I quit because it interfered with my bar-hopping schedule, that's the big deal. I want better for you, Dee!"

Hmm. There has to be some reason other than college for her to be acting like this. "Okay, what's *really* going on, Mom?"

A squirrel dashes onto a rock. She watches as it scrambles up a tree and says, "Nothing. It's just . . . maybe I should have listened to Madeline and sold the campground. She called yesterday to let me know that Chuck is putting in *water slides* next year, according to his Web site. Water slides! How can we compete with that?"

Ah. My grandmother, who is living the high life in her snooty Floridian RV resort. That explains Mom's mood, and the bags under her eyes. She pulls at the sleeves of her vintage Go-Go's shirt that shows off her muscular arms. "Madeline also told me about a bad review we got online just because of a few potholes, but when I told her we can't afford blacktop, she made me feel like a horrible business owner, so I got upset and hung up, which *you know* is going to come back to haunt me. Lord, I wish . . ."

Mom doesn't finish, but I know the rest.

She wishes Dad was here. He was the charmer, the one who made her laugh and who could always calm the storms in her mind, a role I try to take over—emphasis on *try.* "Well, up hers, Mom! She doesn't own the campground anymore, so you had every right to be upset. And so what if Chuck adds water slides? He'll also raise his prices again. A lot of families can't afford his rates, so where are they going to go?"

"They'll come here," Mom finishes for me as soothing pink rays from the rising sun shoot through the trees. "You're right. Thanks, baby."

I wrinkle my nose at her and say, "*That's* why you need me around, to keep you sane. Besides, who else could bring you fabulous morning coffee like I do?"

"Our friend at site fifteen." Mom smiles, pointing to the tent site below where a twenty-eight-year-old we met yesterday had pitched his Coleman. "He seems willing to fetch my beverages, poor kid."

"Aw, I know! He was so smitten with you at check-in that he couldn't remember his truck's tag number! But jeez, Mom, you're not the cougar type, and besides, it'd be such a *pain* to carry around a diaper bag with you everywhere you—" I stop, the rest of my teasing abandoned as clumsy silence blankets us. Mom slowly twists her wedding band and I stare into my coffee. This is the first time we've ever talked about her with another man, and even though we're only joking . . . it doesn't feel very funny anymore.

For the rest of the morning, the thought of Mom dating nags at me more than the woman who complained about her neighbor's dog pooping two feet outside of the pet walk perimeter. Why? My mother is an attractive woman. Most attractive, widowed women eventually start dating again, so why should she be any different?

Because. I don't know why.

During craft hour at the main pavilion, my mind keeps wandering and I end up watching fluffy clouds turn lazy circles while the kids go hog wild with the glitter. A gaggle—or is it a skein?—of geese fly by in a lopsided V formation, calling to each other with honking barks as they follow the leader. Is that why I can't imagine a life without the campground, because I'm following my father's lead? Is that why the thought of Mom dating freaks me out, because I'm afraid of change?

"Dee, a little assistance, please," Natalie says from the other side of the picnic table where she is wrestling a glue stick from a five-year-old boy who's trying to eat it. She nods to a girl who has squirted the entire contents of her juice box onto a pinecone. "And where's the paper towels, did you bring them?"

"Oh, shoot, forgot. I'll be right back." I hurry toward the lodge, stepping right in the middle of a puddle from last night's rain shower with my Old Navy flip-flops and feeling the chilly water tickle my toes in the most delicious way.

Puddles are one of life's many overlooked joys.

The Cutson brothers are arguing over a tube of glitter when I return, so I bop them both on the head with the paper towel roll before wiping off the soaked pinecone. "Hey, Nat? Uh, after your uncle Dick died, how long did your aunt Loreen wait until she started dating?"

"Oooo, you said a dirty word!" Tanner yells. "You said—"

Natalie snaps her fingers at him while watching me. "Oh, six days. But she was seeing her dentist long before that, if you catch my drift."

"Did your aunt kill your uncle?" Lyle asks.

"Bet she blew his head off," Tanner says, taking a fuzzy red pom-pom and field-goal kicking it with his finger. He throws his arms up and screams, "Score!"

Craft hour turns into craft chaos as the kids flick glittery pom-poms at each other, but I'm thankful for the distraction. Otherwise, Natalie might realize my question has something to do with Mom, and I'm not ready to talk about it. The glue-eating boy is happy for the distraction as well, but Lyle still notices him squirting Elmer's on his fingers. "Hey, dork-face, don't eat that! It causes cancer!"

The boy turns to Natalie with fear.

She nods. "Yep, that's how poor Uncle Dick died."

Soon it's time for Roxanne's training. Yippee. There's no way out of it, though, so while Natalie changes into a glitter-free shirt, I head to the store, where we sell camping supplies, food and drinks, toys, and crafts made by local artisans. Ivy is sitting behind the counter, gazing out the window with a pair of binoculars and dressed for this weekend's wild west theme in jeans and cowboy boots. "Miss Ivy, what are you doing?"

"Oh, covering the store while your mom helps some know-it-all park his RV." She lowers the binoculars and turns to me with red marks under her eyes. "I also defragged the computer and started some virus scans. You need to watch the cookies, kid."

"Right, I'll tell Nat." Natalie is the computer pro, not me.

I grab a bag of pistachios and hop on a bar stool Dad made out of wood cut from a fallen oak. He also installed the rustic cedar paneling and copper countertop that give the store a relaxed, homey feel, as does the cowboy Celtic music softly playing on the stereo. Ivy hands me the binoculars. "Site thirty-two. The fool man almost backed into a tree."

I give them a try, but my gaze first falls on Jake's garage, where he's getting ready for tomorrow's race. As he wipes his hands on a rag, I have to admit, there's something so *real* about a guy who spends his day off working on an engine instead of his Call of Duty score. And he wasn't ashamed to tell me about both his parents being laid off a year ago and how they sold their farmhouse in order to buy a smaller home in town, which is why he uses our garage. Now he races on a shoestring budget with his own money against rich guys like Danny Reynolds, one of Blaine's friends and Rex's son, whose equipment is nothing short of top-of-the-line.

I admire Jake for that . . . even if he is a jerk sometimes.

Okay, time to put away the binoculars if they're going to make me think philosophically about Jake—who just yesterday told me how I would love his races because there's plenty of guys for me to drape myself over. I set them on the counter next to a book on bird-watching that is open to a glossy photo of a Baltimore oriole. "Uh, bird-watching, Miss Ivy? I thought you hated any activity that requires a closed mouth."

Ivy slams the book shut with a backhanded swat. "Ha, ha, very funny. And yes, it was a bad idea. Whoever developed the concept is a complete moron. If I felt the need to see an oriole up close, I'd go to Camden Yards."

"Then why did you buy it?"

"My idiotic therapist," she says wryly. "He believes it's 'cathartic.'"

Cathartic? Yeah, right, just like the knitting, the yoga, and the Sudoku puzzles, all of which only agitate her more. Ivy used to be a workaholic until the investment firm she'd devoted most of her life to forced her into early retirement three years ago.

She had never married, never had kids, never knew *anything* other than work, so when her therapist suggested traveling, Ivy took his advice to the extreme by selling her condo and buying an RV. Nothing is working, though, judging from the way she's staring at Mom's overflowing in-bin like a shopaholic stares at a clearance sign. "You know what is cathartic, Dee? *Work* is cathartic, so why won't your mother let me help her with the bills and paperwork?"

I know perfectly well why, even though Ivy always helps for free. Because Mom thinks it would prove Madeline was right— that she can't do it all. So I avoid Ivy's question by inspecting my pistachios and saying, "Hey, have you ever noticed how Jell-O Pistachio Pudding is made with mostly almonds and only two percent pistachios? If it's made with mostly almonds, why didn't they call it almond pudding?"

Ivy contemplates this, the muscles in her jaw tensing as I shake a few nuts onto her palm. "Oh, I don't know," she says after a few moments. "Maybe some male corporate hotshot at Jell-O thought pistachio sounded better. And who knows, maybe a female co-worker suggested they call it Almond Pudding, but *noooo*, Mr. Hotshot trashed her idea."

Her hands twitch as she angrily crunches on a nut. "And then Mr. Hotshot told Miss Almond Pudding that perhaps it was time for her to retire, even though she had dedicated her *entire life* to the firm. But when she said no, I'm not ready for retirement, Mr. Hotshot pushed her out anyway and replaced her with a busty twenty-nine-year-old, that's why."

Oh, my.

Remind me to never bring up Jell-O around her again.

Thankfully, a trio of girls burst into the store to pay for a round of putt-putt before Ivy can crack a tooth on a shell. As they fight over the pink golf ball, Ivy sulks by the window until they leave—with three pink balls. She softens, though, when she sees something outside. "Well, well, well, and here comes another Miss Almond Pudding now."

Huh? The only person I see is Roxanne Swain meandering down the stone-lined path, kicking stray rocks and going about as slow as a blood-filled tick. "Who, Roxanne? Yeah, right, how is she a Miss Almond Pudding?"

Ivy studies Roxanne with laserlike intensity before glancing at the clock hanging above a display of handmade pottery. Eleven-twenty. Roxanne is late. "Hmm," Ivy says. "Maybe because she's being forced to do something she does not want to do."

What, work? Oh, boo-hoo, I work every day. And it's hard to muster sympathy for someone who—no matter how nice I am to her—only speaks to me when necessary, like during our brief *Hey, I need to buy a bag of ice* and *Okay, they're two dollars each* conversation.

However, her mother, Victoria Swain—a woman whose idea of dressing down is wearing Liz Claiborne casual wear—loves to talk. While spending a fortune yesterday on wind flags, awning lights, and tiki torches to liven up their sterile site, she told me all about Dr. Martin Swain's position at Johns Hopkins Hospital. And how it was her idea to rent a motor home for the summer after their house in Baltimore sold faster than expected, leaving them homeless until Rex is finished building their new house. I forced myself to nod politely after learning that—*fabulous*—Roxanne is going to live on what used to be *our* beautiful land, but when Mrs. Swain said how nice it would be if Roxanne and I became friends?

Yeah. I don't exactly see that happening.

The bell above the door jingles as Roxanne steps in, letting the screen slam shut behind her. She shoots me a bored look that makes me feel both awkward and stupid at the same time and then cringes when she hears the cowboy Celtic. "Uh, are you serious? I have to work *and* listen to that?"

Ivy ignores Roxanne's rebel angst routine—maybe because of her Miss Almond Pudding theory. "Welcome! I'm Ivy Neville, but you can call me Miss Ivy. Now, why don't you come here and Dee and I will show you how to use the register?"

Roxanne cracks her gum. "Fine, *Ivy*, but I'm going to the bathroom first."

Big mistake, girl, big mistake.

Pudding or no pudding, Ivy doesn't negotiate with attitude. She frowns, straightening her spine to her full height—all five feet, eleven inches. "By all means, go ahead," she says, her voice like candy-coated barbed wire. "In fact, why don't I grab the cleaning supplies and show you how to freshen the ladies' room while you're there, how would that be?"

Give it up, Roxanne, you will NOT win this battle!

She must not realize this by the patronizing way she says, "Fine, *Miss* Ivy."

Oh, boy, I can tell it's going to be a long, long day. Especially when a yellow Isuzu Trooper with Mardi Gras beads hanging from the rearview mirror pulls up moments after Ivy and Roxanne leave. A woman in a pink minidress with poufy blond hair steps out and checks her reflection before prancing up the stairs in matching stilettos. She's probably a salesperson or an artist wanting to sell her merchandise in the store. The woman enters, bringing in a cloud of perfume that smells like musky cinnamon. She smiles when she sees me. "My stars, you must be Dee! Aren't you just the prettiest thing?"

She researched my name? Sharp, very sharp. But as much as I love huggers, it's odd the way she strides past the brochure stand to hug me, her large breasts making my small ones feel claustrophobic and her silver bangles clanging as she pats my back.

"Now, sugar. Is your momma here? I'd love to chat with her."

Oh, she must be a friend of my mother's, although—wow—I can't remember the last time Mom had a friend stop by, or even call for that matter. I check out the window to see if she's still helping the man park, but instead, Mom is clinging to her cell as she runs toward the lodge. She bursts through the door, wiping sweaty bangs from her forehead as she says, "Dee, drop everything. I just got off the phone with—"

"Well, hello, Jane! Good golly, it's clear where Dee gets her looks."

Never mind. She's definitely a salesperson.

Mom blinks in confusion as the woman shakes her hand with vigor and then takes a lime green business card from her purse. "My name is Mona Owens, proud owner of Mona's Low-Key Karaoke," she says in a voice that's part beauty queen, part Dolly Parton. "I provide karaoke entertainment for your good neighbor Chuck Lambert on Friday nights, and I thought I'd stop by in case you were interested in hiring me as well!"

Mona curls her lips into a confident grin as Mom shifts anxiously and glances at her watch. "I, uh, appreciate you stopping by, but DJ Drake does karaoke for us on Saturday nights, so—"

"But," Mona says, tapping the counter with a long fingernail that has tiny musical notes painted on it. "I'd bet my old Charlie Pride records that I can provide more entertainment than DJ Drake. And, Dee, you know my daughter, Sabrina, right? She's my assistant, so the two of you could hang out if I worked here. Wouldn't that be wonderful?"

What?

Sabrina as in Sabrina Owens? Mona is her *mother*? No way. I imagined her mom as a vain socialite or someone like Victoria Swain. And Sabrina, here? Over my dead body. I hope Mom will make the connection, but she only stammers, "Um, yeah, sure, if we ever need someone to fill in, maybe we'll call."

Maybe we'll call? I can barely focus on anything else they say. Once Mona finally leaves in a pink, poufy, musky-cinnamon haze, I explode. "Mom, how could you take her card? Don't you realize who she is?"

Mom knows what Sabrina did to me. I told her everything, otherwise she would have worried herself to death trying to figure out why I was so upset last September. But before I can say anything else, Mom grasps my forearms. "Dee, I'm sorry, but right now we have bigger problems to worry about."

Oh, no. Her agitated look reminds me of the time when this idiot mother let her kids play barefoot at the septic dump station and then threatened to sue us because of their chances of getting hepatitis C. "Why, what's wrong, Mom?"

"Madeline called from the airport in Florida. She's going to be here in *three hours*."

The Superflirt Chronicles
. . . blogs from a teenage flirtologist

Saturday, June 19

MY FLIRTLESS NIGHTMARE OF A WEEKEND
MOOD: Anxious, overwhelmed, and highly perturbed
MUSIC: "Blue Suitcase," Erin McCarley

Why the horrible mood?

Because I'm awaiting the arrival of an unwanted guest here at the campground. The identity of this guest is best left undisclosed so pardon my secrecy, but let me say that the mere *thought* of seeing this person makes my stomach ache like I've held my pee too long. You know the feeling, don't you? Of course you do.

And why am I flirtless?

Because the only cute guy here this weekend is younger than me and Miss N and I do *not* flirt with younger boys. Yes, perhaps this is hypocritical. After all, it is acceptable for a seventeen-year-old guy to date a fifteen-year-old girl, but an older girl dating a younger guy? No, sorry, maybe some gals can rock the whole cougar thing, but it's just not for me. Besides, the young dude has another strike against him:

He spits.

I mean, really, why *do* guys spit? They do it nonstop—out car windows, in trash cans, on sidewalks, leaving gross piles for the rest of us to step in. Even pro baseball players spit, becoming role models for a whole new generation of spitters. Why? Is there some physical difference between men and women—besides the obvious—that causes this behavior? Do they have extra phlegm glands or overly large mucus producers?

And please—do *not* give me that lame *it's a guy thing* excuse. Some actions just can't be excused. Like what's going on with our girl Meghan:

Hey, it's Meghan again. I went to the salon and mall yesterday, like you said, but the stylist gave me awful red highlights and a salesclerk convinced me to buy these horrible trendy jeans. When I got home, my daughters called me Raggedy Ann and then accused me of trying to be like a teenager. They were joking, of course, but while I was having dinner with my friend, even she told me that my hair looked bad during the first course. So now what do I do? —Meghan9800

Okay, Meghan, love, I'm sorry, but if your daughters are such experts on hair and fashion, then they should help instead of criticize. And a true friend would never dis your hair in public, so I'm leery of her motives. But chin up, sweetie, all hope is not lost. You just need a better stylist—try getting a reference from someone who has great hair. Then you need to find a store that does NOT employ commission-seeking sales hogs but instead has lovely salesclerks who will dress you in clothes that make you feel beautiful. After that, I want you to go back out to dinner . . . only with a better friend this time.

And as for me, it's time to go back to waiting for our unwanted guest.

Which gives me a sudden urge to spit.

4 ～ Dee

Do I hug Madeline or shake her hand?

Hug or handshake?

I check the store clock. Almost four-twenty. Madeline's flight was supposed to arrive at two-fifteen and we're only an hour away from the airport so they should be here by now. Was there a flight delay or hold-up at baggage claim? No, her visits never last more than a few days, so she should only have carry-on. At least I pray she only has carry-on.

I coil my hair into a bun and then let it down. No, maybe I should keep it up. And maybe I shouldn't have worn these shorts. Maybe they're too . . . short.

"Why are you so uptight, Dee? It's not like your grand-mother still owns the place," Jake asks, while cleaning the grass stains off his legs with baby wipes. He grins and throws a soiled one at Natalie, who is sitting at the computer.

She picks it up with pinched fingers. "Oh my gosh, really, Jake?"

He ignores her scorn and walks behind the counter,

elbowing her in the ribs so she'll share the bar stool. "What's on the Internet menu today, more wedgies?"

Natalie shifts to give him more room. "No, I'm checking my ADRs."

"What's that, your Attention Deficit Registry?" Jake jokes, scratching his elbow and getting grass on the counter that Natalie already polished. She swipes away his mess with an annoyed groan and then explains all about the Advanced Dining Reservations she made a hundred and eighty days in advance—seriously?—for her Disney World vacation. As Natalie launches into detailed descriptions of the restaurants, I think about what Jake said.

Why am I so uptight?

Why did we spend the entire afternoon cleaning like the queen herself was visiting? I mean, it's not as though the campground was a total pigsty or Madeline's opinion matters. But no, every time she visits, Mom and I turn into spineless minions desperate to win her approval, like when she showed up unexpectedly last October and criticized the "tacky" haunted hayrides and trick-or-treating that would never be allowed when *she* owned the campground.

Whatever. We like tacky.

Even so, I can't help but say, "Okay, Natalie—you tidied the store and porch, I took care of the pool, pavilions, and cabins, Ivy cleaned the bathrooms with Roxanne, but what about the laundry room? And did anyone check the arcade?"

Natalie swivels to face me. "Dee. Everything looks fabulous. Chill."

Right. Chill.

Chill, chill, chill.

And everything does look fabulous, thanks to us—especially Jake, who cleaned, mowed, and weed-whacked like a maniac, even though it's his day off. He can be a creep, but when push comes to shove, he's the first to help. And he stopped a near riot at the horseshoe tournament I had foolishly put Roxanne in charge of, by offering the players free ice cream after she read a magazine during the championship round instead of keeping score.

I watch out the window as Roxanne lugs the horseshoes toward the shed, stopping every ten steps to rest and then yelling at a little boy who almost nipped her heels with his Big Wheel. She comes into the store several minutes later looking as happy as a drenched cat with her red hair plastered to her scalp. "I'm taking my break," she proclaims. "You do realize it's against the law not to give employees breaks, don't you?"

Breaks? We don't take breaks here. We bust our butts when it's busy and goof off when it's slow and everything works out even in the end. But before I can tell her to go ahead, take that break, Mom pulls in.

Oh, man.

An icy chill goes up my spine at the sight of Madeline's stiff silhouette in the truck's passenger seat. Once Mom parks, my grandmother steps out wearing crisp linen slacks that don't dare wrinkle and a sleeveless mock turtleneck that emphasizes her leathery Florida tan. Natalie and Jake join me in time to see Madeline survey the campground with her upper lip curled as though she just sniffed an uncovered septic hole.

"Yikes," Natalie says. "My butt cheeks just clenched."

Jake nods. "Yeah, I'd rather suck on a spark plug than be around that woman, so if you attention deficits will excuse me, I'm going to go work on my kart for tomorrow's race."

"You have a laydown enduro kart, right?"

Whoa. Who said that, Roxanne?

The three of us turn in unison and stare at her in disbelief. A pink flush quickly spreads across her face, so even *she* must not believe she said it either.

"Yeah, it's an enduro." Jake gives her that rock-star grin of his as though he's impressed. "Wow, you know about kart racing?"

Roxanne shrugs, and then grips the hem of her baggy shirt. "Um . . . not a lot," she says, giving me a quick glance. "Just that their two-stroke engines have top speeds of a hundred miles per hour, and zero suspension, and how a lot of famous drivers like Chase Elliott and Michael Schumacher started their careers with karts."

Okay, she must have looked this up on the Internet just to impress Jake. But then I notice the rolled-up magazine peeking out from the lower pocket of her cargo shorts. *Auto Trends?* So Roxanne is a—

"Hey, a fellow gearhead!" Jake steps forward to give Roxanne a very enthusiastic knuckle tap. Gearhead, is that some kind of insider term? Jake then hooks a thumb in my direction. "I'm used to *some* girls calling my kart a 'thingy.'"

What? No, I do not.

Oh, wait . . . yes, I do.

Jake grabs a Gatorade from the fridge and tosses two dollars on the counter. "So, Roxanne, feel like getting your hands dirty?

My friend Danny was supposed to come over, but he went to a party instead."

Ugh, Danny as in Danny Reynolds, Rex's son, and one of Blaine's buddies. If that wasn't gag-worthy enough, Danny is also dating Torrance Jones, Sabrina's best friend. I do not understand why Jake would want to hang out with someone like him, especially since they race against each other. And Jake is inviting *Roxanne* to his garage, the girl who's been a total jerk to me from day one? I hope she blows him off, but her stony indifference melts like ice thrown into a campfire when she says, "Sure, that'd be cool!"

Oh, yeah, she'll be nice to him but not to me. Well, fine. There's bigger problems on my plate, anyway, such as a big fat serving of Madeline Barton.

"I love, love, LOVE your grandmother's suitcases, Dee," Natalie says, pressing her hand to the window. "Are they Louis Vuitton? I bet they smell *divine*."

They must be Louis Vuitton, seeing as how Madeline isn't the knockoff type. Wow, her luggage costs a fortune and yet she had the nerve to insinuate on the phone to Mom that she wants to stay in our best cabin for free? She knows money has been tight since Dad died. He did have some life insurance, but it wasn't enough to cover funeral costs and the hideous amount of taxes Mom had to pay and . . .

Suitcases? As in *long, long visit* suitcases?

My heart sinks as Mom sets Madeline's one, two, *three* suitcases on a patch of grass. Mom then stands, rubbing her back and looking around as though she's searching for me. Well, I guess it's not fair to leave her on her own. "I'm going out there."

"God be with you," Natalie says, patting my back.

I force myself out the door. Madeline hesitates when she sees me, maybe because of my strong resemblance to my dad. Right then and there, I decide to go with a formal handshake, but for some insane reason, instinct takes over and I hug her instead, only to get an awkward pat on the back in return. *Shoot. I should've gone with the handshake.*

"Yes, hello, Dee, you've grown since October," Madeline says, her lopsided brows and angular jaw giving her a daunting appearance. Her hair is cut in a severe bob with thin, clumped bangs clinging to her forehead like a brown vulture claw. It sways when she scrutinizes my outfit. "And you've almost outgrown your clothing."

Should've gone with the handshake, should've worn longer shorts.

Mom gives me a warm, lingering hug that seems as though it's more for her benefit than mine. She smells of Taco Bell and peppermint, meaning she comforted herself with burritos on the drive to the airport and then tried to cover them up with Altoids. "Hi, sweetie. Anything happen while I was gone?"

"Nope, everything was smooth sailing, as usual," I say, emphasizing the *as usual* to my grandmother. "We've been so busy, and our customers? They love it here."

Madeline's beady eyes scan the packed swimming pool, the shuffleboard court, and the stream of kids waiting by the wagon for Ivy to fire up the John Deere for tonight's hayride. Everyone *is* having fun, but instead of focusing on the positive, Madeline only notices a guest who stubs his toe on a horseshoe Roxanne must have dropped on the way to the shed. "Well, I see you've been too busy to worry about customer safety."

Should've stuck with the handshake. Should've worn longer shorts. Should've NEVER trusted Roxanne.

The first thing Madeline wants is a tour, so she can report back to my grandfather how we've let the campground go to pot. After stowing her Louis Vuittons in the store, much to Natalie's delight, she primly climbs into the golf cart and grasps the roll bar when Mom hits the gas harder than normal. She does nod approvingly at the picturesque landscaping surrounding the lodge, with its swaying cattail grass and gentle daisies, but when she *tsk tsks* a pothole I tune her out and concentrate on our guests instead. I love how they turn their sites into mini home-away-from-homes. Some campers only need the basics—tent, lantern, cooler—while others go all out with canopies, propane grills, outdoor carpet, and decorations, like the couple from Maine who have white lights and wind chimes hanging from their awning. Or their neighbor, who had fun with this weekend's western theme by using old cowboy boots for geranium planters, making a red bandanna tablecloth, and wrapping green chili pepper lights around an oak tree.

All of which is *completely* gaudy, according to Madeline.

She dusts invisible dirt off her slacks when we return to the lodge. "Now, Jane. I'd like to eat dinner early tonight. And I assume you remember I don't eat red meat?"

Mom turns to me in a near panic. Oh, man, we just sell frozen hamburgers and hot dogs at the store and neither one of us thought to go to the grocery store, so our fridge is near empty, with only a few rotting tomatoes, dill pickles, and condiments.

66

"Well, Madeline . . . we could, um, karaoke starts at seven, so—"

"So we thought you'd like to go to Railroad Diner," I say. "They've added more items to the menu you might enjoy."

Mom gives me a grateful smile as we walk into the store. "Well, I suppose, if eating out is my only option," Madeline says with a grimace. Yep, pretty much, unless she wants a rotten tomato/pickle sandwich. "And what—pray tell—are you doing to my suitcases?"

Natalie looks up from a Louis Vuitton. "Sorry, I just wanted to smell them once more!"

We sit in uncomfortable silence while Madeline studies the menu. I already know my order, seeing as how Railroad serves the best Maryland crab cakes. The jukebox is free, so I pick a few songs, including an Alison Krauss bluegrass one that's Mom's favorite. "The usual, ladies? Crab cakes and side salads?" our waitress, Lou, asks.

"Absolutely," I say. "And a diet Coke with lemon."

"Bud Light for me," Mom adds.

Madeline raises an overly plucked brow at Mom's drink choice and then tosses her menu aside. "Unsweetened iced tea, please, with lemon, and I suppose I'll get the crab cake on a toasted bun. No butter, no mayonnaise, just lettuce and Dijon mustard on the side."

More uncomfortable silence until the jukebox kicks in and Mom's song plays. She squeezes my knee under the table before saying, "So, Madeline, how are things at the RV resort with Arthur?"

"Wonderful. It's the perfect place for retired couples such as us," Madeline says crisply while inspecting her silverware for cleanliness. "It's neat, efficient, and children are only allowed on Sundays."

"Are you kidding me?" I ask in astonishment. "What kind of a campground doesn't allow children?"

"A quiet one." Madeline shudders when a nearby toddler loudly refuses to eat his green beans, and then leans back when Lou delivers our drinks and salads. "So, Dee, what are your college plans? My bridge partner has three grandchildren going to Harvard, which is remarkable."

"Yeah, remarkable," I repeat, squeezing lemon in my soda and imagining some of it squirting in her eye. "But I'm going to Riverside Community."

Madeline reaches for two Splendas, disappointment etched on her bony face. Oh, joy, she's probably going to launch into a lecture on how community college is beneath me, and how she expects more from a Barton, blah, blah, blah. What she says, however, is far, far worse. "Yes, well, that would be appropriate for you."

Appropriate? Meaning I'm incapable of higher aspirations? That I'm not smart enough? Yeah, maybe I'm not. Maybe Riverside *is* my only option, but her verbal confirmation stings like fifty yellow jackets, making me dump too much dressing on my salad and miss half of her dull ramblings about my grandfather's newfound interest in art. But then Madeline changes the subject by asking, "So, Jane, have you started dating yet?"

What? Honestly, Madeline shouldn't even *think* to ask such a question of her son's widow. It's none of her business, but instead of saying so, Mom traces the ring of condensation around her beer and says, "Not exactly."

Hold on.

Not exactly? Wait . . . Is she thinking about dating?

Mom's cell rings. She scrambles to answer it, as though grateful for the distraction. "Hello? Oh, hi, Drake, how are you? Uh-huh? Oh, that's horrible. I'm so sorry. No, we'll be fine. I just hope you feel better soon."

Mom frowns as she hangs up and then takes a long, desperate drink.

"What was that about?" Madeline asks.

"That? Oh, nothing, just business stuff," Mom answers breezily while making a show of unwrapping the paper napkin from her silverware and placing it on her lap.

"What kind of business?" Madeline leans forward and places an elbow on the table. "It sounded as though someone was hurt."

Mom gives a nonchalant wave. "Well, yes, our karaoke DJ can't make it tonight because he threw his back out. But he'll be fine, and really, it's no big deal."

"No big deal? Your guests are expecting entertainment tonight. They've *paid* for entertainment, so what are you going to do?"

"Um, we'll have . . ." Mom shifts in her seat, the wheels turning in her head for a solution. "Bingo! We'll have bingo instead."

"You *cannot* be serious, Jane," Madeline says as Lou delivers our food. She picks up the bun to inspect her crab cake and then flicks away a fry cooked too much for her liking. "If your guests expect karaoke, you should provide karaoke. Surely you have a backup plan, don't you? Any good business owner would. Chuck Lambert would."

Oh, man. That's low, even for Madeline. Mom swallows hard, sinking in her seat. But then her panicked look slowly morphs into a confident smile as though she had everything under control all along. She sits up straight. "Yes, of course. I just have to call her."

Her? What her?

Oh, no. No, no, no! Not *that* her!

My heart thumps as Mom pulls out her cell and dials. I nudge her with my foot—hard—as she says, "Natalie, it's Jane. Oh, hello, Roxanne, I forgot you're working until seven. No, don't get Natalie if she's helping a guest, I just need a business card that's in the drawer beneath the cash register. It's green, I think."

Mom moves her feet away from me. "Yes, that's it, for Mona's Low-Key Karaoke. Can you see if she can fill in tonight? Thanks, dear, and . . . Oh, what's that? Yes, you may use the Internet if things are slow in the store."

Mom drops her cell back into her purse and picks up her crab cake, smiling in relief. Now it's my turn to panic, because not only am I *very* against the idea of Roxanne snooping around our computer, but in all of today's commotion, I never told Mom who Mona is. And what did Mona say? That Sabrina *always* works with her.

My appetite is gone. Sabrina might be coming to the campground—*my* campground—tonight. I stare at my plate, saying nothing, until Madeline goes to the bathroom. "Dee, what's wrong, why did you kick me?" Mom asks.

"You can't hire Mona Owens," I say, trying to stay calm.

"Why not? She is a bit . . . loud, but what was I supposed to do? Let Madeline keep talking to me like that? Besides, one night won't be all that bad."

"Yeah, but—" My throat locks up tighter than a rusted camper hitch.

"But what, Dee? What, *what?*"

Maybe I should just shut up, but I can't. "*Sabrina Owens* is Mona's daughter, so please have Natalie cancel and do bingo instead!"

Mom's exasperation softens. She drops her shoulders and says, "Oh, Dee, I'm so sorry. Had I known that, I never would have called her, but it's too late now and besides—maybe it's time you stood up to Sabrina."

"What, like you stand up to Madeline?" I snap, instantly regretting it.

We pick at our food until Madeline returns, complaining about a cracked toilet seat. Lou sets our check in the middle of the table. "Are we having problems, Dee?" Madeline asks while pushing the check in Mom's direction. *Yes, Madeline, problems.*

And I'm guessing that's what you wanted all along.

5 ～ Sabrina

God, this Meghan woman should just lie down and die already!"

Bridget Carson stares at the screen of my laptop and shakes her head. Two of her favorite activities are eating and gossip hunting, both of which she's been doing for the past hour, scanning tabloid Web sites on my bed with a bag of potato chips and relaying important facts such as which celebrity got a boob job or who dared to wear the same outfit twice.

Torrance gathers her long hair and stares at her reflection in my bedroom's full-length mirror. "Who needs to die, Megan Fox?" she asks, keeping both eyes on her slim frame while she goes through a series of poses with her lips pursed and stomach tight as though she's on *America's Next Top Model*.

Bridget shoves a handful of chips in her mouth and licks salt off her fingers. "No, not Megan Fox the actress, although seeing her croak would be fabulous. Meghan from this ridiculous blog called The Superflirt Chronicles."

Surely I didn't hear her right.

"Did you say super *fart*?" I sit down beside Bridget. Oh, gross, she's gotten crumbs on my bed, which is even more annoying than Mom's habit of drinking from the milk jug. Before she can plunder for more chips, I snatch the bag away. "And I swear, Bridget, must you? It's so unfair how you can binge like a total hog and not gain weight."

"Jeez, sorry. And no, Super*flirt*. It's written by some teenage flirtologist chick." Bridget points to a hideously girlie blog that reeks of estrogen with its lime green border and hot pink cheetah print. She brushes crumbs off her snow white polo shirt and says, "Meghan is this old divorced woman who's, like, *desperate for love*. She's in her forties. Why even bother?"

As Bridget starts to ramble about her forty-two-year-old single aunt who is headed for Spinsterville, I read the so-called Superflirt's latest entry about her unwanted visitor—snore—and how she thinks Meghan's daughters should help her find appropriate clothes. Yeah, right, whenever I try to get *my* mother to dress appropriately, she raids my closet for miniskirts. But even though Superflirt is probably just a pathetic, mousy wallflower living vicariously through the Internet, I have to agree—the way Meghan's friend dissed her hair was a deliberate attempt to knock her down a few pegs, maybe because Meghan looked better than she did. It's only one of many tricks we ladies play on each other.

And if anyone should know about tricks, it's me.

"Enough with the blog, already," Torrance whines, turning to the side and staring in the mirror with her back arched and palms clasping her hips. "Let's talk about tonight's party. I *still* can't believe Blaine isn't taking you, Sabrina. What's his excuse this time?"

Speaking of tricks.

Torrance Jones's favorite thing to do: display her passive-aggressive wit.

However.

After spending a miserable day with my father's wife and her evil daughter, Angela, I'm not in the mood for Torrance's potshots at Blaine. But it's my turn to be the pre-party hostess, and drive, now that my car is fixed, so I keep my cool and say, "He doesn't need an excuse, Torr. He has plans with his father."

And really, I didn't mind when Blaine told me how he wanted to spend time with Larson. Tomorrow is Father's Day, so I think it's sweet. Still, I must have sounded icier than expected. "Relax, Sabrina, I didn't mean anything. It's just that he's been breaking a lot of plans with you lately, that's all."

Bridget knits her forehead in concern. "Did you guys have another fight? Torrance told me all about what happened at McDonald's last week."

I'm sure she did.

Torrance drops her hair, letting it fall down her back in a golden cloud. She tosses me a sweet, concerned look and then turns to Bridget. "Did I tell you? Sabrina doesn't want to talk about how Blaine drooled over that girl, right, Sabrina?"

Yeah, more tricks. Torrance may act concerned, but I know what she's up to. She's slamming the ball in my court, waiting to see if I can return it. Bridget might be satisfied with her lower ranking, but Torrance and I have been volleying for control ever since we met in sixth grade, and now that senior year will soon be starting—*senior year*, the most important year ever—I am not about to back down. So I swing my racket hard and say, "Who *wouldn't* check her out, Torr? She was hot—a guy would be totally gay not to notice. Besides," I add with a sly smile, "it's not as though we ladies don't do our share of scoping. We're just not dumb enough to get caught."

Bridget laughs. "Yeah, she's got you on that one, Torrance!"

Ha. Serve returned, no point.

Torrance yawns as though it doesn't bother her. "Well, *Danny* would never do that," she says, flouncing to my closet to rummage through my clothes.

Bridget and I exchange knowing glances. Of course Danny Reynolds, Torrance's boyfriend of only two weeks, wouldn't check out another girl. He's too focused on racing, and when he's not hanging out with Blaine and Prescott, he's at some track or in his garage. Torrance had asked Danny out because she thought it'd be glamorous to go to races and wave checkered flags like models sometimes do. But all she did last weekend was complain about the noise and dirt, so I can't help but grin as she pulls out the brand-new Hollister skirt I got on eBay for the wonderfully low price of five dollars instead of the retail sixty.

Winning that auction felt amazing.

Almost as amazing as when I get a new client for my consignment business or if I score a big commission. And if there's one thing Mom and I have in common, it's our bargain-hunting skills, although she spends too much on bargains instead of important things like, oh, getting the air-conditioning fixed. At least it's cooler tonight and Mom is on a date with an ex-military barber instead of trying to gossip with us. Or worse, telling my friends about our mutual eBay love. They would think it's tacky, so I keep it to myself, not because I'm ashamed or that Torrance's occasional jabs about our small house embarrass me. Shame and embarrassment are signs of weakness and weakness will get me nowhere.

Neither will expressing any doubts over my boyfriend.

Torrance tries on my skirt and does a few more poses, but a small photo album sticking out of my faux Kate Spade bag captures her attention. She opens it without asking and turns to a picture of a nine-year-old girl in a softball uniform with my father's arm around her shoulder. "Sabrina, is this your stepsister, Angela? She's adorable. And wow, it's like she could pass for your father's *real* daughter."

The ball lands once again in my court and hits me right in the gut.

Hard.

I look out the window to the faded shed where Dad used to park his Chevy Suburban. Because he didn't see me last Friday and our next custody weekend is a week away, we made pre–Father's Day plans to hang out in Harpers Ferry having lunch and biking the C&O Canal. But when I arrived at his house in West Virginia early this morning, Dad was loading that Suburban with ball bags, folding chairs, and coolers.

"Honey, I'm so sorry, Angela has a makeup game today," he said, after giving me a warm hug. "Is it okay if we go? You and I will have plenty of time to talk, but I'd understand if you'd rather skip it."

Had it not been for the fact that it rained yesterday, I would have believed Angela planned it deliberately, judging from the victorious glare she shot me from the backseat in her bright red softball uniform. What I wanted to say was no, Dad, let's keep it just us, but that would have only made me sound like a total diva so I sucked it up and said, "Sure, no problem."

"That's my girl. It'll be fun."

Despite the fact that Angela's teammates chanted nonstop with these annoying, high-pitched shrieks and parents kept grumbling over bad calls, it was fun hanging out with him, just like it's fun hanging out with Torrance when she's not starting a pissing contest. Dad and I got to talk—really talk, about school, Blaine, and of course, my mother.

"I want you to know, Sabrina," Dad said from where we sat underneath a canopy that shook with every strong breeze, "how frustrated I was when your mother went against our custody agreement last weekend."

So was I, but something about his curt tone worried me. "Are you going to tell your lawyer?"

Dad waited for a nearby dad to stop cheering over his daughter's base hit and then leaned close, squeezing my hand. The familiar smell of Old Spice aftershave swept over me, making me yearn for the days when the scent lingered in our bathroom long after his morning shower. "Honey, your mom has . . . issues. She's still angry at me and doing that will only make it worse, so let's just be tolerant for now, okay?"

The canopy shook again. I swallowed hard and said, "Okay."

Maybe that was the best option. And it is decent how he's always patient with Mom. So why wasn't I relieved? But then

Angela trotted over in her cleats and grabbed a Gatorade from the cooler. "Hey, Dad, did you see me steal home?"

Oh, the little jerk.

She knows perfectly well how much I hate her calling him that and it didn't help when Dad, *my dad*, gave her a high five and said, "Good job, Ang, that catcher didn't even know what was going on."

Angela shot me another one of her preteen smirks before hustling back to the bench. Fine. Congratulations, home stealer.

Score one for you.

But unlike the catcher, I knew her game. Same with Belinda, my stepmother, who stopped working at the concession stand long enough to bring us both hot dogs even though I despise them. Still, I took a small bite of mine and tried not to gag when Belinda kissed my father hard on the lips. I hate seeing them kiss. For some reason, it makes him seem more like a man rather than my father.

Belinda sat in the empty chair beside him and pulled off her baseball cap, fluffing her high/low highlights that I suspect cover a boatload of gray hair. "Sabrina, I'm sorry you missed Angela's birthday party. We even had a small gift for you so you wouldn't feel left out," she said with enthusiasm, as though I should be grateful for my consolation present or for my "bedroom" in their basement that's nothing but a glorified dungeon. But I didn't realize last weekend was Angela's birthday. That would have been a *nightmare*, so okay, even though Mom was totally in the wrong for making me stay with her . . . it was a slight blessing in disguise.

Very slight.

Belinda pulled a small photo album from her bulging Vera Bradley bag and tossed it to me. "Want to see the pictures? The flowers were so gorgeous—your father picked them out. And hey, they're doubles, so you can keep them, Sabrina, in case you'd like some current pictures of your dad."

Keep them, was she kidding me? Her offer might sound innocent, but I knew what she was up to. The pictures of the three of them were a reminder that Dad is a member of *their* family now, not mine. And she was probably hoping I'd refuse them in front of him, making me the bad guy once again. So I squinted at a photo of them taken near a floral arrangement and said, "They are gorgeous, Belinda! My mother *adores* tiger lilies. They're her favorite, so I'll be sure to show her these."

She frowned as I casually tossed the album in my purse.

My mother does love tiger lilies, that part is true, but I will *never* show her these pictures. That would be too cruel, no matter how angry she makes me. However, seeing the realization that the flowers Dad had picked are my *mother's* favorite pass over Belinda's face made being forced to watch another softball game so, so worth it.

Score one for me.

Torrance, Bridget, and I are almost ready for the party when the front door crashes open and footsteps pound across the kitchen floor hard enough to make the windows rattle. Great. Mom's home early from her date with what's-his-name so my bedroom will be her first stop after seeing Torrance's BMW parked out front. Sure enough, Mom with her perpetual desire to be a teenager again bursts through the door seconds later.

"Sabrina, I'm in, sweetheart, I'm *in*!"

As Mom grabs my hands, I notice Torrance giving Bridget a *good thing she's not my mother* look. I try to pull away but Mom squeezes harder. "Jane Barton called and they need a replacement, so let's get cracking, young lady!"

What? Oh, no, I don't think so.

It was bad enough that Mom stopped by Barton's this morning despite me telling her how Chuck may not appreciate her soliciting his competition—true—and how it's been rumored that Jane Barton discriminates when hiring employees—which, okay, wasn't true.

It was also bad enough that Mom complained to me on my cell during Angela's entire sixth inning about how Jane hardly paid attention to her. But now Mom thinks we're going anywhere near Dee's home, let alone *working* for her? Oh, no. Absolutely no.

"Well, you should cancel, Mother, since she was so rude to you today. Besides, I have plans. We're going to Prescott's party."

Normally, any mention of Prescott, whose *single* father is the mayor of Riverside, would cause Mom to nonchalantly finger a lock of hair while asking how that nice Prescott boy is doing and wouldn't it be fun if we all got together? But she ignores me and makes a dive for my closet instead, rifling through my clothes as though the Royal Ball is in one hour and her fairy godmother is stuck in traffic. "Are you crazy, Sabrina, and miss an opportunity like this?" she says, looking at me over her shoulder with a sparkle in her eye. "Don't worry—after one night, Jane will love me, so cancel them plans, sweetie. And wear something western. They got a cute Wild West theme going on tonight. Ooo,

I'll wear my cowboy boots! And where's that new skirt you bought on—"

"Torrance is wearing it," I quickly say before she can let out my eBay secret. "And you *really* want me to miss Prescott's party? Prescott *Mannings*?"

Mom stops rifling, her expression fiery as she points at me with one of her Billy Joel nails that are painted black with white musical notes. "Sabrina, I want to make a good impression tonight, so you, young lady, will be there, am I clear?"

I know from experience that Storm Mona is about to blow, and how the humiliating damage in front of my friends would be far worse than any eBay confessions. So I concede by saying, "When are we leaving?"

Mom smiles, the danger gone. She gives me a Billy Joel thumbs-up. "Twenty minutes. And don't worry, sweetie, tonight's going to be such a hootenanny you won't miss any party! And stop calling me Mother!"

After she flounces out of the room, taking my brand-new Old Navy tank that won't survive her D cups, Torrance stares at me in disbelief. "Hootenanny? What's a hootenanny? And don't you *dare* tell me you're bailing on Prescott's. We're supposed to go *together*, remember, because Blaine has other plans and Danny is spending the night getting ready for his race tomorrow."

Like I have a choice. But the last thing I want is for them to go to the party and gossip about me, so it looks like I'll just have to play a trick of my own. "Well, girls, you might want to come with *me*, considering who else will be there."

"Who?" Torrance says, still sulking as she reaches for her Coach purse that, unlike my Kate Spade, is definitely not faux.

"Desperate Dee."

Torrance's eyes light up, enough to make her stop fishing for her keys. "Dee Barton? That's right, I totally forgot she lives at a trailer park. We could have fun with that, couldn't we?"

"Exactly. And—" Time to lay down my last card. "Her friend, Nose-Pick Natalie, might be there as well. So are you in?"

Torrance seems intrigued, her pretty face scrunched up in concentration over the possibilities. But then she says, "No, we'll stick with Prescott's. Bridget and I will be thinking of you, though."

By the time Mom settles on an outfit and redoes her makeup, we are fifteen minutes late. She climbs into the Trooper and backs out of the driveway. "By the way, Sabrina, I forgot to tell you. Blaine called while you were loading the equipment."

I pat my shorts pockets. Empty. Seriously, I *have* to stop leaving my cell within her reach! "He did? What did he say?"

Mom hands me my phone and then throws the Trooper in drive before cranking up her favorite Tanya Tucker song. "Oh, he wanted to know what you were doing."

Panic shoots through me as she shimmies to the beat with the wind from the open window already starting to frizz her blown-out hair. "Mom, did you tell him where we were going?" I half shout.

Please say you didn't. I do *not* want Blaine to know we're working at Dee's in case he decides to stop by. But that's ridiculous. If I were a guy, I would never go to my ex-girlfriend's home with my new girlfriend.

Unless . . . I still had feelings for my ex.

"Darling, do you think I'm stupid?" Mom huffs out an exasperated sigh just as a bug slams against the windshield. "Of course I told him, in case he wanted to see me perform. And do you know what that sweet boy said? He said he wouldn't miss it for the world!"

My stomach drops.

She told him. How could she do that? Now I almost wish I hadn't hid Belinda's photo album before she could see it.

Almost.

The Superflirt Chronicles
. . . blogs from a teenage flirtologist

Saturday evening, June 19

WEEKEND FLIRT REPORT TAKE TWO
MOOD: Determined
MUSIC: "Shine," Laura Izibor

Well, well, well, things certainly have gotten rather interesting here at the campground.

Mercedes is here.

Yes, you read that correctly. Mercedes, the jerk who once made me feel bad about myself. Bad, guilty, insecure, ashamed, paranoid, and hopeless. The scum who took my heart, rolled it in dirt, and jammed it through a paper shredder now actually has the nerve to set foot on *my* turf.

But wait—it gets worse.

Mercedes is here with his evil *girlfriend*.

Yeah, I know.

So, if you will excuse me, I think I'm going to leave the store and run to my bedroom for a good long cry before burying myself in a canoe-sized tub of Cookies 'N Cream ice cream. No, Rocky Road. Yes, Rocky Road ice cream, and then *another* good cry.

Hmm.

Surely you don't believe that, now, do you?

Good. Because what I'm *really* going to do is give Mercedes his own Rocky Road by finding myself a cute but gullible dude to flirt with right in front of him and make that jerk perfectly aware of what he's missing because—sorry—Evil Girlfriend's legs will *never* be as good as mine. Or, better yet, I might fight off my gag reflex and flirt with Mercedes myself and *then* move on to my cute but gullible dude. After all, the song "Shine" does say, "Let the sun shine on your face."

My sun is *so* ready to shine.

Until then, please allow me to make the following public service announcement for all women out there who have either been through or who are currently in a bad relationship:

Ahem.

Relationships are supposed to make you feel good.

Relationships are NOT supposed to make you feel bad.

Or guilty, insecure, ashamed, paranoid, or hopeless.

Good.

So when a relationship makes you feel bad, guilty, insecure, ashamed, paranoid, or hopeless, end it. Get over him. Move on.

Flirt.

6 ∽ Sabrina

Excuse me, lady, can I sing this?"

Sweat trickles down my back as I heave a speaker onto its stand. A little girl in a saggy-bottomed yellow swimsuit holds out a song selection slip, but I hardly pay attention to her or any of the other campers who are clustered around the song books like vocal vultures.

I can't believe Blaine.

I can't believe he doesn't see *anything wrong* with his being here. When Mom and I drove in earlier, there he was, leaning against the fender of his Mercedes with his ankles crossed and his elbows on its hood as though we were meeting at the mall and not at his ex-girlfriend's.

"Hey, lady, can I sing this song, huh?"

The girl pulls at my shorts, pleading, with grape Kool-Aid stains around her lips. Ugh, it's going to be a long night. I snatch the slip from her and read it. "'Shake That' by Eminem? Did your mommy give you permission to sing this?"

"Uh-huh, honest."

The little liar. I crumple her request. "Oh, no, that song is for grownups."

"Sabrina, honey, that's not how we talk to our guests," Mom says, clicking over in her high-heeled cowboy boots, silver concho belt, and matching earrings that could double as drink coasters. She plugs in a speaker wire and gives the girl a toothy grin. "Sweetie, you can sing whatever your little heart desires!"

"Mom," I hiss before following her to the Trooper. "She can't sing that! It's not appropriate for someone her age."

"Don't be such a fuddy-duddy, Sabrina, it's just a song." Mom leans over to check her reflection in the side mirror, wiping cherry red lipstick from the corners of her mouth and smoothing her flat-ironed hair. "Oh, why did I straighten my hair tonight? I should have worn it curly. I always do better when I'm curly."

Come to think of it, she does do better when she's curly. But instead of mentioning this, I grab a speaker and motion to her low-cut shirt. "Yeah, and maybe you'll do better if you button up, too. We're not at Chuck's, remember?"

This place is different—more traditional, more like a campground instead of an outdoor nightclub, so Mom's cleavage may not go over as well. She sighs and fastens two buttons. "There, happy now? Lord, you *are* a fuddy-duddy, Sabrina."

Blaine pulls the last of the equipment from the Trooper and gives me an amused wink. "Yeah, Sabbie, don't be a fuddy-duddy."

I fight off the urge to smack him. It's one thing for him to show up here, but it is quite another to take my mother's side. You just don't *do* that. Mom, of course, loves it. She pinches his cheek and says, "Oh, you sweet boy! And what do you think, Blaine, is my hair okay straight? Or should I have done it curly?"

"You look wonderful either way, Ms. Mona."

"Aw, such a charmer, just like your father!" She waggles a Billy Joel at him and then nudges my arm. "Better hold on to this one, Sabrina. And be a dearie and get your momma a soda, will ya? Might help calm my nerves. Tonight's an important night and I'm as nervous as a pig at a livestock auction!"

She walks away before I can tell her that caffeine isn't exactly a good relaxer, but I've been fuddy-duddied enough. Instead, I go to the back of the Trooper and open the cooler. Blaine wraps his arms around my waist, his breath hot on my ear as he says, "You heard the woman. You better hold on to me."

I concentrate on pouring Mom's drink into the tumbler she always uses with a straw to keep her Crest White-Strip teeth from staining and say nothing, not trusting myself to speak. Blaine kisses my neck, causing electric shivers to run up my arm. "Hey, is that the only kind of soda your mom has, generic?"

Yes, it is, because we're on a budget and generic is just fine.

"Eh, no big deal, I'll get my own later." Blaine squeezes me. He must feel my body stiffen, though, from the way he asks, "Sabbie, are you mad at me?"

Don't start a fight, don't start a fight.

The last thing a girl should do when her boyfriend happens to show up at his ex-girlfriend's place is start a fight. But despite my best efforts, I can't help but blurt out, "No, I'm not mad, but it's real funny how once you found out we were working here, lo and behold, those plans with your father changed."

His arms become rigid. He steps back, the spot on my neck

where he kissed me turning cold as he gives me a wounded look. "Babe, I canceled my plans *before* your mom told me because I knew you wanted to spend time with me. But now I'm not so sure."

"Blaine, I never said that—" I stop myself from reassuring him that *of course* I want to be with him. Blaine is so good at this, turning my words around to make me feel like the guilty one. "Look. It's just . . . well, wouldn't you be upset if I wanted to spend the evening at an ex-boyfriend's?"

"No, I wouldn't." Blaine shoves his hands deep into his pockets. "But I trust you. So maybe I should leave if you're going to be like this all night."

Panic shoots up my spine as he takes a step away.

Why didn't I keep my mouth shut? For the past month, I've done nothing but push him away. "Blaine, no, don't. I'm sorry—I'm being way too sensitive."

He wraps his arms around me once more, the scent of his lemony Armani cologne almost as comforting as Dad's Old Spice. "Okay. Only if *you* promise to trust me."

For some reason, I think about how Mom struggled to quit smoking years ago. Sometimes she'd go for weeks without a cigarette, sometimes only an hour. But then she watched the movie *Dead Again* where Robin Williams played a psychologist who said, "Someone is either a smoker or a nonsmoker. There's no in-between. The trick is to find out which one you are, and be that." Mom kept rewinding and playing that line over and over until she decided: she was a nonsmoker. And she hasn't had a cigarette since. It's time for me to do the same. Either I'm going to trust Blaine once and for all and stop nagging him or I'm going to lose him.

I choose trust.

"Of course, sweetheart," I say, pressing my body against his and giving him a lingering kiss. "I'm glad you're here. You'll make it fun."

Blaine's lips tickle when he nuzzles my ear. "It'd be more fun if we got out of here early. Dad's out on a date so we could have the entire place to ourselves."

It's as though the heavens sent me a sign. I made the right decision. Blaine *does* want to be with me. I long to kiss him hard, but Mom calls me over to the pavilion. She thanks me for the soda and then gestures toward a grassy knoll overlooking the common area where two skinny twin brothers wearing fake sheriff's badges and belted toy guns are picking teams for kickball. "Sabrina, honey, you see that girl sitting by herself? Be a sweetie and take a song book over and introduce yourself. Poor thing must be bored."

I follow her gaze to a lone girl with short-cropped red hair and a hideous outfit straight out of a Tomboys 'R Us catalog. Haven't I seen her before? Oh, yeah, at the house being built beside Blaine's. She looked like a whiny pouter back then and she looks even more whiny now. "Uh, Mom, I don't think she's going to be interested in karaoke."

"Now, honey, you can't assume that." Mom places a song book in my hands. She spins me around to face the girl and gives me a nudge. "Go on, it's not nice to make people feel like outsiders."

Please, it's their *choice* to be outsiders. People like her are so annoying, the ones who mope from the sidelines rather than make an effort to fit in. I'm not from a wealthy family nor do

I have the right pedigree, but I'm among the most popular at school *and* I was Prom Queen. Things like that don't happen from luck. You have to work for it and, yes, sometimes put up with a little crap. But I guess it is decent of Mom to want her to be included, so I force myself to walk over.

"Hey, I'm Sabrina. Do you, like, want a song book?"

"Hey, *like*, I'm Roxanne and no, *like*, I don't."

Well, if she isn't quite the charmer.

Mom is still watching, though, so I say, "Fine, then, *Roxanne*, if you change your mind, you know what to do."

She lets out a condescending snort. "What, did your mommy send you over?"

Okay, maybe so.

But does she really think she's intimidating me? Not hardly. She's a minnow compared to the sharks I'm used to swimming with. Before I can tell her that yes, my mother was nice enough to want to include her—stupid, right?—a blur of blond catches my attention. It's Dee, walking past us to join an older woman by the main lodge. She looks different than she does at school. She looks like . . . like *summer*, in her pink shorts and white shirt that shows off her golden tan.

Roxanne's face darkens.

Well, well, perhaps I'm not the only one who doesn't have much love for Dee Barton. Part of me wants to get far, far away from this toxic tomboy, but a bigger part of me wants to find out as much information about Dee as possible.

Know thy enemy.

"So, I take it you know her?" I ask.

Stupid question. Dee lives here, so of course Roxanne knows

her. But she doesn't call me on it. Instead, she sneers at Dee and says, "Yeah, I know the Super Slut. I know all about her, now."

What? Super Slut, are we talking about the same person? Dee might have been a total stalker but I didn't think she slept around, or has even *dated* anyone since Blaine. Unless this girl knows something I don't.

Obviously, she does. The corners of her mouth turn up. "Oh, man. Let me guess. You're Mercedes's evil girlfriend."

Mercedes's evil girlfriend?

"Who are you talking about, Blaine, my Blaine?" I demand, anger swelling like hot lava in my stomach. "That's his name, *not* Mercedes, and how dare you call me evil? Or, wait . . . did *Dee* call me that?"

Roxanne catches the ball when a boy kicks it out of bounds and holds it against her chest instead of throwing it back. "Maybe she did, maybe she didn't, but hey, I do have some free advice for you *if* you want it."

One of the twins yells for the ball.

Roxanne ignores him.

Oh my gosh.

The last thing I want to do is humor this horrible person any more, but before I can stop myself, the words "Yeah? And what's that?" come tumbling out.

Roxanne tosses the ball in the air a few times before drop-kicking it over the twin's head. She nods toward the pavilion where Blaine is sitting beside my mother, nursing a soda with—what?—his eyes focused on Dee.

"My advice," she says while walking away, "is to watch your man."

Barton Family Campground Bulletin Board
CORRECTION FOR TONIGHT'S SCHEDULE:

Due to an unfortunate injury, DJ Drake will not be joining us, but he would appreciate your prayers and thoughts!

In his place will be Mona's Low-Key Karaoke. See you at 7:00!

7 ~ Dee

I've had bad dreams before, especially right after Dad died. The worst one was when I dreamed I was a steak—yes, a steak, a T-bone to be exact—sitting on a white plate with a bunch of campers hunched over me with knives and forks. Natalie said it came from feeling vulnerable without my dad, but as horrible as that dream was, it can't compare with the nightmare of having Sabrina, Blaine, *and* Madeline here at the same time.

"Well, there's what's-his-name, Brent? Blake? Booger?" Ivy says, even though she knows perfectly well what his name is.

"Blaine. Can you believe he had the nerve to show up?"

We both glance at him sitting at a picnic table beside Mona Owens, oblivious to the fact that he no longer belongs here. Ivy hollers at a kid for riding his bike on the sidewalk and then says, "Well, unfortunately, toots, there's no law keeping him from coming here. But I never did like that turd of a boy."

I almost choke on my own spit. "Ivy! You can't say that."

"Why, is there a rule that old people are supposed to like all kids?" Ivy asks, her purple tunic billowing in the breeze. She pushes a lock of gray hair behind her ears. "I do believe the Bible says *Thou shalt love thy neighbor,* but nothing about *liking* him."

I can't blame Ivy for feeling this way. While Blaine wasn't exactly rude to her, he wasn't polite either.

"And although I don't condone the way you're always chatting with different fellows," Ivy says, pausing long enough to take in my outfit and makeup, "it's better than being with him. He's not good enough for you, kid, so it wasn't necessary to get all gussied up."

"What? I'm not gussied."

Ivy raises her eyebrow. Okay, so I am a *little* gussied.

After we got back from dinner thirty minutes ago and I saw Blaine waiting for Sabrina by his Mercedes, my first reaction was to stay in my bedroom—all night long. Natalie, however, disagreed. When she saw me in bed with my face shoved in a pillow, she struck a determined pose that would have made Beyoncé proud and said, "Oh, no, we are *not* having this."

"I'm not going out there and you can't make me."

Natalie ignored me and opened my closet, pulling out my favorite yellow capri pants. She tossed them aside and said, "Nope, these won't do." Natalie then yanked out red shorts, only to throw them on the floor. "Too long." She pulled out a short, pleated skirt next. "No, too *trying-too-hard.*" When she found my pink shorts with a cute pink and green belt—my favorite colors—she nodded. "Yes, perfect. And please tell me your new white shirt is clean, the one that makes your arms look super muscular?"

"Natalie, what part of *I'm not going* don't you understand?"

She put her hands on her hips. "You mean the *I'm going to be a total wuss and hide* part? Is that it?"

"I'm not a wuss."

"Oh, yes you are, Dee." In one fluid motion, Natalie with her low tolerance for whiners leaped onto the bed and put her feet on both sides of my waist, jumping up and down until my head flopped against the pillow like a landed trout. *"Wussy, wussy, wussy,"* she sang.

"Cut it out, Nat!"

Natalie jumped even faster. "Aw, am I annoying you? Well, I can annoy you all night long, my friend, because this is *not* proper behavior for the mighty Superflirt."

Superflirt? I didn't feel super or flirty and definitely not mighty, but Natalie refused to let up. She kept jumping until my crab cake threatened to make a reappearance and the pile of papers I was hiding fell to the floor. "Dee, what are those?"

"Nothing."

Natalie hopped off the bed and snatched up the college brochures and a copy of Blaine's letter. "Really, Dee? Have you been agonizing over this letter *again*? And what's with the brochures? I thought you said you're going to Riverside Community just like I am until I transfer to Penn State."

Right, Natalie is transferring to Penn for her journalism degree, but dumb people like me? "Yeah, well, evidently that's all I'm capable of, according to Madeline."

Natalie shook her head. "You know what? I'm real sorry, but—" She tore the letter into small pieces, letting them fall to the floor.

"Natalie!"

She ignored me and tore up each brochure. "Girl, I love you, but you spend too much time worrying about what people who *don't* love you think. Like Madeline. Roxanne. Blaine. Sabrina. And you're up here hiding, which I don't understand, considering you see the last two at school all the time."

That was a good point. But I had an even better reply. "At school, I always felt horrible, like I couldn't be myself. I don't want to feel like that *here*, in the one place where I can truly be me."

Natalie dropped the brochure pieces and sat beside me. "Look. I want to be compassionate, Dee, I really do. But if you stay in this room, Sabrina will think you're nothing but a coward and a—"

"Wuss," I finished for her. Natalie was right. Why *should* I hide? No, I was going to show Sabrina that she didn't break me. I was going to make that jerk Blaine see that I'm just fine without him.

And now, from the way he's checking me out from the pavilion, I can tell I have accomplished that goal. *Thank you, Natalie, thank you, pink shorts.*

"Testing, testing, one—two—three, can y'all hear me?" Mona Owens taps the microphone with her ridiculously long nails.

"What do you know about her?" Ivy asks, eyeing Mona's outfit that is *way* too tight, but does match our theme. Have to give her credit for that.

"Not much, other than that she works at Chuck's on Friday nights." Oh, and her daughter hates me. Can't forget that part, especially with Sabrina glaring at me. What *is* her problem? Blaine dumped *me* and then gave me that oh so sweet birthday present by starting to date her. She *won*, although he's hardly a prize, so if anything, *I* have the right to be angry.

Ivy scratches her forehead. "Chuck Lambert? Hmm, working for that walking hormone isn't a credible reference. Want to split some Skittles? I have the feeling we're going to need some comfort junk food."

Ivy leaves before waiting for my answer because—duh—of course I want Skittles. Victoria Swain passes her on the lodge porch wearing a prim black sheath dress instead of the standard campground uniform of shorts, tank tops, and flip-flops. Okay, why, exactly, is Mrs. Swain camping here if she has no intentions of, well, *camping*? I've never seen her enjoy the pool or any activities, and Dr. Swain's only form of socializing is stopping by the lodge for the Wi-Fi code Mom changes twice a week.

Mrs. Swain sees me and waves, tiptoeing gingerly toward me so her heels won't sink in the grass. "Hello, Dee! My, you look very attractive tonight. Special occasion?"

Oh, man, maybe I am too gussied.

Mrs. Swain fingers the sleeve of my shirt with a wistful sigh. "I *wish* Roxanne would dress like this instead of wearing those horrible clothes she gets at Goodwill—Lord knows who's worn them before her. I keep asking her to go to the mall with me so we can begin collecting her summer wardrobe, but she always says no."

Yeah, shocker. Can't say I blame her, though.

Mrs. Swain looks at her diamond-trimmed watch. "Drat,

I'm late for our hospital charity event. But thank you, Dee, for showing Roxanne the ropes today."

"Sure, no problem. And hey . . . can I get you an activities schedule? We have tons of fun things to do here that you might enjoy. Like karaoke, maybe?"

This is a shot in the dark, seeing as how Mrs. Swain doesn't seem to be the karaoke type. But to my surprise, she sadly gazes at the pavilion where Mona is fussing with speaker wires. "Well, no, Martin doesn't sing. Besides, he's at the hospital every day, so I'm stuck with all the work for our new house, and Roxanne isn't very interested in spending time with—" She falters as though she's said too much, and then digs out car keys from her beaded handbag. "But thank you, Dee. It does look like fun."

Okay, another shocker.

Mrs. Swain walks away before I can reply and is halfway to her Lexus by the time Ivy returns with the Skittles. Ivy nods her head toward the pavilion, where Mona is standing center stage again. "Well, looks like it's showtime."

Mona takes the mike off the stand.

Good Lord, are her shirt's top two buttons now undone? Yes, they are. She struts to the front of the crowd, her arms spread wide as she shouts, "Can y'all hear me?"

Oh my gosh. Did Ivy mean showtime . . . or showgirl?

A feeling of dread washes over me. Men gawk. Two little boys stop arguing over a cherry Coke long enough to stare at her mile-long cleavage. The Cutson brothers' father, Frank, holds up a Budweiser and hollers out, "We hear ya!"

"All right then, handsome!" Mona gives Frank a wink, despite the fact that his very tough—like, motorcycle-tough—wife,

Tamara, is sitting beside him. Mona poses like Marilyn Monroe welcoming the troops and says, "Welcome to Mona's Low-Key Karaoke! I'm Mona and this lovely girl is my daughter, Sabrina, who's going to help me get the show rolling by playing some Shania. Hit it, Sabrina!"

Sabrina flashes her mother a look of embarrassment. Huh. I didn't think it was possible for the Ice Queen to feel embarrassed, but there's no time to analyze, not when the opening chords of Shania Twain's "Any Man of Mine" begin and Mona starts shaking her hips to the beat. She sashays over to Frank, making him spill beer on his boots when she lifts his chin with her finger and sings, "Any man of mine better be proud of me."

Oh. My. Gosh.

Mona turns to another male camper and sexily gestures to her profile. "Even when I'm ugly, he's still gotta love me."

Frank yells out, "I'll still love you," causing Tamara, with sparks coming out of her eyes, to swat the back of his head. She isn't the only one annoyed. One mother hauls her young son away before Mona reaches the chorus, and another woman scolds her husband when he starts to clap along.

"Jane is not going to be happy," Ivy says.

Not going to be happy is a severe understatement. But a more terrifying thought hits me. "Where's Madeline? She *cannot* see this!"

"Too late." Ivy points to the tennis court. Madeline is glaring at Mona with sheer disgust. Ivy shakes her head. "Go get your mom, Dee. Tamara is about to blow and we do *not* want that woman angry."

One look at Tamara's muscular crossed arms has me running to the store. But only Natalie is there, sitting behind the counter painting her toenails. I flick her big toe and say, "Nat, emergency, Mona Owens is about to strip. Where's Mom?"

Natalie jerks her feet down. "Stripping? I need to see this for myself. Watch the register, okay?" She hops off the stool, walking with her toes lifted to keep from smudging her pedicure. "Oh, and your mom is out back, talking on the phone to some guy."

All thoughts, concerns, and worries about Mona instantly disappear.

"A guy? What guy?"

Natalie opens the door and says, "I don't know. He didn't give his name."

She hobbles out before I can press for details. Maybe it was a business call. Mom did say she was going to check in with Drake to see how he's doing. But when I peer out the back window and see her seated on the rear porch steps, throwing her head back with a silky laugh and combing her fingers through her hair, I know: Mom is flirting.

Mom's *flirting.*

But with who?

I lean against the wall before she can see me, a painful throb swelling in my chest. Mom, dating? No, I can't imagine it, even though I know perfectly well how my father would respond. He'd want her to be happy. He'd want her to move on. *That's* how I should feel instead of hiding like a spoiled brat, but I just can't handle another curveball thrown at what is left of our family. And what if she gets hurt, like Blaine hurt me?

What if she can't recover this time?

❧

For the next hour, Natalie texts me what's going on outside. After Mona finishes her song and Ivy calms Tamara, all of the karaoke calamities are over until a little girl starts to belt out an Eminem song that's more Playboy than PG. The store is slow, so I'm considering closing early when the bell above the door jingles.

"Hey, what's up, Dee-Dee?"

Blaine. I hate that stupid nickname he gave me.

And I hate the way he casually strolls in, just like last summer when he'd stop by with sun-kissed cheeks and tousled hair after a day of golf. And I especially hate the way he inspects the store and says, "Huh, nothing's changed in here, has it?"

His nonchalant comment makes the blood pound at my temples. It's one thing to break up with me—fine, whatever, I got over it—just don't patronize me by being cordial. But when Blaine motions to the freezer and asks, "You still got ice cream sandwiches hidden in there?" I only shake my head and say, "No, Skinny Cow Fudge Bars. They're low-fat."

Okay, why, exactly, did I feel the need to say that?

Blaine gives me an appraising look, one that goes from the tips of my ears to my toes and back. "Well, the low-fat is working, Dee-Dee."

Of course he would say this. Heaven forbid I should have any extra pounds on me. I think of all the times he'd order Big Macs for himself and salads for me. And why is Blaine trying to have a conversation, anyway? I say nothing as he taps the counter a few times and then strolls to the cooler for a Coke and a Diet Coke. *Is the diet for Sabrina? Does he always buy it for her whether she wants it or not, like he always bought it for me?*

Hold on. Why do I care?

Thankfully, the door opens again and Jake walks in, fresh from the bathhouse with his sandy blond hair hanging in damp curls. His pace slows when he sees who is with me, but he still politely says, "Hey, how's it going, Blaine?"

Blaine doesn't respond. He only gives Jake an amused smirk and pulls his wallet from his pocket. I pound the price of the sodas into the register, remembering how Blaine would blow off guys at school who came from blue-collar families, like Jake. How *dare* he? Jake might be a jerk sometimes, but he's the campground's jerk. *My* jerk.

An idea comes to my mind. A Superflirt idea.

I wink at Jake before dropping Blaine's change in his hand. Most of it falls to the counter, but I pretend not to notice and give Jake my very best hair toss instead. "Hey, sweetheart, I was missing you!"

Please catch on, Jake, please catch on!

He catches on. Oh, boy, does he catch on. A grin sweeps across his face. He rests an elbow on the counter and uses his other hand to graze my forearm. "Well, hello there, Babykins. I was missing you, too."

Babykins? Okay, roll with it. "No, I missed you, Pumpkin Breath."

"No! I missed *you*, Fuzzy Peach Bottoms."

Blaine's face darkens as we banter back and forth, our terms of endearment becoming more and more ridiculous. He angrily pockets his change and grabs the sodas. "Well, guess I'll see you later."

Jake turns as though distracted. "Huh? You say something, dude?"

I rip my adoring gaze away long enough to say, "What? Oh. Later, Blaine!"

After he stalks out, slamming the door hard enough to rattle the deer antlers on the wall, we burst out laughing. "Fuzzy Peach Bottoms, are you serious, Jake?"

"Pumpkin Breath? Oh, yeah, that's a surefire way to win over the fellows," Jake says before grabbing a Snickers from the candy display. He throws a dollar on the counter. "Man, he's such a loser. What did you ever see in him, anyway, Dee?"

I'm not sure.

No, that isn't true. I know *exactly* what I saw in Blaine, and for some reason, I want Jake to know as well. "At first, he reminded me of my father because he was so charming and charismatic," I say, turning to the photograph of Dad on the file cabinet. "You would have loved my father, Jake. Everyone did. If your engine blew up the day before a race, he'd be in the garage with you all night long until it was fixed, you know? So when Blaine asked me out after he died, I guess I . . . You know. And now—"

My throat tightens. *Don't cry, don't cry.* I pick up Jake's dollar instead, absentmindedly folding it into a small square. Jake leans closer, the softness in his voice startling me. "And now you're still not over him, right?"

Is that what he thinks, that I miss Blaine?

"No, not right. He's *nothing* like my father. Blaine always made me feel like I wasn't good enough, so I am over him. But even though I know better—really know better—seeing him makes me feel horrible all over again."

"That's bull, you're plenty good enough, Dee," Jake says, opening his candy bar and breaking off a piece for me. "Great, even, and you know what? We should go out there, dance up a storm, and show Blaine exactly how great you are."

"Yeah, right. You don't dance."

"What? There's a lot of things you don't know about me, Dee."

Apparently there are. And the biggest one is that he thinks I'm great.

8 ~ Dee

Never in a million years did I ever think that Jake Bollinger could dance. Fix a leaky faucet? Sure thing. Pop a tent for a novice camper? Piece of cake. Change a tire? One minute, tops. But move so good that I forget why we were out there to begin with—to make Blaine jealous? I didn't see that coming.

It had started innocently enough: us, walking to the pavilion with my arm linked debutante-style onto his. The next karaoke crusader had just taken the mike, a skinny pale man named Leroy who has a balding head and a love for plaid Bermuda shorts. I feared Leroy would sing some whiny country song, but to my surprise, he started to belt out "Burning Love" with a rich, powerful baritone that would have made Elvis proud.

You go, Leroy.

I pretended to protest with a teasing pout when Jake tried to pull me onto the dance floor. But then I kicked off my flip-flops and joined him, giggling as he spun me in a circle, which, okay, might have been overdoing it, but remember—I was on a mission.

That mission, however, was soon forgotten. Jake played it

cool and reserved at first, but after some coaxing from me, he started to move.

Oh my gosh. Jake Bollinger can dance.

Jake Bollinger can *dance*!

And now, I can hardly focus on my own steps. Good Lord, he's like the guys on those dance shows that Mom and I love to watch. Even Leroy misses a verse when Jake suddenly jumps in the air, landing on his hands and then rolling down on his chest and stomach.

Oh my gosh!

I don't know whether or not Blaine notices us, and quite frankly, I don't care. But as the song ends and Jake draws me close, tipping me back into a deep, sultry dip, my gaze falls on Blaine. A dark fury shadows his face as he gulps down the last of his soda and tosses his empty bottle at a nearby trash can, missing it by a few feet. But his reaction is nothing compared to Sabrina's. Her fists are clenched, as though she's ready to kill both Blaine *and* me.

And she's not the only one.

Glaring at me from the lodge porch is Roxanne.

"Where did you learn to dance?" I ask Jake a few moments later, as we sit near the common area where some sweaty kids are arguing over who won their kickball game.

He yells at one of the Cutsons—Lyle, I think—for throwing grass and then says, "The VFW. When I was younger, my mom used to take me to country line dance lessons so she wouldn't be alone when Dad had to work nights." Jake strikes a debonair pose. "Why do you ask, did I impress you?"

"Well, maybe just a little."

He lightly punches me. "Oh, come on, Dee, admit it. You were wrong when you said I don't dance, weren't you?"

"Okay, fine. You were right. You're an excellent dancer," I admit.

Jake puts a hand behind his ear. "Pardon? Did you say *I* was right?"

I punch him back. "Yeah, and you'll *never* hear me say that again."

At the pavilion, the older campers clap with nostalgic appreciation when Natalie starts to sing a Patsy Cline song. Man, she's got such a beautiful voice. Even the cute guy who's delivering pizza to Mona stops counting out change long enough to check her out, but Natalie only blushes and turns away. *Nat, Nat, Nat, what am I going to do with you?*

And she calls me wussy.

I'm trying to think of a few ways to get my girl to stop being so flirt phobic when Jake leans back on his elbows and stretches out his long, muscular legs.

"What?" Jake asks when he notices me gazing at his thighs.

Oh, shoot. I jerk my head back up. "Nothing. I was just wondering. How's your go-kart thingy, are you all set for tomorrow's race?"

Saying the word "thingy" reminds me of how Jake invited Roxanne to his garage, but his dance moves have redeemed him. Jake laughs and throws a handful of grass at me. "First of all, please do not refer to my kart in such a girlie manner. And no, I'm not ready, so I'm going to bail instead. Maybe hang out here or something. You got any plans?"

"Hey, didn't you just yell at Lyle for throwing grass?" I'm

just about to retaliate with a handful of my own when I realize something. "Oh, man, Jake, you're not ready because of all the yardwork you did for us today. I'm sorry, I never should have—"

Jake shakes his head. "No, it's not that. My tires are shot and I need another paycheck before I can buy a new set, so it'd be a waste of race fees if I went. Last weekend, I almost lost my heat because of poor traction at the corners." He brushes off the sympathetic look I give him and says, "It happens. Racing is not a poor man's sport."

I lean back beside him and nudge his elbow. "Hey, you won your heat, right? And didn't you tell me that you placed second in the race against Danny, who can afford the best with his daddy's deep pockets? That means you're *twice* the driver he is, and I'm not just saying that because Danny's an even bigger jerk than Rex."

Jake shrugs. "Yeah, I guess. But Danny isn't all that bad. You've just got to get to know him."

Uh, hello? I know Danny. He's dating Torrance Jones, a bona fide mean girl straight out of the movies, and he's the third member of the trio with Blaine and Prescott. But instead of bringing this up, I only say, "Well, you're still a better driver than him."

We lock eyes.

My heart jumps.

My heart jumps? What's wrong with me? This is Jake for heaven's sake, who, okay, is being a total sweetie tonight. And sometimes we do have nice conversations without any bickering. Like when we sat on the fishing pier one night talking about his parents' layoffs and how it made him even more determined to get a drafting and design degree from ITT Tech so he can one day take care of them. But Jake is also the guy who makes me feel like a total moron sometimes.

And I have zero interest in any kind of relationship.

No thanks, I've already been down that road with Blaine. That long, miserable, painful road where in the beginning everything is sunshine and butterflies, but by the final turn, I'm a paranoid wreck and the author of *Dear Blaine, please say we're not breaking up. Why, Blaine? What did I do wrong, or is it what I haven't done? I told you I wasn't ready, but I'll do anything to get you back. Anything.*

Never again will I be that stupid.

It's safer to just flirt.

And NOT with campground employees.

So when I see Mom hustling back and forth from the woodpile with sweat beading at her temples, I use it as an excuse to bolt, reaching her just as she drops the firewood into the pit. She pushes back her bangs, leaving black smudges by her hairline.

"Mom, let me help you."

She dusts off her hands and then leans over to wipe her face with the bottom of her faded Rolling Stones T-shirt. "No, I'm fine, sweetie, there's no sense in both of us getting dirty."

Uh-oh. Something's wrong, I can tell.

"No, you're not fine. What's wrong, did Madeline say something?"

Mom slumps down on one of the four log benches circling the pit and kicks at a stone with her hiking boot. "Oh, let's see. According to her, I'm a horrible businesswoman for hiring Mona—which, okay, was a huge mistake. And then she grilled me about your dancing with Jake, so I told her he was your boy-friend to get her off my case."

"What? Why did you do that, Mom?"

"Because I'm stressed out, so forgive a few white lies, okay?" she says, biting down on a fingernail and then cringing when she remembers how dirty they are.

I don't see what business it is of Madeline's who I dance with, nor do I believe her lame excuse about wanting to visit us to get away from the Florida heat. I mean, come on, after all the years she's lived there, she can't take the heat when it isn't even July yet? But now is not the time to argue. Now is the time to make Mom smile. "Hey, I have a great idea. How about you start the fire, I'll take care of the snacks, and we'll tell the kids scary ghost stories, okay? One of them will be about an evil ex-mother-in-law who angered the wrong campers and was burnt to a crisp in a bonfire."

"Dee Barton! That's so inappropriate, young lady."

But I do see traces of a grin.

Inside the store, I fill the large percolator-style coffee urn with water and then put boxes of hot chocolate, graham crack-ers, Hershey bars, and marshmallows onto a rolling cart. As I pull the paper cups from the storage closet, the back door opens.

"It's going to be a while before the water's hot, Mom," I say, slapping a pack of hot chocolate against my thigh and tearing it open. "And hey, have you ever wondered what the difference is between hot chocolate and hot cocoa?"

Instead of Mom's voice, a deep male one answers. "I don't know. I've never really thought about it."

Blaine. He walks toward me past the display of beaded necklaces.

I drop the drink envelope, dusting my feet with a light brown powder. Blaine picks up the wrapper and tosses it into the trash. "You okay?" he asks.

"Yes, of course, why wouldn't I be?" I straighten the cracker boxes even though they were already perfectly aligned. "What are you doing here?"

"Just visiting." Blaine leans against the countertop, propping his elbow on the polished wood before motioning to my cart. "Still doing the Saturday night special: double servings of hot chocolate and s'mores for two dollars?"

"Three," I snap. "Things have changed."

I've changed. I am no longer interested in casual visits with Blaine, so I push the cart toward the door and say, "Now, if you will excuse me—"

"What's your deal with Jake Bollinger?" he asks abruptly.

I almost crash the cart. How dare he ask me about Jake? How dare he ask *anything*, after what I went through? Our breakup. Sabrina passing out my letter like it was free candy. Guys mocking me. Girls from the softball team who I thought were my friends saying stuff like "Seriously, who would be stupid enough to put that in *writing*?" I should leave. Right now. But a part of me wants so badly to take advantage of this moment.

I deserve it.

And getting a little revenge on Sabrina would be a bonus. So I do what I do best.

Flirt.

I coyly let my hair fall forward, exposing a bare neck that

Blaine used to love to kiss. My posture changes from employee to enchantress as I lean against the counter and say, "Why are you asking about Jake, hmm?"

Blaine studies the small mole on my collarbone. "No reason. Are you, like, dating him or something?"

"Maybe. Maybe not." I reach out to smooth an imaginary wrinkle on his designer shirt, letting my fingernails graze his chest. With my voice dropped to a near whisper, I say, "You're not jealous, are you?" while looking at him dead in the eyes.

One . . . two . . . three.

I expect Blaine to deny it. I expect him to say something snide about Jake being a grease monkey before he goes on his merry way back to Sabrina-ville. But instead, he leans closer. "Yeah, maybe I am. I—I miss you, Dee."

Gotcha?

Oh my gosh. I swallow hard, trying to digest this knowledge as he reaches for my hand. "I mean it, Dee-Dee. I miss you."

For one brief moment, I feel that familiar pull, that weakness in my knees that came whenever he was close. But this is Blaine—conceited, egotistical Blaine, the one who could weave a tapestry with his words. I pull away and turn. "Well, I don't miss you."

"Dee, wait. I'm sorry. I shouldn't have said that." Blaine holds my hand again, this time more gingerly, sending chills up my spine. "It's just that seeing you tonight—I've never seen you so confident, so . . . *different.*"

How many times after our breakup have I prayed for this? And here he is, standing in front of me, and the more his brown eyes drive into mine, the more I remember how it felt to have strong arms wrapped around me and the security it brought. I want that security, that feeling of safety, the same one I used to get from my father. I miss it so much.

So damn much.

Blaine misreads my hesitation and steps forward. "Man, you're so hot tonight."

Hot? Did he say hot?

I'm such a fool. Such a stupid fool. Blaine doesn't miss me. He never did. I just look good to him right now, like an old sweater thrown in the back of a closet might look if it gets cold enough. Only now, my old sweater days are long gone.

"Leave me alone, Blaine. Go back to Sabrina. You two deserve each other."

I back away from the cart and run outside, trying to catch my breath. I don't want to be there when he comes out, so I bolt past Roxanne, of all people, who is sitting on the porch swing, and take the steps two at a time to the recreation room. The second floor is thankfully empty, so no one can see me slump against the wall, my heart pounding.

One minute later, the door creaks open.

"Why are you following me?"

Blaine shuts the door behind him. "Hey, forgive me but I thought we made a connection downstairs, Dee. I thought maybe we could talk."

"No, I told you to leave me alone, remember? But okay, you want to talk? Fine. Then tell me how Sabrina got my letter."

My question knocks him off guard. "W-what?"

I step closer. "Don't play stupid, Blaine. I wrote you that letter because I was hurt and confused and you never even bothered to respond to it. Instead, you got yourself a new girl-friend who made it her duty to show it to everyone else."

Stupid tears start to brim in my eyes. I blink them away, refusing to cry. Blaine studies his feet as though they can help him come up with a good answer before saying, "Dee, I never showed it to Sabrina. She found it when she went through my things, and after it got out, I was sick to my stomach."

Yeah, so sick that he kept dating her.

"And I'm sorry things ended the way they did, Dee. You just needed me too much, maybe because of your father—"

"It had nothing to do with my father!"

"Let me finish!" Blaine puts both hands on my shoulders. "I'm just trying to say that I should have been more understand-ing. I should have realized you were being so clingy because you lost your dad."

Outside, I think I hear light footsteps coming up the stairs, but I can only focus on the pounding in my skull. Clingy? Was that how he saw me? Or did Blaine do it again—flip the situation around so *I* feel guilty, like *I* am the one who should be apolo-gizing? But before I can brush away his hands, the door swings open.

"WHAT THE HELL IS GOING ON?"

I jump back.

It's Sabrina.

Standing in the doorway like a bull about to charge.

"Answer me! What's going on?" She angrily strides toward us, her face bloodred and fists clenched. I stand speechless as Blaine gently takes her by the forearms and pins them to his chest.

"Sabbie, relax, babe! Dee and I were just talking. I swear!"

For once, he is telling the truth, but Sabrina wrenches her arms away. "Don't Sabbie me, Blaine. And you—" Sabrina points at me, venom spilling from her lips. "Who do you think you are, playing your games, huh? I know your story. Someone already told me, just like they told me you were up here with *my* boyfriend."

"What? Who? It's not true, I never—"

Time slips into astonishing slow motion as she lunges for me. I avoid her by stepping back, and then brace myself for her next attack.

But instead, Sabrina stops.

She turns to Blaine.

"How could you?" she whispers, before running for the door.

He rakes his fingers through his hair, not bothering to go after her until we hear a shriek and the sound of someone falling. I run out to the deck and down the steps, kneeling beside Sabrina where she lies at the bottom.

"Are you okay? Are you hurt?"

"Get your hands off me!" Sabrina hisses, clutching her left wrist. She stands, leaning against the railing for support. "I'm fine—I only tripped, so stay away from me, Dee, I swear, you better stay away from me *and* him."

Blaine pushes me aside and grabs Sabrina by the elbow, leading her toward his Mercedes and giving me one last glance as she stumbles before getting into the passenger seat. I stand speechless, still watching the road after his taillights disappear, only to discover someone else is watching me.

Jake.

9 ∼ Sabrina

Well, I made it home okay, no thanks to you," Mom says as she storms into our house at eleven and slams the door. She tosses her purse on the end table and slumps onto the leather recliner, kicking off her boots and letting them fall to the carpet. Her mascara is smeared to a hazy gray and her once perfectly straightened hair is now a frizzed blond cloud. She was right. She should have worn it curly. And she should *never* have opened her big fat mouth and told Blaine where we were going to be tonight.

If she hadn't, none of this would have happened.

"I thought it was agreed that you were going to work tonight, Sabrina. But who had to pack up everything by herself? Me. And who ended up dropping a very expensive speaker on the ground? *Me*, so a little help would have been nice."

Yeah, well, you're the least of my problems tonight.

I rub my sore wrist and bury myself deeper into the sofa cushions. Starting an argument would be a bad idea, so I mumble, "Sorry, I was having a bad night."

"You think you were having a bad night?" Mom fumes. "The nerve of that Jane Barton, telling me she wants someone more neutral to work at her campground, the *nerve!* Well, if she wants 'neutral,' she should take a peek in the mirror. I've never seen a woman with a more dire need of highlights in my entire life!"

She flops her head back and whimpers, glancing at me from the corner of her eye as though she's waiting for me to ask what happened. I pretend to watch a home design show until her next whimper tapers off with a few sniffs. Fine. Might as well get it over with. "Gee, Mother, what happened? Do tell me all about it, please!"

And don't you worry about me, okay?

"About time that you asked." She kicks her feet down and leans forward with her elbows on her knees. "Well, after my last song, I went to Jane and said—all polite-like—how it was a pleasure to work for her. And then she's like, 'Oh, that's nice,' and gives me a check without a 'thank you, you did great,' *nothing!*"

Why am I not surprised?

Mom pats her messy hair. "So then I told her I was available while DJ Drake recovers, bless his heart. Of course there would be a small price increase—a girl can't work for nothing, you know—but guess what she told me?"

I'm in no mood for guessing games. All I can think about is Blaine telling me on the car ride home how it was Dee who lured him upstairs because she wanted to talk. How he shouldn't have been so stupid, but he felt he owed it to her to hear what she had to say. At the time, I was too furious to listen. But now . . .

Maybe I should have believed him. Maybe I shouldn't have

slammed his car door and told him that I never wanted to see him again.

What if he was telling the truth?

"Are you listening?" Mom pouts, hitting her palm on the coffee table and causing a pile of Harlequin romances to fall to the floor. "How dare that Jane woman fire me! You were there, Sabrina, her campers loved my show!"

Right. The male ones did, but certainly not the women, although I suspect it was a combination of her nerves and caffeine that turned her usual flamboyance up about twenty notches.

"But no, she told me I made some campers uncomfortable, can you believe it? That woman fired me because a few cows were jealous." Mom leans back again, as though her outburst exhausted her. "Well, you just wait, honey. Your momma is going to be the most popular karaoke queen in all of Riverside and then I'll get my revenge. She'll beg me to work for her and *I'll* be the one who turns *her* down."

Mom sniffs, waiting for me to respond. When I don't, she asks, "What's wrong with you, anyway? Why are you so grumpy?"

I give her an annoyed look. "My wrist hurts, okay?"

"What happened?" She leans forward to study my face. "And how did you get that bruise?"

I know better than to tell her the whole story about Dee and Blaine together. She'd only confirm my fears by saying I overreacted. Again. So I just tell her about falling down the Bartons' steps and leave out the part about stumbling at Blaine's car and hitting my forehead. Mom clucks her tongue and nods. For a second, I think she's going to comfort me, but she only says, "Well, it's a small bruise, but you don't want that handsome Blaine to see you like that. Don't you worry your pretty little head, though, your momma's here."

She disappears down the hallway and then returns shaking a concealer bottle. "This here is my miracle cream, baby, it covers everything you want to hide." She dabs some on my forehead and blends it with a makeup sponge before holding a small mirror to my face. "Perfect! You can't see a thing."

She's right, the bruise is gone, but I can feel it, just like I can feel the ache in my heart from seeing Blaine with his hands on Dee's shoulders. And what else would they have done if Roxanne hadn't told me where they were?

Late the next morning, my wrist feels like someone slammed a door on it. I roll over in bed and stare at the photos on my dresser. One is from prom, with Blaine and me posing with our newly won crowns. Another is of Dad and me before the divorce, standing by the Christmas tree. I touch the diamond stud earrings he gave me that year, wondering what he's doing right now. Is he watching CNN and eating bagels, his usual Sunday morning routine? Is Angela sitting beside him on the sofa, reading magazines like I used to when he lived with us? Those are the moments I miss the most—those random, casual moments we used to have without Belinda or Angela around, making me feel like an outsider in their home. Those times were when he truly felt like my father.

My cell phone buzzes. I hope it's Blaine, texting to apologize, to say it was a huge misunderstanding and please, forgive him. But it's only Mom, asking if I'm awake. I ignore it and throw the covers over my head.

I must have fallen back asleep, because the sun is shining full force when Mom walks in later with her face covered with a blue purifying mask. "Sabrina, are you finally up? I brought you some breakfast, sugar."

Mom, bringing me breakfast? There has to be some ulterior motive.

"What do you want now, Mother?"

"Oh, hush, baby," she says in a comforting tone. She sets a tray on my nightstand and pulls a baby wipe from her robe pocket, using it to clean away the heavy concealer I didn't bother to wash off before going to bed. "There, that's better. Let's show off that bruise. And how's your wrist, sweetie, does it still hurt?"

Wow, this is a switch from last night when she couldn't have cared less. I shrug as she hands me a mug of coffee. "Yeah, a little."

Mom pats my thigh. "Good, we'll take a little trip to the hospital, then. But first," she says with her lips freakishly frozen now that her mask is drying, "where's your camera?"

"It's in my purse, why?"

"Just trust your momma, okay? Have I ever steered you wrong?" she asks, yanking my covers back. When she sees my face, Mom lets out an exasperated breath. "Well, maybe a few times. Just get it, okay?"

Fine. I trudge to our kitchen, which is decorated like a '50s diner with black-and-white-checked tiles and bloodred walls. My purse is on a table by the window, where Mom's old computer is moaning. She must have been performing her usual Sunday morning routine of drinking coffee while reading blogs and forums full of angry, jilted women, since she doesn't have many friends or family members to talk to.

Something about the word "blog" strikes a nerve.

A big, fat, tender nerve.

Bridget. Bridget was reading a blog yesterday. What was it called? The Superflirt Chronicles, where the writer talked about an unwanted visitor at . . . at a *campground*. And Roxanne. She called Dee "Super Slut" before warning me to *watch my man.*

I grab the mouse, cursing Mom's ancient RAM as the computer slowly comes to life. My anxious fingers keep making clumsy typos while I try to Google the site, until finally, the Pepto-Bismol pink blog fills the screen. I sit, slamming my knee into a table leg, but the pain is soon forgotten.

An icy chill goes down my spine as I read the latest entry.

It's about getting revenge on a Mercedes.

My Mercedes.

This is *Dee's* blog. She's writing about Blaine. About me—I am Mercedes's evil girlfriend, just like Roxanne called me, so she must know about the blog, too, and—oh God, last night was nothing but a cruel joke planned out by Dee. Blaine *was* telling me the truth, Dee *was* the one who lured him upstairs, and I didn't believe him.

I can't think. Can't speak. But I do know one thing:

Dee Barton is a dead girl.

Sunday, June 20

OH, WHAT A GLORIOUS MORNING!
MOOD: Validated
MUSIC: "So What," Pink

You know what they say: *LIVING WELL IS THE BEST REVENGE!*
THE DUDE: Mercedes
THE GRADE: A+
THE BREAKDOWN: Surely you don't think the A+ is for Mercedes, do you? No, darlings, it's for me, for proving to my ex that I am, indeed, living well without him, thanks to the efforts of a certain race car driver who came in handy on the dance floor. And the best part of the evening? Getting Mercedes away from his evil girlfriend and hearing him admit how much he misses me.

Well, guess what, Mercedes?

I don't miss you.

As for the evil girlfriend, I do feel partly responsible for an unfortunate mishap on her behalf. But, dear readers, would you feel horrified if I confessed to feeling a tingle of delight over her finally getting what she deserves?

Barton Family Campground Bulletin Board
NONDENOMINATIONAL
CHURCH SERVICE

Pastor Mike's sermon from the book of Romans will be
starting today at nine o'clock at the main pavilion. Come as
you are! Free doughnuts and coffee will be available, but if
you'd like to make a small donation toward a local women's
shelter, that would be wonderful. See you there!

IO ~ Dee

Church is different at a campground.

There's no singing, no pulpit, no pews, just Pastor Mike speaking gently from where he sits on the top of a picnic table, dressed in plaid shorts, Nike sandals, and a JESUS IS MY HOME-BOY T-shirt. Campers face him in their folding chairs, eating doughnuts and sipping coffee, a few still in pajamas. An intoxicating breeze causes Ivy to nod off beside me. I'm halfway there myself, after hardly sleeping last night, until Pastor Mike quotes from Romans: "Do not take revenge, my friends, but leave room for God's wrath . . . if your enemy is hungry, feed him; if he is thirsty, give him something to drink."

I sit up. Did Pastor Mike look at me when he said that? Did he really mean, "If your enemy shows up with his girlfriend, do not take revenge by dancing in front of him with another guy"? But no, he's preaching about the dangers of road rage because of a major accident in town yesterday. The more I think about what happened, though, the worse I feel, regardless of how horrible Sabrina may be. What if she was badly hurt? And if I had never danced with Jake, then Blaine wouldn't have followed me upstairs and she wouldn't have fallen.

That's the bottom line.

Mom rolls her eyes at Madeline, who is listening with utmost attention with a Bible she's probably never read past Genesis open on her lap. Earlier this morning, when I brought coffee to the porch, instead of Mom I found Madeline perched on Dad's chair, already dressed and coiffed for the day.

"Why, thank you, Dee," she had said, reaching for Mom's mug like I brought it for her. "But could you get me more cream?"

Uh, okay, demand much? I fetched the cream and then sat beside her, peering down to where the Cutson brothers were sleepily padding out of their camper with their hair in matted Mohawks. Madeline took a sip, wrinkling her nose at the taste before saying, "So, tell me about Jake. Your mother said he's your boyfriend?"

A squirrel that was climbing down a tree stopped mid-scamper and turned its head to me as if to say, Don't do it, girl, don't do it! Maybe it would have been best to lie, but something about Madeline's steely gaze drew the truth out of me. "Um, no."

She nodded, shifting in her seat. "As I guessed. And what about the gentleman I saw you leaving the upstairs room with, who is he?"

Seriously, how did she know about that? What is she, a stinking fly on the wall—or better yet, a buzzard on a branch? But even though it was absolutely none of her business, those steely pupils continued to hold me hostage. "Uh, my ex-boyfriend? I was up there taking a break and he walked in."

Madeline's lips pursed. "And the young lady? She was in quite a rush to leave, judging by her fall."

Oh my gosh! The buzzard saw that, too?

"Who fell?" Mom asked as she stepped out onto the porch, the screen door clipping her ankle when she saw my grandmother sitting in her chair. Since Mom was both annoyed with Madeline and in pain, I knew full disclosure was my best course of action. So I told her it was Mona's daughter, Sabrina, who tripped—by accident. "*Wonderful,*" she said, her face contorted like she'd bit into moldy bread. "That'll give Mona Owens another reason to hate me."

"Why's that?" Madeline asked.

Mom sank down onto a different rocking chair. "Because I sort of fired her."

At first, Madeline seemed impressed by Mom's gumption. But then she stood and dumped her coffee over the railing dangerously close to that poor squirrel. "Well, then. Let's just hope nothing bad comes out of this, shall we?"

But something bad did come out of it. Sabrina fell. And when Pastor Mike ducks his head in prayer, I keep mine up long enough to see Jake park his truck by the garage.

When I wave, he doesn't wave back.

I need to find Jake after church, to explain what happened . . . No, make that what *didn't* happen with Blaine, but I first have to work in the store. I try his cell, but all my calls go unanswered—as does my page over the intercom asking him to report to the lodge. So as soon as my shift ends, I run to the garage. He isn't there. Neither is his truck. Instead, I see Ivy stretched out on a hammock, reading a John Grisham legal thriller, her favorite kind of novel. Ivy turns a page when I ask if she's seen Jake. "Hmm, he just left for Bender's," she says.

Huh. Bender's Auto Store is only two miles away.

I do have the afternoon off.

No, forget it. Madeline has already taken Mom's truck to the grocery store for "real" food, so I'd have to take my bike. I'm not *that* desperate to see Jake. But then I remember the look on his face after he saw me with Blaine, and the horrible assumption he must have made.

Well, a little exercise won't hurt.

Ivy is happy to oblige when I ask if she'd help Mom if she needs it. So I grab my bike and head toward town, not slowing until Rex's development comes into sight. Like always, the pretentious brick entrance makes my chest ache, both from the fact that I was stupid enough to date a guy who lives here and from the memory of how beautiful this land used to be before my grandparents sold it to Rex. Rex also bought land from Chuck Lambert, who used the money to transform his campground into the ridiculous carnival that it is now. Word is, Chuck wants to sell another parcel to finance the water slides he's putting in, but the zoning board won't allow it.

Good.

And Rex certainly isn't about to get any more of ours.

By the time I hit the city limits, my shirt is plastered to my sweaty back and Lord knows what my hair looks like, so I'm thankful that Jake's truck is the only vehicle in Bender's parking lot. A blast of air-conditioning makes my breasts ache when

I open the door and step into the dank smell of motor oil. Mr. Bender, an elderly man with a stubble beard and grease-stained work shirt, nods at me before shuffling to the stock-room. On the walls, vintage Goodrich and Valvoline posters hang among the cobwebs, and a dirty table fan rotates on the counter. Jake yanks two bottles of Coke from an old-fashioned soda machine. He pops the caps off with the rusted metal opener and hands one to a person sitting on a cracked bar stool held together with duct tape. Roxanne.

Jake's with *Roxanne.*

His eyes widen when he sees me. "Dee? What are you doing here?"

Are they on a date? That's not possible—Jake usually doesn't hang out with guests. But Roxanne is into racing. Maybe he's attracted to that and— *No, it doesn't matter if they're dating.* I just need to think of an intelligent reason that explains why I tracked him down like a crazed stalker, which is hard to do with Roxanne looking as though she wants to slam me upside the head with a tire iron.

"Oh, I was on my way to meet Natalie at the movies and I saw your truck. Can I, uh, talk to you? Alone?"

Roxanne turns away, mumbling something underneath her breath—something I'm sure isn't good. Jake doesn't seem pleased either, but he still excuses himself and leads me to the other side of the store where tires are stacked nearly to the ceiling. He faces me with his chin raised and says, "Okay, so, what do you want, Dee?"

Oh. I wasn't prepared for this.

Jake has been abrupt with me before, but this is different. Before, there was always a teasing undercurrent. Now there's something else, something I can't identify.

"Jake, about last night. I wanted to explain—"

His cell buzzes. The corners of his mouth turn up as he reads his text and walks back to Roxanne. "Hey, Danny just texted from the racetrack. He came in second, but the guy who won got eliminated because of his piston."

I don't want to stand by myself like an idiot, so I follow him. Mr. Bender hobbles to the counter, spitting his chewing tobacco into a trash can. "Fool boy." He swipes a finger behind his lower lip to get all the remaining black bits before saying to Roxanne and me, "The piston is an engine part, girlies."

"Riiight," Roxanne says as slowly as the condensation rolling down her Coke. "You mean the same part that the top three finishers always have inspected by race officials in case the compression ratio is too high, which is probably why that fool boy got eliminated?"

Mr. Bender grunts, a fleck of tobacco still clinging to his lip. He studies her and then says, "Yeah, well, sodas are fifty cents. I ain't running a free-for-all."

After he goes back to the stockroom, Jake nudges her arm. "He must like you, Roxanne. He normally charges a dollar."

Had the situation been different, I would have been impressed by the way she handled Mr. Bender's "girlie" comment. But it's clear from Jake and Roxanne's interaction that *something* is going on between them. I should go. Now. But after Jake slides his phone in his pocket, he leads me back to the other side of the shop. "Okay. What about last night, what could you possibly have to explain?"

A lot. There's a lot I have to explain.

He doesn't speak while I tell him about Blaine coming back into the store, about him following me upstairs after I told him not to, about Sabrina walking in . . . and her falling down the steps. The only thing I leave out are those brief moments of flirting with Blaine because, well, I'm not exactly proud of that. "So, I just wanted you to know there was nothing going on, okay? Nothing at all."

Jake acts as though none of this was necessary. "Okay, whatever."

I grab his arm before he can walk away. "No. Not whatever. Stop it, Jake, I need you to believe me, okay? I'm serious. I don't want you mad at me. Not this time."

His eyes soften. He shifts to block Roxanne's view and says, "Dee, it's cool, of course I believe you. And I'm not mad. I was just a little peeved because—"

"Jake!" Mr. Bender hollers from the back. "Come help me before fifty bolts fall down on my stinkin' head!"

Jake stares at me for a moment then runs to help Mr. Bender. Shoot. *What was he going to say?* Roxanne drains the last of her Coke and stands, walking to the wall filled with dusty framed photos of local drivers. She ignores me and concentrates on a picture of Danny standing by his racing kart. Starting a conversation is not a good idea, but as I head for the door, I can't stop myself from blurting out, "Um, tell Jake I'll talk to him soon."

This time, I have no problem hearing what she says.

"Yeah, I'm sure you will."

Okay, what's that supposed to mean?

Roxanne clenches her jaw and tosses her empty soda bottle in a wooden crate. "I'm sure you'll summon Jake again," she says bitterly, "when you need someone to clean the campground or dangle in front of your ex-boyfriend."

My stomach drops. How does she know about Jake's plan to make Blaine jealous? Did he tell her? He must have, but why would he share something private that was just between us? And better yet, why should Roxanne care about Jake helping me out if it was his idea to begin with? But then again, the girl has hated me from day one.

And it's about time I find out why.

"What is your problem with me, Roxanne?" I demand, trying to keep my gaze steady even though my legs feel like jelly.

Her voice reeks of sarcasm as she walks back to the counter with her hands raised in the air. "Me, have a problem with you? Oh, no, don't be silly, you're perfect. *Just perfect.*" She slams two quarters for her soda by the cash register. "So, please, just go on with your perfect little life and leave me alone."

I waver between fear and anger. No one has ever talked to me like that, not even Sabrina Owens. "My life's not perfect, Roxanne. You don't know a thing about me or what I've been through."

"Oh, yeah, you got it real tough. And God, what is it with you pretty girls? You smile and act all sweet and kind—like you're trying to make the world a better place—but what you *really* do is hurt people. And, yes, I *do* know all about you, *Super-flirt.*"

What?

How does she know about Superflirt? I never told Jake about that—did she overhear Natalie and me talking? I stand rooted to the spot, too stunned to respond. Hurt people? Who have I hurt? But Roxanne only turns away, dismissing me by saying, "Whatever. It doesn't matter anyway because things will never change."

By the time I make it back to the campground, I'm a sweaty, stinky, exhausted mess. Natalie is scheduled to watch the store this afternoon, so she's perched on a porch swing with her Disney World planner, a stack of Florida guidebooks, and a bottle of Yoo-Hoo. She chews on her pen as I park my bike and crawl up the steps with my helmet dangling from my fingertips. I toss it on the floor then flop down beside her.

"Rough day?" Natalie asks. "You need a Skinny Cow?"

I shake my head. Not even a Skinny Cow can help me now. It's all too much. Madeline arriving. Blaine. Sabrina falling. Jake. Roxanne all but telling me I am a horrible skank of a person and looking at me the same way Tamara looked at Mona Owens last night.

Oh my gosh, does this mean—

"Do you think I'm like Mona?" I ask.

Is that what I am, some horrible show-off who steals other people's thunder and leaves them stuck with the rain?

Natalie's mouth drops. She swats me with her copy of the *Unofficial Guide to Walt Disney World* and says, "Honestly, where did that come from? Please tell me you're not still worried about last night. First off, Mona has cellulite, which you'll never have if you're like your mother. Have you ever noticed how fabulous her thighs are? And second, Mona flirts with married and/or taken men, which is something you never do. You have principles."

"Uh, hello, aren't you forgetting something?" Natalie knows the truth—I told her everything last night, right down to the *Gotcha* moment with Blaine. Idiot. What was I thinking? No wonder he followed me upstairs. No wonder Sabrina was furious. No wonder I was too ashamed to tell Jake about the flirting part.

"Okay, you need to stop, Dee." Natalie shakes her head and shifts to face me. "So you flirted with Blaine for, like, one minute. Big deal. Did you ask him to follow you upstairs? Did you push Sabrina down the steps?"

"No," I slowly reply.

"And didn't she humiliate you and countless other girls like me, hello, Nose-Pick Natalie? So, yeah, flirting with Blaine wasn't the best thing in the world to do, but you had your reasons. And I'm sorry Sabrina fell, but she didn't die, and after all the pain she's caused, maybe she deserved a little pain herself."

Natalie does have a point. It'd take an hour to list all Sabrina's victims. Natalie hands me her Yoo-Hoo and nudges my arm. "So come on, give me a teeny-weeny smile."

I manage a small one.

"That's my girl," she says, flipping her book back open to a section about Epcot and then motioning to the pool where two guys are throwing a football back and forth in the shallow end. "And as your reward, I'll tell you about the two brothers who checked in an hour ago *and* I'll let you call dibs on the cuter one."

I watch the taller boy's biceps flex as he jumps to catch the ball. Okay, he's hot. Very hot, and worthy of a pool trick or two. I could even try to convince flirtaphobic Natalie to go first. But instead of plotting, I lean my head back and close my eyes. Maybe she's right—maybe last night wasn't entirely my fault. But after this weekend, one thing is for sure.

My Superflirt days? They are super *over*.

The Superflirt Chronicles
. . . blogs from a teenage flirtologist

Thursday, June 24

RAIN, RAIN, SUCKY RAIN
MOOD: Soggy
MUSIC: "Steal My Sunshine," Len

Why did I choose this song? Because it's got the cutest beat ever, and maybe I need a little sunshine after a long week of rain, rain, rain.

Rain + Campground = Dismal, dismal, dismal.

It doesn't help that the unwanted guest I blogged about last Saturday has yet to hop on her broom and fly home. And if that wasn't bad enough, there have been no flirt-worthy guys here all week. Well . . . except for some cute brothers, but Miss N and I threw those little fish back in the water. So, my lovely readers, I've decided to take a flirt break. Clear my head for a while. Take a breather. Chill. But don't you dare assume that things are going to get boring here at the Chronicles. Allow me to announce something new: The Superflirt Book Club. Here is my first selection:

How to Win Friends & Influence People by Dale Carnegie.

What, were you expecting some kind of bodice-ripping romance? Oh, please.

And, okay, the book is from the 1930s. But guess what Dale

Carnegie says is a simple way to make a good first impression? To smile. Hello—Flirt Rule #1! And he believes that the secret of dealing with people is to give honest and sincere appreciation. Uh, Flirt Rule #3 anyone? So get yourself a copy—book discussions start in two weeks! Until then, here's an update from our friend Meghan:

Hey, Superflirt, I just don't think I'm cut out for all this flirting stuff. This one guy, Joe, did ask me out, but on the night of our date, both of my girls became horribly ill. It's just as well—my place is at home with them. I do thank you though for trying. —Meghan9800.

Darling Meghan, your daughters were not ill. They were faking so you'd cancel your date and it worked. Bravo for them, they deserve an Oscar. But I don't think you would have gone, regardless of their performance. Why? Because dating Joe might have made you happy and you don't think you deserve to be happy. Well, guess what, Meghan. You do. So maybe it's time for you to start living for yourself for a change.

As for everyone else, I feel that I should address the petty comments that have been posted recently, like these:

Seriously, the thought of someone as old as Meghan flirting is so gross! She's like, what, forty? She should just die now and get it over with. —BridgetRocks.

Better watch what you say, sweetheart, because there will

come a day when you turn forty and karma kicks your rocking butt for making such a cruel comment! —LovinMy40s.

Ladies, *ladies*, love and sisterhood means for *all* women, both young and old, remember? Come on, shouldn't we support each other?

Welcome to the Barton Family Campground's
SUMMER SCHOOL WEEKEND!

Friday, June 25:	7 pm	Clarksburg Strings, a local three-piece orchestra
	8 pm	Tonight's movie: GETTYSBURG, a lesson in our nation's history
Saturday, June 26:	10 am	Kids' spelling bee, please register in advance
	3 pm	Adult Swim
	3 pm	For the kids—meet with a local career counselor
	7 pm	Adult bridge tournament, please register in advance
	8 pm	Tonight's movie: SUPERSIZE ME, on the horrors of fast food
Sunday, June 27:	9 am	Nondenominational church service

II ～ Dee

What in the world?" Mom demands early Friday morning. We dodge a massive mud puddle and run up the lodge steps to where my grandmother is standing by the bulletin board. "Madeline, adult swim? Spelling bee? *Bridge tournament*, are you serious?"

"There you two are!" Madeline aims her dry-erase marker at the new schedule she wrote as though it's the Sistine Chapel ceiling and she is Michelangelo. "Isn't this wonderful? And I think it's high time that bridge is re-introduced into society."

"No, no it's not!" Mom shakes her head, the thin streak of gray hair at her part seeming to grow wider by the second. "It's our Kids' Holiday Weekend, one of our most popular, and despite the weather, we're nearly booked solid!"

The rain finally stopped last night, but everything is still a wet, dismal mess. The campground has been gloomy all week, making my flirt ban easy to follow with an empty pool, abandoned playground, and our permanent summer guests sequestered in their RVs. It got even worse when Madeline decided to extend her stay because we are apparently in desperate need of help. She straightens the bulletin board and steps back to survey her perfect penmanship. "Yes, Jane, but if you're going to have a kids' weekend, what's more important for today's youth than education?"

"Today's youth will hate this," I say. "And adult swims are stupid. Pools are always empty during them except for that one guy who'll leisurely paddle around in his inner tube, watching the kids with a *ha ha, losers* look on his face."

Madeline replies with a snippy *hmph* and heads for the store with us following behind. "The concept of adult swim is to force the kids to take a break and not exhaust themselves in the water. And the concept of studying over the summer might be of benefit to you, considering your last report card."

Well, bite my butt.

I might get the occasional B, but it's hardly anything to be criticized for. Besides, when did she see my report card? I find out after Madeline points at Mom's once overflowing in-bin, which is now empty. "I made myself useful and did some filing, since the task has been ignored for quite some time. That's where I found your report card, young lady. And, Jane, perhaps you need help with the bookkeeping? I noticed you paid your last insurance bill rather late."

Wow. In one fell swoop, Madeline managed to tap into Mom's fear of being a bad businesswoman—*and* a bad mother. Mom doesn't reply, but when Madeline asks if we'd like to take flowers to my father's grave, Mom looks out the window and whispers, "No, we mourn in our own way."

I used to visit my dad every week to pull any weeds and to

fill the vase with wildflowers picked from the mountains. But it didn't feel right—the grave was too quiet and dismal, everything he wasn't. Mom, however, didn't stop going until about one month ago, and—

Wait.

Does it have something to do with her *not exactly*?

The next few days pass in a blur of chaos and commotion. Mom takes the marker from Madeline and returns the schedule to our Kids' Holiday theme, with DJ Drake back on board, although his announcement that he's soon moving to Denver to be near his grandchildren throws us for a loop. The sun comes out in full force by the afternoon, bringing with it a steady stream of campers, pop-up trailers, and trucks loaded with tents, bikes, and—of course—kids. A *lot* of kids. It reminds me of the scene in *Chitty Chitty Bang Bang* where all the children escape from Baron Bomburst's prison and swarm the banquet hall. Madeline reminds me of the prissy Baroness Bomburst, but to her credit, she does help, although she grumbles about the candy Natalie hides for the flashlight treasure hunt, and she doesn't give awards to the relay race winners until they correctly spell "victory." Roxanne helps as well, just not with any kid-related activity after she yells at a child for throwing a water balloon at her. She takes care of the store mostly, but when I go in for hula hoops, I could swear I see her reading Natalie's copy of *How to Win Friends & Influence People* before she hides it behind the counter.

Once Sunday night rolls around, everyone is exhausted. Jake vows to never give another hayride again, and after being bombarded by cannonballing kids while trying to take a quick dip, I decide that maybe adult swim isn't a bad idea after all. By Monday, though, most of the weekend guests have left.

So now, my Tuesday afternoon plans include a bikini, a copy of *Glamour* magazine—love their Dos and Don'ts—and a lounge chair, seeing as how Natalie is spending the day with her grandmother to finalize their Disney plans. As I head to the pool, though, I consider stopping by Jake's garage. Just to hang out or something . . . as long as Roxanne isn't there. But while passing the playground, I see her on a swing, digging her bare feet in the sand and reading a graphic novel as the Cutsons run by with Dorito-stained lips and fingers. Lyle stops long enough to squat near a toddler who is sticking his sandy fingers in his mouth and yell, "Hey, don't eat that, you stupid ding-dong! It causes cancer!"

"Sand doesn't cause cancer, Lyle," Ivy tells him as she falls in step beside me with a container of Tide and a full laundry bag.

I motion to the dirty sock poking out of the top. "Got a hot date with Mr. Maytag?"

"Mr. Grisham, actually," Ivy says, motioning to another legal thriller tucked under her arm. "I took it from my therapist's office today."

"You stole a book from your shrink?"

Ivy grins and turns onto the sidewalk leading to the laundry room. "Borrowed, Dee, borrowed, although considering the hideous amount he charges for services that haven't done me any good, he owes me more than a few—"

She stops.

A patrol car is creeping up the drive.

That's odd. The sheriff often stops by at night to make sure no campers are out of line, but never at this time of day. Mom walks out of the store and watches him approach from the porch. The sheriff parks and steps out, wearing a wide-brim hat low on his forehead and dark sunglasses. He strides up to Mom with his gun bouncing on his hip. "Ma'am, you are Jane Barton, correct?"

"Of course, Wesley, you know I am."

"I know, Jane, I'm just following procedure," he says, handing her a large envelope before tapping his hat brim and walking back to the patrol car. She opens it and reads the first page as he drives away.

The blood drains from her face.

"Mom? Are you okay?"

She takes a shaky step back, and another, until she reaches the porch swing. She sits, tears gathering and her breath quickening as she continues to read. "Jane?" Ivy asks as we run to join her. "What is it, what are those papers about?"

When Mom composes herself enough to speak, her words come out in a whisper. "Dee, did you—did you—shove Sabrina Owens down the steps?"

"What? Why, what's going on?"

She turns the papers around. Across the top is fancy script letterhead that reads "Wyatt, Hyatt & Smith."

"Dee, Mona Owens is suing the campground for two million dollars."

12 ～ Dee

Ivy drops her laundry and takes the papers from Mom's shaky hands. Her gray hair falls in her face as she reads them. "This is a summons and claim citing physical and emotional damage caused by," Ivy pauses, long enough to give me a worried glance, "by Dee Barton and campground negligence."

Physical and emotional damage. Caused by me.

Ivy shakes the papers in the air. "And it's from the law firm of Wyatt, Hyatt and Smith, of all places. Those bastards!"

I sit, gripping the swing's armrest so hard my knuckles turn white. *This is not happening. No, this has to be a joke, a cruel, twisted joke.* Mom stifles a sob with the same stunned expression she wore the day my father died. She doesn't blink until Madeline strides around the corner and says, "What's going on? I saw the sheriff's car."

Ivy reluctantly hands her the papers. Madeline skims the first page with her lips pinched. "I knew it. I knew the moment that woman walked on this property she'd be nothing but trouble. You should never have hired her to begin with, Jane."

"Do you *really* think I need to hear this right now, Madeline?"

She ignores Mom and turns her rage to me. "And according to this, the plaintiff's boyfriend was lured to an upstairs room by you, Dee, and you became physically violent when confronted."

"*What?* No! Ask Blaine, he'll tell you what happened! He came into the store. We talked and I got mad, so I ran to the rec room. Blaine followed *me*, even though I told him not to, and when Sabrina came in later...she got upset and left, and she tripped when she ran down the stairs."

Madeline frowns, as though I'm nothing but a frivolous, lying twit. She turns back to Mom. "Jane, you need to contact your lawyer right away. You do have a lawyer, don't you?"

Mom wipes the tears from her face. "Of course I do. He helped me when John died. Carl Bedden."

"Carl Bedden?" Madeline asks. "Do you mean *Judge* Bedden?"

Whatever thin slice of composure Mom was clinging to dissolves like a tissue in tepid water. "What? He's a judge now? That's right. I completely forgot! So that means...no, I don't have a lawyer!"

Ivy takes Mom by the elbow and pulls her to her feet. "Let's talk in the store. Roxanne! Come over here and stand guard in case any campers have an emergency. And later on, there's a guided hike scheduled for three o'clock. I'll need you to grab a map and take care of it."

Roxanne.

I forgot that she was at the playground, close enough to

hear everything. She must be loving this, getting to witness firsthand how right she was—I am nothing but a stupid, horrible person who hurts people.

"Me?" Roxanne asks. "You want *me* to lead a hike?"

"Yes, step up to the plate and handle it, girl," Ivy barks, opening the store door and leading Mom inside before Roxanne can respond. Ivy locks the deadbolt and turns the sign to CLOSED before facing us. Gone is her normal air of bored retiree. Gone is the woman who would spend hours deliberating whether she should learn how to crotchet or go to bingo with other senior citizens. Instead, she looks controlled. Fierce.

Powerful.

"Jane, don't panic," Ivy sternly says, pulling down the blinds on the front windows. "Ninety percent of lawsuits never make it to trial and are not winnable, okay? So, here's what you're going to do. You're going to calmly contact your insurance company and report to them how you received the summons and at what time. They are the ones who will provide a lawyer for you. That's why you have insurance."

Mom's eyes widen. She runs over to the files and jerks open a drawer so hard the entire cabinet rocks. "The insurance bill. I just paid it Monday a week ago," she says, rifling through the folders. "It was late, but I had misfiled our statement and didn't remember it until I found the late notice, and—oh my gosh, Madeline, why did you have to rearrange everything?"

The air turns stagnant.

The payment Mom said she had to drop by the insurance office that Saturday. But the office was closed, so she couldn't pay until Monday.

Ivy presses a hand to her mouth. "Jane. How late was it?"

147

Madeline races behind the counter, elbowing Mom aside and finding the insurance folder in a different drawer. She thumbs through the papers and then turns to Mom with her mouth held aghast. "Jane. How could you?"

"What? I paid the bill."

"But you didn't respond to their late notice!" Madeline holds up a sheet of paper, her dark Florida tan turning crimson. "Guess what happens when you don't respond to a late notice, Jane? *Your policy is canceled and you're not covered!*"

Mom snatches the notice from her. "What are you talking about? They're not going to drop me over one late payment, are they?"

"No! Of course they won't drop you over a late payment. But if you *read* the notice, you'd know they only gave you a ten-day extension while waiting for payment. That extension expired on June 18, meaning that on June 19, the night Sabrina fell, you had no insurance. No insurance, no coverage. Which means, *no lawyer.* And judging from your bank account balance, you can't afford one either."

"So because I made an accounting mistake—"

"Mistake? Is that all you can say, Jane?" Madeline picks up an activities schedule and shakes it in the air. "You'll take the time to plan themed weekends, but insurance? No. You'll pay for wireless Internet, but insurance? *No!* After all the hard work my husband and I put into this campground, you didn't even bother to protect it!"

Mom slumps in a chair. She twists the gold band around her finger and stares at the photo of my dad holding up a ten-pound bass he caught at the Susquehanna River before saying,

"John always did the bills, okay? He was so much better at it than I am."

Madeline closes her mouth.

We are silent until Ivy steps forward. "I know you both are upset, but we need to calm down, because everything will be okay. I promise."

"How, Ivy?" Mom asks. "I'm being sued for two million dollars and I can't afford a lawyer, so how is it going to be okay?"

Pain swells in my chest, making it hard to swallow or breathe. The reality of what is happening crashes upon me like water from a broken dam. First we lost Dad. And now, we could lose the campground. The room blurs as I start to sob, pinching my eyes shut until strong hands grasp my arms.

It's Ivy.

"Dee, you listen to me," she says, with a strength I've never heard from her before. "Everything will be fine, I promise. You hear me, Jane? Everything is going to be fine. But first, Dee, I want you to tell me the absolute truth, right here and right now. Did you touch that girl *at all* on the stairs, even briefly?"

Her abruptness makes me question everything that happened that night. Was I to blame? No, I might have done some things wrong, but "I never touched her, Ivy. I was inside the rec room when she fell."

"Okay, then. Okay." Ivy nods. She steps back, still nodding, and peers at her reflection in the small mirror hanging behind the chip display. Ivy reaches up to touch her messy hair and then grimaces at her plain yellow T-shirt. "Okay, then," she repeats, walking to the door and flipping the deadbolt. "Jane, listen. You know how the worst thing a lost hiker can do is panic and run wildly through the woods? No, she should stop, be calm, and stay in one place. That's what I want you to do right now, stay calm, because you *do* have a lawyer. You have me."

Hold on.

It takes a moment for her words to make sense.

"You're an *attorney*, Ivy?" Mom asks in complete shock.

"Yes, I was . . . I mean, I am. And after I take care of a few details in town, we're going to get down to business and make this all go away, I *promise*. So stay calm, I'll only be gone for two hours, maybe three."

She leaves before we can say anything, and we hear her firing up her truck outside.

Ivy . . . Miss Almond Pudding herself, a *lawyer*? No, I can't wrap my head around it, not with the words "personal injury" and "emotional distress" churning in my brain like a bucket full of blue gills. Mom puts away the insurance folder then leans her chin on the cabinet, staring at the photo of Dad again. Madeline makes coffee and pours herself some, only to dump it after just one sip.

I can't sit still.

I can't stay calm. I have to do something. Something other than listen to the ticking clock or Madeline's aggravated sighs or Mom's occasional sniff. I grab the inventory chart and go to the first aisle, trying to lose myself in the mundane task of tallying butane lighters and waterproof matches. Mom joins me, kneeling to count the coils of extension cords, water pressure gauges, and surge guards, but I can tell she can't concentrate.

Neither can I.

Madeline sighs again and walks over to where Mom and I

are counting the spare camper parts. When she reaches for the sewer caps, Mom's body stiffens. "I wish you wouldn't do that," she says.

Madeline ignores her and starts counting.

"I said," Mom repeats, "I wish you wouldn't do that."

"And I wish you paid your bills on time," Madeline says. "Maybe then you'd have a *real* lawyer to call instead of us waiting for Ivy and God only knows what."

Mom stands, her muscles flexed. "You want to talk about wishes, Madeline? Okay, then, here's mine: I wish you were more supportive of my decision not to sell the campground after John's death. Maybe then I would have done better. I wish you had *helped* me, instead of throwing all my mistakes in my face. Maybe then I would have done better. I wish you had mourned John's death *with* me instead of *against* me. Maybe then we *both* would have done better."

"This has nothing to do with his death, Jane."

Mom steps past me, almost knocking the hose clamps from my hands. "This has everything to do with John's death. You blame me, don't you? You think I should have forced him to go to the hospital. You think it was me who said ignore those chest pains, honey, go ahead and take a nice long drive."

Madeline turns away.

Mom forces my grandmother to face her. "Don't you think I tried? Don't you think I asked him to go to the doctor? But no. John didn't think guys like him had heart attacks. And he was right, they shouldn't. They shouldn't. *They shouldn't!*"

I drop the clamps.

I never knew this. I didn't know there were warning signs—I

thought the heart attack he had while driving to the hardware store was sudden. But I can imagine Dad shrugging it off, keeping his hands on the wheel through the storm that claimed him in the end.

Madeline's lower lip shakes, her aloof demeanor threatening to crumple. She quickly composes herself. "So, the campground being sued is my fault, I suppose?"

"No, I didn't say that. But you certainly didn't help!"

I slap the clipboard on the counter. They are not to blame. It's my fault. *All of it is my fault.* Sabrina tripped because of me. Mona is suing because of *me.*

Suddenly the room feels like a sauna.

I want to leave.

I want to run through the woods until my lungs ache. I want to get in a boat, cut the rope, and let the river take me away. Instead, when I go onto the porch and see Ivy's dirty clothes on the sidewalk, I take them to the laundry room, hoping to find comfort in the sound of agitating water and the sweet smell of drying clothes. But by the time her last pair of shorts is folded, my mind still feels as dizzy as a pinwheel in a tornado.

Natalie. I need Natalie.

By now, she is probably knee-deep in Disney discussions, but twenty minutes after I send her an urgent text, Natalie arrives, driving her grandmother's minivan. She sits beside me on the porch steps. "You want to talk about it?"

I shake my head.

"Okay, Dee. We'll just sit here, then."

So we sit.

We stay that way for thirty more minutes, watching fluttering alfalfa butterflies and a little girl playing hopscotch with a hot dog in her hand, dripping ketchup on her arm with each jump. Roxanne soon limps around the corner, sweaty and damp, with a troop of clammy hikers behind her. Her pace falters when she sees me. Natalie shoots me a curious look when Roxanne says, "Um, we kind of got lost, so our one-mile hike turned into five. Sorry."

Guess she doesn't know about Ivy's *stop and be calm* policy. And if it didn't feel as though my life is destroyed, the surprise of her talking to me without a slur would've sunk in. Instead, I only say, "Oh. Well, thanks for taking care of it."

She shifts her weight and brushes back her soggy bangs. "Okay, then, I better get back to my—" Roxanne stops when she notices a shiny black car with sparkling chrome-rimmed tires pulling in. For a second, I think it's Blaine, coming to tell me not to worry—he'll tell everyone I never pushed Sabrina. But it isn't a Mercedes.

"Whoa," Roxanne says. "That's a BMW 335i Coupe!"

The black car sweeps into a parking spot. We watch as the door opens and a slender foot in a navy sling-back heel emerges, stepping down with a loud click. The driver stands tall, wearing a slim-cut skirt and tailored blouse. She pulls a leather briefcase from the backseat and turns, her hair swinging in a classy curve across her cheek. The smell of perfume sweeps over us as she walks up the porch stairs, takes off her dark sunglasses, and says, "Roxanne, close your mouth, kiddo, the car is only leased. Natalie, you drive Jake to the dealership in town so he can bring back my truck. And, Dee? Get those scumbag lawyers Wyatt, Hyatt and Smith on the line. Now I'm ready to kick some rear."

Ivy.

Well, goodbye, Miss Almond Pudding, hello, Miss Hotshot.

Inside the store, Ivy, her gray hair now cut in a sleek, elegant bob, opens her briefcase. She tosses me her cell. "Dee, tell them that Ivy Neville, Esquire, would like to speak to her former boss, Aaron Wyatt."

"You were with Wyatt, Hyatt and Smith?" Madeline asks. "But I thought Jane said you used to work for an investment firm."

Ivy pulls out a legal pad. "It is an investment firm—they invest in themselves. And they never made me partner, which is why they were able to 'encourage' me into retirement. Afterward, I did maintain my license," Ivy says, reaching into her new purse for a pen. "But I felt too depressed and too old to keep practicing . . . until now."

I thought about the clues. Reading John Grisham novels. Never backing down from an argument. Her inability to feel relaxed despite her therapist's many attempts. And now, Ivy Neville is *our* lawyer.

Maybe hope is not lost after all.

The receptionist answers on the fourth ring. When I ask for Aaron Wyatt, she informs me with a snotty voice that he's unavailable. I relay this to Ivy and her eyes narrow to angry slits. "Hmm, he's not taking my call, is he?"

She strides over and takes the phone. "With whom am I

speaking? Oh, hello, Sheila. This is Ivy Neville. Yes, I'm well, thank you, how are your husband and kids? Good, good. Now be a dear and put me through to Aaron. No? He's in a meeting?"

Ivy shifts the phone to her other ear.

"Well, then, perhaps we should start this conversation over, shall we? Hello, Sheila, how are you? And how is Steven Jones, the associate you slept with at the Christmas party four years ago?" *Nod, nod, pause.* "Oh, Aaron is available now? Wonderful, thank you, Sheila. Give my love to your family."

Ivy clicks open her pen. "Dee, I promise. Everything is under control. Oh, and call my therapist. Tell him he's *fired.*"

13 ～ Sabrina

Everything *was* under control.

After I discovered Dee's blog that Sunday morning—and after Mom dragged me to the hospital for X-rays that showed my wrist was sprained—I drove straight to Blaine's and told him I was an idiot for not trusting him, and that I should have known it was Dee who came on to him instead of the other way around. He stopped packing his suitcase long enough to wrap his strong arms around me and say he was sorry, too, so as far as I was concerned, that whole stupid mess was over, and for the rest of the summer we were going to do nothing but have fun together.

Well, once he returns from his New York trip with Larson, that is.

As for Dee Barton, my first intention was to tell everyone about her stupid blog *and* see to it that her life is a total nightmare when school starts. But after reading all of her entries, I realized that everyone—especially the guys—would think the blog was *hot*, unlike her desperate letter to Blaine. Dee's status would skyrocket to iconic levels and I'd be forever known as the evil girlfriend. Uh, *not happening*. My best course of action was to just let it go, regardless of how mad I was. Bravo, Dee, you got your revenge . . . and maybe I did deserve some of it.

So life *was* perfectly under control.

Until, of course, Mom screwed everything up.

Now, not only is everyone going to find out about Dee's blog, they will also find out how my mother filed a tacky suit against her mother, seeking restitution for my hospital visit and a little extra. I won't be just the evil girlfriend. I'll be the pathetic, poor, *and* evil girlfriend, much to Torrance's amusement.

And what will Blaine think?

In our backyard on Wednesday evening, I yank on a ragweed that is choking the marigolds and almost fall on my rear when it pulls loose. Mom and I have an arrangement—she plants and I weed, which is fitting, since I'm always the one who gets stuck with her messes. I toss the weed into a plastic tub and pull off my gloves, sifting my fingers through the chalky gray mulch that used to be a fresh black. I can't even imagine how to break the news to Blaine when he gets back from New York. *Hey, guess what, sweetie, my mother is suing your ex-girlfriend's mother, now give me a big kiss.*

As I put my gloves back on to attack a cluster of ground ivy, my cell rings. I hope it's Blaine finally calling me back. Then I can get it over with and tell him about Mom's latest scheme, but when I answer, a shrill voice screams out, "You witch, why didn't you tell me?"

It isn't Blaine. "Torrance?"

"Of course. I *cannot* believe you let me find out this way!"

157

Oh, man. She knows about the lawsuit. My throat tightens, like the ragweed is now choking me. I've been dreading this ever since Mom barged into my room on the Monday after the horrible Dee incident looking like a possessed airline stewardess in a lime green skirt and pastel sweater. She pulled out a blue sundress from my closet and said, "Change into this and put your hair up all nice and pretty, sweetie. We have an important meeting that's gonna change our lives forever!"

My first thought was *Oh, no, she's dragging me to another one of those whacked-out psychics.* The last time Mom saw a psychic, she was depressed for weeks after the phony told her she'll never remarry and will die alone.

"Come on, Sabrina, chop-chop!" Mom bellowed from the hallway.

My wrist was aching, so I was in no mood for her chop-chops, but I threw the dress on anyway and coiled my dark hair into a messy bun. Mom cocked her head and sighed when I met her at the front door. "Aw, you look like an angel, sweetie. Now let's go!"

We climbed into the Trooper and she floored the accelerator before I even had a chance to put my seat belt on. "Where are you taking me, anyway?" I asked.

"I'm not telling, sugar, it's a surprise!" Mom then lifted her giant fringed purse onto my lap and said, "Now dig in there for another little surprise, will ya?"

The only thing in her purse that could pass as a surprise was a country classics CD, unless she meant her hair-ensnarled brush or collection of super-sized tampons. "Yep, that's it," Mom said, taking the CD and popping it into the stereo. Twangs of steel guitar came through the speakers and Mom rocked to the beat. "You remember this one, Sabrina? 'Harper Valley PTA' by Jeannie C. Riley? It's our theme song for the summer." She started to sing. "I wanna tell you all the story 'bout a Harper Valley widowed wife."

Seriously.

"Please, Mom, please don't," I begged. "And you're not a widow."

She kept singing, tapping the steering wheel with her Donald Trump nails that were painted hot pink with glittery green dollar signs. Trying to tune her out, I watched a group of cyclists wearing spandex pants, but it was impossible to ignore Mom as she caterwauled about a sexy widow who was criticized by the PTA members of her daughter's school for wearing short skirts, drinking, and running wild with men. The widow gets them back, though, by barging into the PTA meeting and exposing everyone else's dirty little secrets.

"Mom, enough! Tell me what's going on!"

"Sugar, I've received some friendly legal advice that's going to make our life a heck of a lot easier, trust me," Mom said over the music, before singing, "That day my mama socked it to the Harper Valley PTA."

When she swung into an elaborate brick professional center and parked beside a WYATT, HYATT & SMITH sign, my heart sank. Oh, fabulous. She had a meeting with Aaron Wyatt, her weasel-like lawyer who represented her through the divorce and always smells as though he just returned from a spa. Was Mom dragging Dad back in court for more alimony or for full custody? But then she repeated the last line of her ridiculous song, adding a little twist:

"That day my mama socked it to the Barton Family Campground."

Dad wasn't her target—Jane Barton was.

And now, while on the phone with Torrance, I try to stay calm because how everyone at school reacts to the lawsuit will depend on Torrance's opinion, and if she thinks it's lame I might as well kiss my senior year goodbye. "Oh, yeah, how did you find out?" I ask.

"From the article in today's *Herald*, of course! Your mother is suing? Nothing this cool has *ever* happened in Riverside! Well, except for when Bridget's mom sued her hairdresser for that disaster highlight job, remember?"

I should feel relieved that Torrance thinks it's cool. But what article? Mom never said anything about a newspaper article.

"Hmph, that stylist got what she deserved," Torrance continues in true diva form. "Those orange highlights surely were the reason her membership application at the Riverside Golf Club was denied."

With my gloves on, I run to the front of the house, feeling the dry grass scratch my bare feet. The morning paper is still propped against the mailbox post. As Torrance rambles about highlights, I open it to see Mom on the third page, wearing a prim cardigan, with the headline "Mother Sues Local Campground" printed above her head.

"Sabrina, are you listening to me?" Torrance demands.

I mutter a quick *uh-huh*, and start to read. "Mona Owens,

Riverside resident and owner of Mona's Low-Key Karaoke, has filed suit against the Barton Family Campground on behalf of her minor daughter, Sabrina Owens, citing physical and emotional damage from negligence."

Oh, no, she didn't.

Emotional damage? Mom never said anything about emotional damage. She told me she was only suing for our medical expenses!

"Owens offered this statement through her lawyer, Aaron Wyatt: 'I did not want to do this—Lord knows there are enough frivolous lawsuits swamping our legal system these days. But I put my own concerns aside and thought only of my traumatized daughter, who I had to comfort for hours after she was pushed down those rickety stairs. It was very hard on me.'"

Pushed? Dee never pushed me.

And traumatized? Comforting me for hours? All she did was cover up my bruise with her miracle cream. She didn't even think about taking me to the hospital until the next day, when she barged into my room after surfing the Internet all morning. Aaron. Maybe she called Aaron and he told her to get X-rays taken, and to take a picture of the bruise on my face, even though it wasn't from the fall.

"Sabrina—*hello*—give me the details! Like, did Dee really push you? Did it have something to do with Blaine? Tell me!"

I mumble something incoherent and read the last line. "Ms. Owens is seeking two million dollars for her daughter's physical damages and emotional distress."

Three words jump out at me like a brick to the forehead.

"*Two million dollars*, is she serious?" I yell.

"I know, isn't it fantastic?" Torrance squeals. "Just think of all the shopping we'll be able to do, and oh! You could go to San Diego State with me instead of that stupid Riverside Community College, so come *on*, tell me what's going on, talk!"

No, it's not fantastic. And yes, there is someone I want to talk to. A bleached blond forty-two-year-old Harlequin Romance addict who assured me *nothing* like this was going to happen.

"Torr, can I call you later?" I ask while rushing in the front door.

"Oh, no," she demands. "Not until you tell me everything. I'm your best friend, *remember*? At least, I thought I was."

Great. If Torrance gets annoyed with me now, I will be about two steps away from total social homicide. Inside the house, Mom is at the kitchen table, nursing an iced tea and applying a top coat to her Donald Trump nails. Perfect, she can help me get rid of Torrance again. I give her a knowing gesture and point at my cell. "Of course you're my best friend, Torr," I warmly say, while motioning at Mom. "And I'll tell you everything."

"Finally," Torrance murmurs.

I pause.

My mother takes a long sip of tea.

"Mom!" I mouth.

"Oh. Right." She waits a second and then hollers, "Sabrina! Can you get off the phone, honey, and help me?"

It's about time. *"Sorry,* Torrance, gotta go, but I promise to call you later, okay?" I hang up without waiting for her reply. "Mom, I can't believe you!"

"Fine! Get your own self off the phone next time, then."

"No, not that." I slam the paper down and jab a finger at the article. "Two million dollars, are you insane?"

Mom smiles, putting down her nail polish and clapping her hands excitedly. "Well, my stars, I thought they were running this tomorrow! Oh, joy, my picture turned out good, huh? But look at your dirty hands, Sabrina. How can I scrapbook this with mulch stains on it?"

Scrapbooking? She's worried about *scrapbooking*? "Screw your scrapbook, Mother, would you mind explaining?"

"Watch your language, young lady. You know I hate being called Mother," she says, taking a sip of her tea. "And, sweetie, the article was my lawyer's idea. Who are we to question his judgment? And don't get your panties in a pickle over the amount. We're not *really* suing for two million. We're just bartering."

"Bartering?"

Mom heaves an impatient sigh. "You know, like in Mexico when a vendor says a necklace costs ten dollars but you barter back and forth until he agrees to sell it for three? Vendors are insulted if you don't barter with them, honey, don't you know that?"

Oh my gosh, does she actually think Jane Barton would be insulted if she doesn't sue for so much money? Unbelievable. But there is an even bigger topic we need to discuss. "What about Dee pushing me? You know that's not what—"

Mom cuts me off with a sharp look. "Hey, why did you run down those steps and fall? Because Dee was with *your* boyfriend, getting revenge like her blog said, so don't get hung up on a technicality, sugar. Besides, this will all be over in a matter of weeks."

"What's that supposed to mean?"

Mom notices a smudge on a cuticle. She dips an orange stick in polish remover and dabs at it. "The case will never go to trial, that's what, so it doesn't matter whether or not Dee pushed you," she says, waving the stick at me wandlike. "Trust me, her insurance company will be more than happy to settle for much less. And, just think, Sabrina. If your momma gets herself some money, then we can replace your car with one that isn't breaking down every five minutes, and . . . your dad will pay less alimony."

Her enticing words dangle in the air.

I never should have told her how Dad worked most of the time during our last weekend together, just like I never should have told her about Dee's blog. But at the time, I was too angry and Mom has always known how much I hate Dad's schedule. Less alimony would mean less work for him and more time for me. So maybe her orange stick wand does have magic powers, because I find myself saying, "Fine. But I refuse to lie about anything. That's just not right."

Like any of this is.

"Of course not, sugar," Mom purrs, just as the doorbell rings. She pats my face and then sashays to the foyer to answer it, coming back later with an enormous bouquet of her favorite tiger lilies. She buries her nose in the middle of one and breathes in deeply. "My, my, what a lovely surprise. I wonder who they're from."

Does it matter? Whichever fool sent them will only stop calling in a week, although I am impressed by the bouquet's volume. She fluffs them with amazement and reads the card. "Oh, my . . . now this *is* a surprise."

I wait for her to coyly make me guess who they are from.

The short-order cook? The barber? The UPS delivery guy she flirted with at the mall? Or, gag, Chuck Lambert? But instead, she folds the card with a Cheshire cat grin and quietly goes back to her nails. Good, I don't want to hear about her latest love interest, not when there are bigger things to worry about.

Like Blaine.

He answers my call this time on the fourth ring. Sounds of laughter and talking accompany his quick "Hello?"

"Hey, sweetie, how are you?" I ask while walking to my room.

"What?" he says loudly over the noise. "Who's this?"

"Blaine, it's *Sabrina*."

"Oh, sorry. What's up?"

What's up? *What's up?* That's something a guy says to his buddies, not a girlfriend. But maybe he's near his dad and wants to sound manly. So I twirl a lock of hair around my finger, hoping to sound carefree and lighthearted while saying, "Oh, nothing, sweetie, there's just something we need to talk about."

"What, about the lawsuit?" Blaine asks. "My father showed me the article in today's paper."

It suddenly feels as though someone has reached down my mouth and yanked out my lungs. *He already knows.* Is that why he didn't call from New York, because he's mad? Even though some of my ex-boyfriends were terrible, I would *never* wish a multimillion-dollar lawsuit on any of them. But then again . . . Blaine doesn't *sound* mad. He sounds . . . completely indifferent. Dee Barton is a horrible person, but wow, doesn't he have any feelings for her at all?

Wait—I don't mean that.

If anything, I should be relieved because his blasé attitude toward her welfare proves once and for all he doesn't still have feelings for her.

But how could he have read the article if he's in New York?

"Um, Blaine, where are you?"

"Home, but not for long. Prescott and I are going to the driving range in about twenty minutes."

Anger swells in my chest. He's home? And going golfing with *Prescott*? Prescott is more important to him than me? No, don't get upset. *Be calm, be calm.*

"Oh, really? And when were you planning on calling me, huh?"

Yeah, real calm, Sabrina.

Blaine gives me his *here we go again* sigh. "Sabbie, we got in this afternoon, and since you don't like going to the range, I planned on calling you later."

My pulse quickens from the possibility that he has blown me off—again. But I'm not going to bicker, not after we've already made up. No, we are going to have a wonderful summer together, so I force myself to say, "Well, welcome home, baby. Have fun tonight and call me when you're done, okay? I want to hear all about your trip and—"

Larson's booming voice cuts me off. "Blaine, time to get off the phone."

"Fine, Dad. Sorry, Sabbie, I gotta go. But I'll call you later, okay?"

He hangs up before I can say goodbye, leaving me to wonder if Blaine used his father to get me off the phone. Oh, no, he better not. I *refuse* to be played that way, even though, technically, I just did the same thing to Torrance.

"I'm going to Blaine's," I tell Mom while walking back into the kitchen and trying to ignore the fact that she has her bare feet propped on the table.

"Dressed like that?" She clucks her tongue as I open the side door. "You don't want Blaine seeing you all grubby, do you, baby?"

Screw it. Blaine is leaving in twenty minutes, so there isn't time to change. But after I get in the Honda and turn the key . . . there's nothing. Only a grinding moan.

Son of a . . .

"Need a lift, Sabrina?" Mom asks from the open doorway, dangling the keys to her Trooper. "I feel like taking a spin."

No, I'm not that desperate to see Blaine.

Oh, who am I kidding. Of course I am.

14 ∽ Sabrina

When we pull into Blaine's driveway, it feels as though we have interrupted a Ralph Lauren photo shoot. Larson, Rex Reynolds, and a posh couple in their forties are lounging on the porch in designer clothes with a pitcher of sangria on the table between them.

Mom was right. I should've changed my clothes.

She certainly did. Even though she's only dropping me off, I had to wait for her to throw on black capris, heeled sandals, and a tight Baltimore Ravens jersey. "Okay, Mom, thanks for the ride, I'll see you—"

"Don't be silly, Sabrina," Mom says, opening her door and gazing upon the sangria social scene. "I can't leave without saying hello, now, can I?"

Right, like politeness is her only motive.

Larson waves at us from where he is sitting on a wicker chair with his legs crossed. "Sabrina, Mona, what a lovely surprise! Come meet our new neighbors, Dr. Martin Swain and his charming wife, Victoria. They're building the house next door."

Blaine's Mercedes is still in the garage, thank God, so I'd rather go find him, but Mom clutches my arm and pulls me toward the porch as though I'm her two-legged security blanket. I feel like complete scum in my gardening outfit compared to Dr. Swain's gray trousers and Mrs. Swain's silk tunic, but I fake a confident smile as Mrs. Swain makes polite small talk about seeing us the night we worked at Barton's Campground. Larson then motions to Rex. "You both know Rex Reynolds, right?"

Sure, Mom's ex-boss and Danny's father. Rex greets us, his slightly crooked teeth, broad face, and stocky build making him look like an ex–football player who's more comfortable drinking beer than sipping cocktails—which is odd, considering the swanky development he designed. "Hello, Sabrina. And, Mona, how are you doing?"

"Fine and dandy, couldn't be better," Mom answers, keeping her eyes on their drinks as though she is dying for an invitation to join them. She then tilts her head toward the lot next door. "And I don't know much about construction, but I can tell that house is going to be just gorgeous, Rex!"

Larson uncrosses his legs and reaches for the pitcher, his tall runner's body reminding me so much of Blaine. "I'm glad to hear you're doing well, all things considered. I read today's article—horrible situation, just horrible. Sangria, Mona?"

I can't tell what Larson means. Horrible, as in she's horrible? But at the word "lawsuit," an odd look creeps over Rex's face, one I can't decipher.

Is it . . . intrigue?

Just as Mom drops her purse on the floor and starts to sit,

Rex stands. "Would you like a tour of the Swains' house, Mona? I'd be happy to show it to you."

Mom obviously doesn't want to go, not when she just scored an invite, but when Rex holds out his hand, she takes it. "Why, thank you, Rex, that'd be lovely."

I'm about to hunt down Blaine after they leave, but something Dr. Swain says stops me in my tracks. "Well, regarding the lawsuit, I, for one, am not comfortable staying at Barton's Campground any longer if the owner is negligent. So I spoke with Chuck Lambert. He's offered us a discounted rate for the rest of the summer."

Oh, man. I didn't think about Dee's mother losing business.

Mrs. Swain isn't pleased either. She grips her necklace and says, "Martin, we can't move! I've already bought decorations for this weekend's Fourth of July best-decorated-site contest. Besides, Chuck's campground is so distasteful. And I was hoping we'd, you know, start spending more time with Roxanne. They have so many lovely activities we don't take partake in. Like hiking. Or maybe we could try karaoke. Wouldn't that be fun?"

Dr. Swain regards her as though she suggested they go streaking in a cactus forest. "Right, Victoria, like you'd ever do something so redneck as karaoke."

What?

As he casually adjusts his gold Rolex watch, Mrs. Swain glances at me, her face ashen. Larson shakes his head, as though pleading with me not to react, but no, I don't think so. It's okay for me not to be a big fan of Mom's business. But it's definitely *not* okay for someone else to insult her.

"My mother owns a karaoke company, Dr. Swain. Do you think *she's* a redneck?"

Dr. Swain stammers for something to say, but any lame apology from him is not worth listening to. Not when Blaine is leaving soon. I turn back to Larson. "If you will excuse me, I'm going to see Blaine now."

Larson swirls his sangria, ice clinking against the crystal glass. "Uh, I'm sorry, Sabrina, but he isn't here. Prescott picked him up and they went to the driving range a while ago."

Great.

I missed him, so all of this was for nothing. Well, fine, I'll just find Mom and we'll take our redneck rears home. I mumble my goodbyes and step off the porch, but before I can make it past the fragrant roses lining Larson's sidewalk, Mrs. Swain catches up with me. "Now, Sabrina, you know my husband didn't mean any disrespect with his comment."

Uh, yes, he did.

"And while you're here, do you go to Riverside High?" she asks, guiding me almost forcefully past Mom's Trooper and around the side of Larson's house. She smiles when I nod and leads me toward the river where a girl is sitting on a pier with her feet dangling in the water and the warm sun beating on her face. "Then come meet my daughter, Roxanne. She's about your age and I'm *sure* she'd love to meet you!"

Before I can tell her no, we've already met, Mrs. Swain calls out to Roxanne. She is dressed in knee-length camouflage cut-offs and a huge black T-shirt. Wow, if Dr. Swain thinks karaoke is redneck, he must be horrified with her.

"Roxanne," Mrs. Swain purrs, linking her arm in mine.

"This is Sabrina. She goes to Riverside High, just like you will, although I'm sure she's not taking those horrible auto mechanics classes. But why don't you two get to know each other and then you'll have someone to eat lunch with, how's that?"

You've got to be joking.

Why is it that grown women—who have already been through the miseries of high school and should vividly remember how mortifying it can be—still manage to embarrass their own daughters? This sounds like the perfect topic to be discussed on The Superflirt Chronicles . . . if I were even remotely interested in that stupid blog.

Which I'm not.

"Well, I'll leave you two alone," Mrs. Swain says, before taking away a half-empty bag of Doritos that Roxanne must have been eating. She then steps back cautiously, like someone who has just finished building a house of cards and is afraid it will come crashing down with one false move.

Roxanne glares at her mother's retreating back and then turns all of that angry and—quite frankly—*boring* teenage angst onto me. "Well, I'm sure you're quite pleased with yourself," she says, as though she's been counting the days for the chance to say that.

Pardon me?

"What are you talking about, your mother? Hey, I never asked to be dragged out here like some—"

"Don't play dumb with me," Roxanne says, kicking her legs back and standing. She jams her wet feet into her Converse sneakers, which are old and beaten with the back heels flattened like clogs. "*Your* mother. The lawsuit. *That's* what I'm talking about."

That's right.

I had completely forgotten. Roxanne was there that night. She was the one who saw me looking for Blaine after he told me he was only going to the store for another soda. She was the one who called out to me from the porch swing, and who pointed up the stairs.

Did she also see me fall?

Does she know the truth, that Dee didn't push me?

Oh, my stupid mother. Of all the stupid things she's done, this is the absolute stupidest by far. It's too late now, though, so the only thing I can do is get me *and* Mom through the legal proceedings as unscathed as possible, although once again, Mom has left me to deal with the weeds. Only now, that weed is Roxanne Swain.

"What do you care about the Bartons?" I ask, planning my words carefully so I can find out exactly what she knows. "You were the one who called Dee Barton a super slut, so *you know* from her blog about the games she plays. You were the one who made me paranoid with all that *watch your man* stuff. And you were by the steps, so I'm sure you know what happened!"

Or what *didn't* happen.

"So," I continue, "you might as well tell me everything you saw before my mother's lawyers grill you." *Or Jane Barton's do.*

Roxanne shifts her weight, grasping an elbow with her opposite hand as she looks down the riverbank to where two girls are fishing. Her concrete shell seems to weaken and crack when the two friends burst out laughing, as though she longs to be with them—the same way Mom wanted to be with Larson's crowd earlier. "I know what you're up to," she says. "You want to know if I saw Dee push you. Well, no, I didn't. I couldn't see from where I was sitting, does that make you feel better?"

She's telling the truth.

But no, I don't feel better. Especially when the rest of Roxanne's rigid façade melts just enough for her to say, "And . . . I only told you where they were because I was mad at Dee for dancing with Jake. He's a nice guy who didn't deserve to be used like that just to make her ex jealous. And yeah, I did see her flirting with Blaine in the store, but when Dee ran upstairs, she seemed . . . she seemed upset, like she wanted to be left alone, not like she sounds on her blog."

So does this mean Roxanne feels *guilty* over what happened? And Dee—upset? Why would she be upset if she was getting exactly what she wanted?

"But." Roxanne faces me with her shoulders squared. "I may not like Dee, but I don't believe for one second that she'd push anyone. Steal someone's boyfriend? Sure, I wouldn't put it past her. Flirt with her teacher for a better grade? Why not. But push someone? No. No way."

A piece of driftwood floats toward us. So Roxanne is suspicious of me, after all. Okay, that's fine, I'll just have to persuade her to keep those suspicions to herself. "Look," I say as gently as the water lapping against the pier's green-stained posts. "My mom has no intention of going to trial for the full two million. She just wants a fair settlement, so all of this will be over by the time school starts. And speaking of school—"

"What are you going to do, Sabrina, put in a good word for me? Tell the A-Listers not to torture the weird new chick? What makes you think I need your help?"

Girl, you should NOT have asked that question.

"Well, let's see," I begin, motioning to her new house under construction. "I'm guessing you were forced to move away from your old home and you lost your friends as a result, judging from the way you keep watching those girls fish and the way your mother is dead set and determined to play matchmaker."

Roxanne says nothing, but from the way she watches that helpless driftwood until it's pulled around the bend, I know I'm right.

"And about your parents. Your mother snatched away your Doritos, and your father is a judgmental snob, so I'd say they don't exactly approve of your weight, your clothes, and those 'horrible auto mechanics' classes, right?"

Roxanne bites the inside of her cheek.

Check, check, and check.

"So no, I'm not going to invite you to my lunch table, Roxanne. But I can certainly make life a lot easier for you when school starts *if* you're interested in helping me make the settlement happen as quietly as possible."

On the other side of the river, a circling buzzard is spiraling over some poor dead animal. Roxanne watches as it flies lower, and lower, and lower, until it disappears from sight.

She turns back to me. "Okay. I'm interested."

At first, I feel victorious as I leave without saying goodbye and go back to the front of the house where Larson is showing Mom his roses. But through his open garage doors, I see something resting against a workbench that makes my blood run cold.

Blaine's golf clubs.

Welcome to the **Barton Family Campground's**
FOURTH OF JULY WEEKEND!

Friday, July 2:   7 pm   Red, White & Bluegrass with Butch and the Boys

    8 pm   Tonight's movie: SCHOOLHOUSE ROCK: AMERICA

Saturday, July 3:   10 am   Kids' Crafts: Felt Uncle Sam hats

    3 pm   Horseshoe Tournament

    5 pm   Hayride

    6 pm   Announcement of the most patriotic campsite!

    7 pm   God Bless America Karaoke

    8 pm   Tonight's movie: THE INCREDIBLES

    10 pm   S'mores & cocoa by the community fire

Sunday, July 4:   9 am   Nondenominational church service

    9 pm   Riverside Fireworks!

15 ~ Dee

After an article accompanied by a photo of Mona Owens posing Queen of Sheba–style came out, news about the lawsuit spread quicker than a marshmallow catches fire.

"Did you hear someone filed a lawsuit against this campground?"

"No, really? Why?"

"Because the owner's daughter—that girl who checked us in—hit another girl. Smacked her right in the nose!"

"How awful!"

The two women who were gossiping in the arcade while their children played skee ball last Wednesday jumped when I came in to refill the claw machine with stuffed animals, but I was grateful we still *had* guests. Chuck has been taking advantage of our situation by advertising how his campground is "safe," and he's even offered discounted rates to some of our permanent summer guests, which upset Mom almost as much as Madeline's decision to postpone her return home—again. The only time I've seen Mom truly happy this week was when a florist delivered a bouquet of her favorite gerber daisies on Thursday evening with a card that read, "Hang in there," and no name.

Were they from her *not exactly*?

Maybe I don't want to know. And even if I did, there's no time to ask. Despite the lawsuit, we're sold out for the weekend and packed to the gills by Friday afternoon. Most guests made their reservations months in advance and the competition for the most patriotic site is downright brutal, turning the campground into a temporary sea of red, white, and blue. Of course, Madeline thinks this tradition was not something anticipated by our founding fathers, but even her persnickety frown lifted when an elderly veteran saluted the flag.

And then there's Uncle Sam.

"Wow. You're so *old*."

Jake turns from the mirror mounted on his garage wall, wearing red-and-white-striped pants, a royal blue tuxedo jacket, and a white stovepipe hat with blue stars. "Look," he says, the attached Uncle Sam beard jiggling with his every word, "I better get paid extra for this. And I am *not* judging next year, I'm telling you that right now."

He stares at the many containers full of cookies, brownies, and cupcakes that are scattered among the tools and unassembled parts on his worktables. Poor Jake. Word somehow leaked out that he is this year's judge for the best decorated site so he's been sucked up to more times than a casting director on audition day.

I grab a cupcake and sit on a bar stool, breathing in the pungent smell of motor oil and dirt and feeling the dampness of the concrete blocks chill my arms. I never really thought about it before, but Jake's garage is kind of cool, with racing schedules posted on a bulletin board, classic rock playing on the radio, and battered tool chests covered in bumper stickers lining the wall. What I like the most, however, is that Roxanne isn't in here, although the reason *why* she's absent does make me nervous.

Earlier today, she was lingering by Ivy's leased BMW parked in front of the store, her head sticking through the open window and her chest expanding as though she was inhaling the new car scent. "She's a beauty, isn't she?" Ivy asked.

Roxanne jumped, crashing her head against the car frame as Ivy walked down the porch steps with me, carrying files for her meeting with Mona's lawyers.

"I wasn't stealing anything!" Roxanne said. "I just—I just was coming to the store to ask you something."

Ivy opened the BMW's back door and tossed her briefcase inside. "Of course you weren't, Roxanne. Surely you'd be smart enough not to take anything in plain sight, so what is it that you want?"

As I put Ivy's files on the backseat, Roxanne shuffled from side to side, ignoring my gaze as she said in a surprisingly polite voice, "Yeah, uh, I wanted to know if you needed any help with the case. It would, ah, look good on my college applications."

What? Jake told me how Roxanne wants to go to Lincoln Tech to study auto mechanics—a plan her parents aren't exactly thrilled about—so assisting Ivy wouldn't matter one bit on her college applications. Ivy seemed suspicious as well, but she only twisted her lips to the side and checked her watch. "Well, I have a three o'clock appointment with Aaron Wyatt. Do you have your driver's license, Roxanne?"

Roxanne stepped back. "Uh, no, just a learner's permit. Why?"

"Because you're driving, that's why," Ivy said.

Driving? Her BMW, are you kidding me? But even though I was completely annoyed, I couldn't help but notice the jubilation that spread on Roxanne's face. It reminded me of the day when Dad announced he was teaching me how to drive. Of course, I was six and it involved the John Deere tractor instead of a BMW, but the feeling was the same.

So when Jake takes off the Uncle Sam jacket and says, "Hey, think you can fix this before tomorrow?" while showing me a small rip on the left cuff, tears gather in my eyes. This was Dad's costume. He always had so much fun wearing it, pointing at guests and saying, "We want you." And my gosh, Dad always made the best Santa for our Christmas in July weekend. He was so magical, perched on the wagon as Mom pulled it with the tractor, bellowing out a *ho ho ho* that could rival any Santa at Macy's. He had a way of making every child feel special. Especially me.

But what would he think of me now?

What would he think about his daughter flirting with guy after guy every weekend and how his campground is now at risk because of it? What would he think of the way I dress, all skimpy and showy, enough to make girls like Roxanne hate me from the start?

I know what Dad would say—he'd say that life is full of messy mistakes that help us grow into better people—but what would he *think*?

"Dee, you okay?" Jake asks.

I wipe my damp cheeks. "Yeah, sure. I'll mend this tonight."

Jake pulls off the stovepipe hat. "No, you're not okay. Is it about the lawsuit?"

Duh. *Everything* for the past week has been about the lawsuit. Pain burns at my temples from trying not to cry as Jake pulls up a stool beside me. "Hey, come on, now, it's not that bad. Ivy has everything under control."

That's exactly what Ivy told me before leaving for the meeting—and also that Mona's lawyers don't have enough evidence to back up her ridiculous claim. But it still doesn't change who started all of this to begin with. Me. "So what, Jake? I'm a horrible person for letting this happen."

Jake swats at a persistent honeybee that's circling his soda. "Dee, you're not a horrible person and you know it."

"No, it's true. I am a horrible person who does stupid pool tricks, and who drapes herself over guys, just like you said, remember?"

He winces and holds up his hands. "Okay, that was a low blow on my part, but come on, Dee. You'd take a bullet for your mom. And I bet if I quizzed you, you could tell me the name of every camper staying here this weekend. Why? Because you genuinely care about people."

I mentally run through the names of guests who have checked in so far. The Ogles, who own a convenience store. The Tacketts, who are celebrating their twentieth anniversary, and the Sibles, who once rode their Harleys cross-country, but so what? And yeah, I'd do anything to protect my mom, but what daughter wouldn't?

Jake nudges my knee. "In fact, the only major complaint I

have is about when you told that loser you were a Red Sox fan. That's like saying you—"

"Technically," I interrupt with a smile of my own, "I never said I was a Boston fan. I do have my limits, Jake."

"See? So things aren't all that bad," he says.

I suddenly notice the closeness of our knees and how he must have gotten a haircut, judging from the tan line along his forehead. For some weird reason, I have an urge to trace it with my finger and—

Honestly. Where did that come from?

Maybe I'm going through flirt withdrawal.

Or maybe it's because when he's nice like this, it's so . . . nice. And, my, my, the way he danced that night. Afterward, he did ask me if I had any plans for the next day. Was Jake asking me out? No. No way. Besides, he's never—

Jake's cell buzzes. I watch the corners of his mouth turn up into a slow, sexy grin as he reads his text. Who is it from, Roxanne? He hops off the stool and grabs a gym bag off the counter. "Hey, I'm off to take a shower, unless you want to talk some more."

Oh, man, I'm such an idiot.

Jake has a *date*, so of course he's not interested in me. Sure, he's being nice, but deep down he's still the guy who thinks I'm nothing but a silly tease. Just as I am about to tell him no, so go on your stupid date, Ivy's urgent voice comes over the loudspeakers. "Dee Barton, please report to the main lodge. *Now.*"

Ivy is back from the meeting.

And it does not sound as though it went well.

∾

When I get to the lodge, I see Ivy inside pacing up and down the hardwood floors, Mom bingeing on Taco Bell—not a good sign—and Roxanne standing awkwardly by the counter. A wave of trepidation sweeps through me, making it hard to walk in the store. As soon as I do, Ivy whips around. "Dee, didn't I ask you to tell me the truth, the *whole* truth, and nothing but the truth, so help you God?"

My heart pounds. Of course I told her everything. Twice. Three times, even. "Well, yeah, I did, Ivy—"

She cuts me off. "And didn't I say that anything pertinent to the case better be disclosed to me *before* I met with those two-faced lawyers? But no, you chose not to tell me about your Superflirt blog, the one that outlined your plan to flirt with Sabrina's *boyfriend* in order to get revenge *and* all but claimed responsibility for her fall."

What? "Ivy, I—"

"Don't interrupt me, Dee! This supports Blaine's statement that *you* were the one who asked him upstairs. And they're going to try to enter some letter you wrote him as evidence of your instability!"

No, this is not happening.

The case was supposed to turn our way and Blaine was supposed to tell the truth—that *he* followed *me* upstairs. And there was something else—

"Ivy, what blog? I have no idea what you're talking about."

Spike. Check Mate. Bull's Eye.

Every single guy I've ever flirted with. McMuscles, a martial arts champion. Cannonball, a guy who kept jumping in the pool until he crashed into the ladder. John Deere, an FFA member who made farming sound hot.

Beater Boy. Sox.

Mercedes.

They are all there in black and white for my mother, Ivy, and Roxanne—*Roxanne Swain*, of all people—to read about. And I know exactly who put it there.

"Natalie wrote this, Ivy, not me."

I can't believe it. Why would Natalie do this, why would she write a blog pretending to be me? No, this has to be nothing but a big fat joke because Natalie wouldn't do this. *She wouldn't do this.*

"Natalie?" Roxanne blurts. "You're telling me that *Natalie* wrote this and you had absolutely no idea it existed?"

My blood instantly boils at Roxanne's nerve, her *audacity* to stand over my shoulder, reading the blog, instead of doing what any decent person would do and leave. It's bad enough she got to watch the lawsuit being served. Now she gets to witness my mother discovering exactly what kind of miserable person her daughter is?

"Why are you here, Roxanne, to enjoy the show? Is that why you conned your way into Ivy's car earlier today?" I snap, whirling around to face her. I expect to see gloating pleasure or smug happiness because, after all, this blog proves her right. Instead, she looks . . . surprised. Completely surprised.

But then a bigger realization hits me.

"Wait a minute . . . you knew about this, didn't you? Yes, you knew all about this and you were probably the one who told Sabrina, *weren't you?*"

Roxanne shakes her head. "No, I mean, yeah, I did find the blog on the night you had dinner with your grandmother, but I never showed it to Sabrina, I swear, but I did—"

She stops when Ivy steps in between us. "Ladies, now is not the time for this conversation."

I slump in my chair and face the computer again. Mom reads an entry out loud about how guys look so hot in dirty uniforms—especially "Jeter," a guy who resembled Derek Jeter and arrived at the campground last April still dressed from baseball practice. I wait for her to ask me if any of this is true, if I really did flirt with these guys, but she never does—which means she probably knew all along.

She must be so disappointed in me. And Madeline, what will she think?

And Jake.

Mom exits out of the Internet, as though she's had enough. "So, what does this mean, Ivy? Will the judge allow this to be used against us?"

"I don't know, Jane, but Lord knows the prosecution is going to try." Ivy takes off her glasses and rubs the bridge of her nose. "Lawsuits are being served by the hundreds against people who make slanderous comments on their blogs, but seeing as how this was written by Natalie . . . I just don't know. But you better believe I'm going to find out."

There is something I need to find out as well.

How Natalie could do this.

I get my chance when she breezes into the recreation room later that night, just as I am loading a *Schoolhouse Rock* movie into the DVD player for the row of kids sitting on the sofa. "Get this, Dee, my brother just called, and apparently he wants this girl he met in Ocean City to come to Disney with us!"

For hours, I've been rehearsing what to say to Natalie, but now that I see her face—one that I've always gone to for guidance and for comfort—my words disappear. She picks up the movie case and puts it back on the shelf while saying, "Seriously? After all the planning my grandmother and I have done, he thinks he can just spring this on us six weeks before the trip? Unbelievable! It will completely screw up my ADRs!"

The DVD whirls. I hit the play button and stand, not yet trusting myself to speak.

"Dee? What's wrong?"

It's impossible to talk. I walk outside and grip the deck railing, hearing laughter and the sound of Butch and the Boys playing James Brown's "Living in America" with a bluegrass flair. Natalie steps up beside me and yanks twice on my shirtsleeve. "Hey, did something happen at today's meeting?"

I turn to face her.

"The Superflirt Chronicles? How could you, Natalie?"

She drops her hand.

"Dee, no—please, let me explain."

"Explain! What's there to explain, Natalie? For *ten months* you've been posting things I thought were just between you and me. Is that all I am, good blog material? Is that why you always dared me to flirt, because I'm some journalism project?"

Tears brim in her eyes. "Dee, that's not true! And I kept the blog anonymous. No one was supposed to know!"

"Oh, and that makes it okay? Roxanne knew about it.

Sabrina knew about it—that's why she said I lured Blaine up here, because of what you posted about that night, how I did it for revenge."

And maybe she was right. Wasn't that why I was dancing with Jake?

"Dee," Natalie chokes out. "I'm so sorry. I never meant for this to happen. I started it for fun, you know, and I had no idea it would turn into something so big. But I swear, I'll delete everything. I'll post another entry telling people that it was all a lie, a big stupid lie."

Even though it wasn't.

"Natalie, don't you understand? The damage is already done, and Ivy said that if you take the blog down now, it will only make us look *more* guilty," I cry, tears now streaming down my face as well. "But what I don't understand the most is why you didn't tell me about it. Why keep it a secret from me? From *me*?"

Natalie presses her lips together and looks down at the grassy common area where two preteen girls are practicing a cheerleading routine. It's not until Butch finishes his song that she says, "Because . . . it was my chance to be Superflirt. My chance to be *you*, the star of the show, the pretty girl everyone notices."

I step back, my mind reeling. "What are you talking about? I'm not the star. At least I never try to be. If anything, I'm always trying to get *you* to flirt and—"

"—And I always chicken out," Natalie interrupts, with a deep self-loathing. "And I know you don't realize it or do it deliberately, but come on, Dee," she says, first pointing to my chest and then her own, "you're the star and I'm the sidekick and you know it. So this blog was my chance to shine, because in the real world, it's not easy for most girls. We can't all be perfect like you."

A jolt runs through my body, like someone kicked me into an electric fence. Isn't that what Roxanne said to me in the auto store, that I was *just perfect*? It was clear that Roxanne didn't mean it as a compliment.

And I don't think Natalie does either.

"What's that supposed to mean, that I'm some horrible show-off? That I think I'm special? Because you of all people should know I don't."

Natalie shakes her head. "Of course you don't, Dee, you never intentionally show off."

"So, what, I *un*intentionally show off?"

Natalie holds a hand against her forehead and paces the length of the small deck. "No! I didn't mean—*God*, I'm saying everything wrong!" She stops and stares at a nearby aspen tree just as a strong breeze ruffles the green and silver leaves, causing them to twist and quiver in a frenzied dance. "Dee, it's just that ... You don't understand. Everything comes so easy for you. Your looks, your figure, your hair. The way you can talk to anybody, the clothes you wear. It's like you're a magnet when you walk into the room."

I cannot believe my ears.

"But, Natalie, you pick out half of my clothes! You encourage me to flirt!"

"I know, I know!" Natalie exclaims. "And that's why we're such wonderful friends, because if I didn't know you, I'd completely hate you."

Oh my gosh.

There it is, the cold, hard truth.

If I didn't know you, I would hate you. That's what I would expect girls like Roxanne or Sabrina to say to me, but Natalie? No, that can only mean one thing. I am a show-off. I wasn't being paranoid, all those times I worried about talking too much or laughing too hard or acting like a total jerk. Jake was only being nice earlier today, trying to make me feel better, but the harsh reality is that while I might have been a flirt, I was never, *ever* super.

16 ~ Sabrina

Dear Blaine,

I had a wonderful time last night at Prescott's party, ~~even though you spent more time playing poker than being with me, and I really don't think I brought bad luck by standing behind you~~. I know you're busy practicing for the golf tournament, but I thought it would be fun if we got together tomorrow for the Clint Eastwood marathon on TV, ~~which you would know about if you bothered to read any of my texts~~. So give me a call—or text, e-mail, whatever—~~because I feel like I am losing you and that would break my heart~~.

"What are you reading, Sabrina?"

I jump at the sound of Bridget's voice and nearly fall off my chair when she throws open one of Macy's dressing room doors and almost catches me trying to write a letter to Blaine. "Oh, nothing," I lie, "just, um, something from my dad."

"Aw, how sweet!" Bridget says, stepping toward the floor-to-ceiling mirror. "My father never sends me anything."

Neither does mine, come to think about it. Even his Christmas cards are signed by Belinda. I shove the letter deep into my purse, in case Bridget asks to read it, but she has already moved on to a more interesting topic. Herself. "What do you think of this?" she asks, while posing in a size one dress.

Another stall door opens and an overweight woman steps out with an armful of clothes that don't fit, judging from the way she hangs them on the return rack and then frowns at her reflection. Bridget winks at me. "Do I look fat in this?" she asks, with her back arched and hips thrust forward. The woman slows her pace long enough to study Bridget's tiny frame with a deep sadness in her eyes. Bridget giggles when she leaves. "Oopsie! I totally didn't mean to say that so loud!"

Right. She knows perfectly well what she's doing. Just like I've always known when I was being mean for fun.

How many people have I hurt like that?

"You know, in London, they don't have separate stalls in the dressing rooms," Torrance says, as she comes out wearing a black halter dress cut to her navel. She gazes at Bridget from head to toe. "Hmm, are you sure you don't need a bigger size?"

Bridget's smugness disappears. She anxiously checks her reflection. *Nice, Torrance, give her an eating disorder, why don't you,* I want to say. But these girls are like wolves. They'll attack at the slightest trace of blood or weakness, and right now I can't afford to be on their bad side. I didn't even want to come along for their Sunday afternoon shopping ritual, not after my neighbor, Mrs. Mason, gave me a ton of curtains to sell on craigslist for a thirty percent commission. But it's almost senior year and I have no intention of spending it as an outsider, not after I've worked so hard to be on the inside. So I reach into my purse and crumple the letter to Blaine that I've been trying to compose for days. There's *no way* I can send him this, even though he's driving me completely insane and—

Desperate.

Like Dee was when they broke up.

Now I understand why she wrote that letter.

"Sabrina," Torrance coos. "When your mother wins the lawsuit, you really should go to London. The crown jewels are spectacular!"

"Yeah, that would be awesome," I say with fake enthusiasm. Torrance doesn't know Mom's lawyers have scheduled another meeting for next week where they plan on asking for a sixty-thousand-dollar settlement instead of going to trial. Because of Blaine's statement and Dee's blog, they are optimistic about getting at least twenty-five thousand, once negotiations are done, but that's still a lot of money. Dee's mother drives a beat-up truck, and Dee doesn't even have a car. How are they going to afford a settlement?

Stop. *Since when do I care about her?*

Twenty-five thousand dollars won't break them, and besides, I read her blog. And Dee did stalk Blaine, both last September and at the campground. Still. At the party last night, I saw Bridget duck into a pantry with Prescott—and I doubt it was for cookies. His girlfriend, Vanessa, would be livid if she found out, but would that justify filing a lawsuit?

"Sabrina, what's wrong with you? You haven't answered me," Torrance says, checking the tag on her dress and not balking at the beefy price. "Are you hanging out at my house for tonight's

Fourth of July party or not? Blaine will be there, unless, of course, the fireworks between you two are gone for good."

That's cold. Even for Torrance.

From the way Bridget's eyes gleam, I suspect she must be planning on sneaking off with Prescott again tonight. *These girls are my friends?* I'm not an expert, but I'm pretty sure friends aren't supposed to make snide remarks about the guy who's breaking your heart, or sneak around with another girl's boyfriend. And what did Dee say on her blog about relationships? How they're supposed to make you feel good and not bad?

"What's wrong, Sabrina?" Torrance asks. "You're not mad at us for teasing you about the book we found in your room, are you?"

Bridget clutches her hands to her chest. "Oh, yeah, *How to Win Friends & Influence People*, how stupid!"

Why didn't I have the good sense to hide that book Dee mentioned on her blog? And better yet, why can't I stop reading that ridiculous Web site? Now the wolves are about to attack, so I have to regain my footing. Quick. Knowing that Vanessa is capable of making Bridget's life miserable, I say, "Oh, really, Bridget, as stupid as, say, hanging out in a pantry during a perfectly good party?"

The color slowly drains from her face as the realization that I know what she did sinks in. She swallows hard and glances at Torrance. "Ah, actually, Sabrina, the book sounds cool. Can I borrow it when you're done?"

"Sure," I say sweetly.

∾

After Torrance drops me off at home, the only thing on my agenda is crawling into bed for a nap, but when I walk into my room, I hear sounds of shuffling inside my closet. Fabulous. My darling mother is once again raiding my clothes, trying to find something skintight to wear.

"Sabrina, is that you?" Mom asks.

"Who else, Mother? And don't even think of wearing my new pink sweater set. It will never fit me after your monster boobs have been in it."

Mom steps out. Instead of her usual video vixen attire, she's wearing a conservative black pencil skirt, a simple blouse that hides her swelling cleavage, and minuscule diamond studs instead of bangle-sized hoops.

You've got to be kidding me.

Surely I'm in the twilight zone.

"Sweetie! There you are," Mom says, her lips now a modest shade of mauve instead of fiery red, and her nails—her trademark nails—painted a pale pink, with no designs, no sparkles, nothing fancy, nothing *Mona.*

As she pushes my leather belt through the skirt loops, it hits me, the reason she's dressed like this. *Of course.* "Are you meeting with the lawyers? Another photo session for the papers?"

Mom looks into the mirror, smoothing a stray hair back in place. She gives me a demure smile. "No, sweetheart, I have another date tonight. And is it okay that I borrowed your belt? I don't have any that are quite right."

Oh, no. I recognize that spark in her eye, the one that means she has fallen hard for a new guy—probably the one she's seen every night since she got those flowers last week. But she has never, *ever* changed her appearance. Not Mona Owens, who doesn't give a rat's behind about the unofficial *no miniskirts over thirty-five* rule. And since when has Mom ever asked permission to borrow my belt? Normally she just swipes whatever she wants and then *la, la, la*, goes about her merry way.

This is strange. More than strange.

"Yeah, that's fine," I say.

"Thanks, toots. Well, how do I look?" Mom asks, turning away from the mirror and waiting for my response. There is something about her, something so different from her usual devil-may-care attitude. Insecurity?

"Um, you look nice, Mom. Really nice."

She breathes out deep with relief and then encases me in a huge hug. "Thanks, sweetie. Now for heaven's sakes, I gotta get going before I'm late!"

I follow her to the foyer, where she grabs a small leather clutch instead of her favorite purse. Another bouquet of tiger lilies is sitting on the entry table. "More flowers, are they from the same guy? And why are you being so coy about who he is?"

Mom grips the doorknob, pausing long enough to nervously say, "I'll tell you later, sweetie, I promise, once things are . . . once I'm sure, okay?"

Sure? Sure of what?

And since when does my mother not brag about her dates?

The Superflirt Chronicles
. . . blogs from a teenage flirtologist

Tuesday, July 6

AN APOLOGY
MOOD: Miserable

MUSIC: "What Can I Say," Brandi Carlile

D—I'm so sorry. Please let me explain.

N.

17 ~ Dee

I should talk to Natalie.

I should end the silence between us that has done nothing but make me feel miserable all weekend. Even watching the fireworks with Mom on Sunday night didn't bring me any joy, not when I knew Natalie was working in the store by herself while everyone else was having fun.

It's not as though she hasn't tried. She's texted, called, e-mailed—everything short of hiring skywriters and renting a carrier pigeon to send me her apologies.

Then there's what she posted yesterday.

And the fact that after reading through every single entry— sometimes twice—it's become clear that her blog was about more than flirting. It was about helping women be stronger.

But if she didn't know me, she'd hate me.

How do you respond to something like that? Do you say, oh, okay, thanks—good to know? Or, gee, glad we're friends, then, huh? And how well do I know Natalie if she thought it was okay to share what was supposed to be nothing but a fun joke between us with the rest of the world? My mother read it. Madeline read it, and judging from the way two women in dowdy swimsuits keep glancing my way while I'm taking a break by the pool on Wednesday afternoon, they must have read it, too.

Jake read it.

And, by the time school starts, every one of my classmates will have as well, guaranteeing that my senior year will be as sucky as my junior.

I slump in my lounge chair and watch as a bunch of guests gather at the sand court for an impromptu badminton game. Jake shows an elderly woman who is clearly charmed by his good manners how to serve. So far, he hasn't ragged on me about the blog, just like he's never once teased me about the letter I wrote Blaine last year, even though he surely must have known about it. And he invited me to his race this weekend, saying how a break would do me good, although he probably invited Roxanne as well.

Or whoever his new little texting buddy is.

The gate behind me creaks. I turn to see Mom walking through, looking out of place in her work boots among the flip-flops and bathing suits. She waves at a sun-soaked, pampered woman from New Jersey and then sits on the lounge chair beside me, wearily stretching her legs out and motioning to the sand court. "Hey, toots, shall we join them?"

Despite my love for badminton, I shake my head. A week ago, I would have reveled in throwing myself right into the middle of that crowd, but isn't that why people don't like me, because I always have to be the center of attention, the star? Forget it.

From now on, I'm a sidelines-only kind of gal. And no more bikini tops and flippy skirts either. Ever since my fight with Natalie, it's been nothing but T-shirts and baggy shorts for me.

At least I don't have to suck in my stomach now.

Mom crosses her ankles. "You know, I can't remember the last time I've hung out at the pool. Isn't it stupid? I have a lovely pool, and I never take time to enjoy it."

No, it isn't stupid. Mom works nonstop, so of course she doesn't have time for pool lounging or manicures like the New Jersey queen over there. What *is* stupid is a daughter like me who does nothing but add to her heartache. I wish Mom would go ahead and tell me how I am a disappointment, how she is ashamed of my behavior, *anything*. Instead, Mom squints at someone swimming crooked laps. "Is that Madeline?"

I nod. If Natalie was here, she would've cracked up over Madeline strolling into the pool area earlier, stretching and twisting in her Speedo swimsuit, swim cap and goggles perched on her head. And knowing Natalie, she would have bribed the Cutsons to cannonball near Madeline's head after her first lap.

Huh. Lyle and Tanner are in the shallow end, dogpaddling like a couple of bug-eyed Chihuahuas. Maybe *I* should bribe them, just to give Mom a well-needed giggle, but it wouldn't be the same. Nothing feels the same. Not the pool, not badminton, and not the campground that has always given me comfort during the darkest times in my life—after Dad's death, after Blaine's breakup, and the letter fiasco.

Now, I feel like an outsider looking in.

And besides, when I look in Mom's direction, she is sound asleep.

The following day, Mom is in our cabin's bathroom rubbing aloe onto her red nose. "Great, I relax by the pool for once and what happens? I turn into a burnt tomato, as though I don't have enough wrinkles already."

"Mom, stop. You're beautiful."

She turns off the light and then joins me in the kitchen where I'm fixing Hot Pockets for lunch. Mom flops down at the small oak table. "Nice try, honey, but I do have wrinkles. And gray roots, and—" She looks at her nails. "Ugh. And horrendous cuticles."

I hate seeing her so defeated and worn-out. Mom runs her finger along a ceramic vase filled with wildflowers. At first, I don't understand her odd expression, until I remember that was the vase her daisies were delivered in. Maybe now would be a good time to ask who sent them, but what if it opens the door to a conversation I'm not ready to have?

God, I'm horrible. I'm thinking of *my* feelings, instead of hers. I'm no better than Meghan's daughters—the woman from Natalie's blog who's divorced and unhappy, whose dates kept getting ambushed because of her selfish children. Mom should date.

She should spend time with people other than me.

I throw a Hot Pocket in the microwave and punch start, not caring if the radiation fries my brains from standing too close. Mom absentmindedly straightens the lace table runner. "Um, honey, we need to talk—about the lawsuit. You know the judge has denied the motion of summary judgment that Ivy filed," she says, her voice strained and tight. "But what I haven't told you is that Mona's lawyers gave us a settlement offer for sixty thousand dollars."

The room begins to spin. My knees weaken.

Sixty thousand dollars?

"Hold on, sweetie, okay?" Mom says. "It's not all that bad. Ivy worked for Aaron Wyatt and knows his tricks, so she's fairly certain they'll settle for much less."

I slump down on the chair beside her. "For how much?"

"Maybe twenty-five thousand dollars."

No, no, this isn't happening. This can't happen! *What have I done?* Teenagers are supposed to do stupid stuff that costs their parents money, like dent a fender or lose a cell phone, but twenty-five thousand dollars?

The microwave beeps.

Mom reaches for my hands and grips them tight enough for me to feel her wedding band. "Dee, it's okay. I wasn't going to tell you until all the details were worked out, but—" She swallows hard. "I'm going to sell four acres to Rex for two hundred fifty thousand dollars. He has generously offered to give me a forty-thousand-dollar usable, nonrefundable deposit, so not only can I pay the settlement, I'll also be able to afford your college tuition, Dee. I can buy you a car so you won't have to ride your bike everywhere."

No. No!

I don't want a car. I don't want college. Rex is only taking advantage of her after trying to get his hands on that land for years. "No, Mom! Dad hated it when Madeline sold land to Rex eight years ago. He hated it when Rex started building those houses and he hated Rex!"

Mom's face pales.

The microwave beeps again, but I ignore it. "What about the bank, can't you get a loan? Did you even try, or Ivy—could you borrow the money from her?"

"Yes, I did try, but after your father died, I had to take a second mortgage to pay off the estate taxes and funeral costs, so they said no, sweetie. I do *not* want to go farther in debt by borrowing from Ivy, so this is my only option."

I jerk to my feet and open the microwave, grabbing the Hot Pocket with my bare hands and then flinging it on the range top when it burns my fingers. I hold them to my mouth and cry, "No, the best option would have been to never have such an idiot of a daughter."

"Don't say that, Dee!"

"Why not? I've ruined everything. I know you're disappointed in me. Will you just say it, huh? Say how you're angry with me, anything!"

Mom stands and pulls me into a tight embrace. "No, Dee, that's not true. And aren't you forgetting that *I'm* the one who didn't send the insurance payment? Are you angry with me for that? Are you angry with your father for not having enough life insurance when he died?"

I shake my head. "That was different—"

"No, it isn't. It isn't, Dee!" Mom says. "You made a mistake. A small, *innocent* mistake, but it's not your fault Mona Owens is taking advantage of that mistake, do you understand? I need you to understand this, Dee!"

"But the way I've behaved . . . Superflirt . . . I know you're ashamed."

Mom holds her palms against my cheeks, forcing me to face her. "Honey, I could *never* be ashamed of my daughter. If anything—I wish I could be more like you."

Like me?

Mom drops her arms and leans back against the counter, staring at a picture on the windowsill of my father holding up a giant catfish. "You're so much like your father, Dee. He was the one who would convince me to dance when I'd rather sit out or make me laugh when I got too uptight. You have that same spirit. That's why it never bothered me to see you talking with boys, because I *never* wanted to do anything that would break it."

She takes a deep breath and then studies the gold band on her finger. "What I wouldn't do to get some of that spirit. Maybe then I could move on."

My own breath catches.

So it is true—Mom does want to date. She wants to be something other than a mother and a widow and a workaholic. She wants to be a woman again.

"And I know you're upset about the land," Mom continues, "but the campground will still be plenty big enough *and* we'll figure out a way to finally beat Chuck Lambert." She then grabs hold of my baggy shirt. "So, I want my daughter to get out of these hideous clothes and go back to being herself."

How can I go back to being the person I once was? No, I'm ashamed of that person. Too much has happened. Too many things have been said. But when Mom looks out the window and says, "By the way, you have some company, honey," my heart melts as I notice someone walking up the path carrying a box of Skinny Cow Fudge Bars.

Natalie.

I throw open the door before she can even raise her hand to knock.

"Dee, give me five minutes, please. I'm so sorry for everything, for the blog, for what I said, because you know, *you know* I love you dearly, for causing the lawsuit, for—"

I wrap my arms around her.

"Stop. You had me at Skinny Cow. You had me at Skinny Cow! And, Natalie, you did *not* cause the lawsuit."

Neither did I. Neither did Superflirt.

And come to think of it, neither did Mona or Sabrina Owens. They are guilty of being complete gold-digging opportunists, sure, but they didn't *cause* the lawsuit. Someone else did. Someone who followed me when I told him no. Someone who lied about being lured upstairs.

That someone is Blaine Walker.

"Give me your cell," I demand of Natalie because mine is dead. Again. She digs her phone out of her pocket with a bewildered look. "Okay," she says. "Normally when friends make up after a big fight, they talk, but sure."

I'm tired of talking. I'm tired of beating myself up each and every day. It's time to put an end to this once and for all.

Blaine answers on the third ring with a sly "Hey, Torrance."

Torrance, as in Sabrina's friend? Blaine is fooling around with her? Unbelievable. "Try again, dirtbag," I say through gritted teeth.

He hesitates. "Dee-Dee?"

"My name is Dee. And I want to know why you lied because *we both know* what happened that night."

Blaine doesn't reply, the gears in his head probably spinning for his next defensive play. It doesn't take long. In one heartbeat, his demeanor shifts from surprise to total control. "Oh, really? Don't you remember flirting with *me*, or are you forgetting that part?"

He's right. I did flirt with him for those brief moments. Maybe that's what caused him to follow me and . . . *No, stop it!* He's only doing it again, making me doubt myself and feel as though *I* should be apologizing instead of him. All it takes is his voice, that confident, con-artist tone he always used to sweet-talk his way out of an argument.

"Don't even try it, Blaine. I'm not falling for that trick."

"Sure you are, Dee-Dee. You always did. And my dad is having a wine-tasting party this weekend, so he needs my help right now. We'll talk later."

He hangs up. The jerk hangs up. *You always did.* Well, not anymore. Before I think twice, I quickly send him a text.

If you want a fight, you got one. Better watch your back, Blaine.
Superflirt is ready to battle.

18 ~ Sabrina

Aaron Noland Wyatt, Esquire, is nothing but a player.

A swanky, meticulously groomed blond player with tweezed brows, gel-shellacked hair, and a butter-soft tailored suit that certainly didn't come from anywhere around here. The smell of his overwhelming cologne nearly makes me dry-heave as he escorts Mom and me into his office late Friday afternoon. It's pompous and pretentious, with bronze fixtures, textured wallpaper, and floor-to-ceiling shelves full of leather-bound law books.

In other words, Mom is entranced.

A month ago, I might have been, too, but now . . .

"Can I get you ladies anything to drink? Coffee? Tea? Perrier mineral water?" Aaron asks, resting his manicured hand on Mom's shoulder.

Mom clasps her hands. "Ooo, Perrier, that sounds lovely, Aaron, thank you! Sabrina, would you like some Perrier?"

I'm too focused on Aaron's lingering hand to answer.

No, no, NO, is he the mystery man Mom has had dinner with

every single night for over a week now? Is he the reason she's dressed like a Sunday school teacher in a prim summer suit with her hair smoothed in a neat bob instead of its usual teased bouffant?

The thought of having to deal with a different man in our house is uncomfortable enough as it is without it being *this* man. I bet he wears robes in the morning. I can imagine him at the breakfast table—chest hair poking out of his robe while he enjoys his cappuccinos and crepes. I'd prefer Chuck Lambert over him. Barely.

"Sabrina, honey, are you okay?" Mom asks.

I shake off the nasty image and nod. Yes, I will be okay once this settlement meeting is over and life goes back to normal. I'll spend the rest of summer having fun with Torrance and Bridget, and maybe I'll try out for cheerleading in August, since my reputation might need a pick-me-up. Blaine and I will patch up the awkwardness between us, and he'll no longer act so distant, like at Torrance's Fourth of July party when he skipped the fireworks to play pool or all this week when he spent most of his time on the golf course instead of calling me.

Aaron admires his reflection in the window that overlooks historic downtown Riverside and straightens his tie. "I'll have my secretary bring your drinks. Take your time enjoying them," he says, giving Mom a wink. "Ivy Neville and her party are already in the conference room, but it wouldn't hurt to let them stew for a while."

Okay, it's official. I'd jump off a cliff if he became my stepfather.

❧

Thirty minutes later, after Mom has enjoyed every last sip of her Perrier—and stated a million times how she has to get a case from Costco—Aaron finally takes us into the conference room where Dee, Jane Barton, and two older women are waiting. I recognize one of them from the campground, but she looks so different now with her cut hair and tailored suit. The other I don't recognize. Dee's grandmother, maybe? They do have the same blue eyes. But what about Dee's father, are her parents divorced like mine?

"Well, well, Ivy Neville, it's good to see a former employee," Aaron says. "How's retirement treating you?"

From the way Ivy's jaw braces, I can tell her relationship with Aaron is not a good one. She forces a smile and reaches out to shake his hand. "Hello, Aaron, always a pleasure, and my retirement is getting longer by the minute considering you've had us waiting in here for *almost an hour.*"

"My apologies, ladies, I had a conference call," Aaron says, pulling out a chair for Mom at the head of the table. Liar. "Would anyone care for a beverage? Coffee, tea, tap water?"

Tap water, huh?

Ivy grabs her pen. "We're quite fine, Aaron. What we would like is for this meeting to start sometime *today.*"

"Suit yourself," Aaron says, sitting on the opposite side.

The other elderly woman raises her hand. "I, for one, would love a refreshment," she huffs.

"Well, then, Madeline," Jane Barton says through clenched teeth. "You should have stayed home and had all the refreshment you wanted."

As Aaron leisurely arranges his papers, I slump down on a chair by the window, trying hard not to notice the way Dee and her mother lean toward each other, as though they are holding hands underneath the table. Man. I can't remember the last time I held my mother's hand. Even if I tried, she would only think I wanted something from her, and to be honest, I'd feel the same way if she held mine. Our relationship is more like Jane and Madeline's, with the bickering, bickering, bickering. Is that how Mom and I are going to be for the rest of our lives?

Yes, we probably will. It's kind of sad, really.

So maybe I was right to be jealous of Dee when Blaine and I started going out.

But not for the reason I thought.

Aaron Wyatt opens a manila folder, his motions fluid and impassive, as though tearing people's lives apart is just another day at the office. "Now, Ms. Neville, we have received your client's settlement offer of twenty thousand dollars."

Ivy nods. "That's right, to be paid immediately."

Aaron leans back in his chair, resting his elbows on the arm-rests with his fingers steepled beneath his chin. His elaborate pinky ring sparkles as he squints and says, "Well, unfortunately, after consulting with my client, your counteroffer is not adequate."

I expected this to happen. I knew Mom would do her Mexican bartering for as much as possible. She told me a few days ago that she would accept twenty-five, so *come on, Ivy, say twenty-five and let's just end this!*

Ivy crosses her arms, giving me the feeling that her retirement wasn't all that voluntary, especially when she glares at him and says, "Not adequate, huh. Well, would twenty-two be more adequate?"

I watch Mom inspect a fingernail, majestic as a queen bee on her throne. She really is enjoying this, her moment of power. She shakes her head, stretching this moment out as long as possible. "No, Ms. Neville, twenty-two is not adequate."

Aaron gathers his papers and stuffs them in a folder as though the meeting is over, causing Ivy's eyes to widen. "Okay," she says. "We're prepared to raise the offer to twenty-five thousand."

Oh, thank you. The magic number. Mom pretends to contemplate this by pressing a nail against her chin. "Well . . . no, it's still inadequate."

Mom . . .

"Twenty-six thousand?"

Aaron grins, reminding me of a cat we used to own who would catch a mouse and bat it back and forth between its paws before killing it. "Actually, Ivy, our client has decided that no settlement offer will be adequate."

Some of the color drains from Ivy's face. "Meaning?"

Mom leans forward, placing her forearms on the table and clasping her hands. *"Meaning* I am proceeding to trial for the full two million."

The room begins to spin.

Someone gasps.

I shoot out of my chair, sending it crashing against the wall behind me. "Mom—you promised we were going to settle! You said this was all going to be over!"

"Not now, Sabrina," Mom whispers.

No, this is not happening.

It feels as though my entire world has been ripped out from underneath me, just like when Dad came into my room on that night so long ago and told me he was leaving to be with Belinda. I sink into my chair, unable to comprehend how Mom can just sit there calmly and not be affected by the sheer terror on Jane Barton's face. And Madeline's.

And especially Dee's.

"What's going on, Aaron," Ivy barks. "You arranged this settlement meeting *yesterday*. What could possibly have changed since then?"

"My client told me her decision earlier today. I'm just honoring her wishes."

Mom brushes lint off her lapel, and then turns to him. "Isn't there something else that needs to be discussed?"

Aaron nods, pulling another folder out from his pile. "Yes, there is. We have received word that the daughter of your defendant, Dee Barton, has threatened one of our witnesses, a Mr. Blaine Walker."

What? She threatened Blaine?

"No, that's not true," Dee says, her voice rising with each word. "I mean—yeah, I did call him, but it was only to find out why he lied, because he did lie, I *never* asked him to come upstairs. I told him to *leave me alone*, so yeah, maybe I did tell him to watch his back!"

"Well," Aaron says with a lofty smirk. "Isn't that the same as threatening?"

Tears start to stream down Dee's face. She swipes them

away with the back of her hand. "No, no, that's not it at all. Blaine lied. And you—Sabrina—"

She thrusts a finger toward me.

"You know I never pushed you. You know. *YOU KNOW!*"

Our eyes lock.

I have to look away.

Ivy grabs Dee's elbow and pulls her down. "Dee, it's okay. Relax."

Aaron slides the contents of the folder across the table to Ivy. She quickly scans the paper, her fury growing with each word. "You're not serious, are you?"

"I'm afraid so," Aaron says. "Considering the possible witness tampering and Miss Barton's violent nature, as proved just now, we're filing a restraining order against Dee Barton."

What?

"She needs to stay a hundred feet away from Sabrina Owens and Blaine Walker at all times."

"How 'bout some coffee?" Mom chirps from the front seat of her Trooper after driving out of Aaron's parking lot. She turns off Main Street and onto a side road, nodding toward the Starry Night Bakery. "We can get some of those fancy chocolate ones, with whipped cream and cocoa sprinkles, yum-yum!"

Yum-yum?

She just dropped those major bombshells at the meeting and now she's casually talking about *yum-yums*? "No, Mom, I don't want any stupid coffee!"

Too late. She puts her blinker on.

"Oh, I *hate* parallel parking," she moans, looking over her shoulder and cutting the wheel. She backs a few feet and then jerks to a stop. Forward, stop. Backward, stop. The truck behind us honks. "Hold your horses, mister! And, Sabrina, it'll be my treat, since you're still a little annoyed."

"Annoyed?" I shoot back. "Annoyed doesn't even begin to cover it, Mother. You lied about going to trial. You *promised* me that would never happen!"

Mom hits the curb with the right rear tire. She spins the wheel hard to the right and moves forward until she hits the curb with her front tire. "Now, honey, you best remember that I'm the adult, and I make the decisions, okay?"

"No—not okay. Why did you change your mind? And the restraining order, how do you explain that?"

Especially when Dee never once touched me, except when she was trying to help. And Aaron told us about Ivy's claim that *Natalie* wrote the blog. Of course, he doesn't believe it and neither does Mom. But if it is true—if Dee didn't even know about the blog like Ivy said—then was she playing games with Blaine or not?

And what did Roxanne tell me? *Dee seemed upset, like she wanted to be left alone, not like how she sounded on her blog.*

This is such a mess. And who really is to blame? Is it Dee, if Natalie was the person who wrote the blog? Roxanne, because she was the one who told me they were upstairs? Mom, for being a total court whore? Or am I to blame, for agreeing to this whole stupid thing to begin with?

"Sabrina, honey, I changed my mind because . . . I changed

my mind, okay?" Mom slams the Trooper into park and gives me a wink. "Besides, the restraining order was Aaron's idea. He thought it would strengthen our case at trial."

I stare openmouthed at her. She clearly has no clue about how all this is affecting me. "You're unbelievable, Mom."

"Thanks, sweetie!" Mom beams, reaching into her purse for a ten-dollar bill. "Now, what do you want, huh? You can have anything at all."

"Fine. A mocha frappe light, no whipped cream," I say, leaning back in my seat.

Mom hands me the money. "Yum. Get me one, too, will ya? But with the whipped cream and no light. Life's too short for light!"

"Me? I thought you were treating?"

Mom flips down her visor, wiping off a stray bit of lipstick that was bleeding into a wrinkle. "Well, I am paying. Now scoot!"

Great.

I slam the door loud enough to startle a woman who is walking out of a nearby florist shop with a large plant arrangement. Then a parked Mercedes on the other side of the street makes me stop in my tracks. No, it can't be Blaine's, *please don't be Blaine's!* He'll think I'm stalking him. But . . . maybe it would be good if he is here.

Maybe I can find out if we're still together or not.

I walk inside the dimly lit bakery with its deep purple walls, painted murals, and a rubber ducky collection lined up on a long shelf. So far, no Blaine, which is a relief. Facing him isn't something I'm prepared for. Not today. A cute, tattooed girl makes my mocha frappes, but as I turn to leave, I remember the back tables. *No, forget it.* The best thing to do is just go home. But once I reach the door, my resolve snaps like a rotten rubber band, making me spin around and almost run into a college student with an armful of books. Sure enough, there he is in the back, sitting with his feet hiked up on a chair.

"Blaine," I say, stronger than I mean to.

He jerks his head up, his handsome face distorted with alarm. He glances at the back door behind him and stammers, "Sabbie! Hey, what a surprise."

I put the drinks down. "Yeah. Today has been full of surprises, so it makes perfect sense to find you here."

There is genuine concern in his voice when he asks, "Are you okay? Do you need to talk about it?"

My heart pounds. I long to kiss him, feel his lips on mine, have him wrap those strong arms around me . . . but there are two cups on the table. One has lipstick on the brim, a pretty coral shade that is somewhat familiar. Which means—

Blaine isn't alone.

Of course he isn't.

I shake my head and let out a bitter laugh. "Wow, I'm so stupid. All this time, I've been so *stupid.* You're nothing but a Mr. Booty-Bagger, aren't you, Blaine?"

"Mr. What?"

"A Mr. Booty-Bagger. Blaine the Booty-Bagger."

Blaine looks at me as though I am absolutely nuts but I don't care. For the second time this month, I think of what Dee—or

Natalie—wrote about relationships on the blog. Whoever it was, she was so right:

> Relationships are supposed to make you feel good.
> Relationships are NOT supposed to make you feel bad.
> Or guilty, insecure, ashamed, paranoid, or hopeless.
> Good.
> So when a relationship makes you feel bad, guilty, insecure, ashamed, paranoid, or hopeless, end it. Get over him. Move on.
> Flirt.

I'm tired of feeling bad, tired of defending him or justifying his behavior because his mother deserted him, tired of needing a guy to be happy, tired of that stupid Sabbie nickname, just *tired*. I want to be happy on my own. I want to have fun. I want to be confident again and get over him. Move on.

Just flirt.

"It's over, Blaine."

He says nothing, his fingers tapping the table as though he's about to put up some kind of fight, some kind of *say it isn't so*—if only to make me feel better. But instead he sips his drink with indifference and says, "Yeah, you're right, especially now that things are going to get weird."

"Weird? What do you mean by that?" I demand.

Blaine doesn't give me an answer.

I don't feel like waiting for one.

"Goodbye, Blaine. And tell your new girl I said good luck. She's going to need it."

Mom is chatting animatedly on her phone when I walk out. She quickly hangs up and checks her watch. "Goodness gracious, what took you so long? I need to go."

"Long line," I mumble before getting in.

Mom whips the Trooper back onto the street, almost cutting off a UPS truck and causing me to spill my drink down my favorite shirt just as we pass Blaine's Mercedes. *My favorite shirt, really?* Was that some kind of omen that I just made the biggest mistake of my life? After all these weeks of worrying that he was going to break up with me, how could I call it off like that, without thinking it through?

I'm going to be sick.

Mom hands me a stack of napkins and stomps on the accelerator. "Lord, child, you're gonna have to change as soon as we get home, okay? I can't have you all messy when my date gets there."

"What does it matter?"

The only thing I want to do is crawl into bed, *not* have awkward conversation with some jerk who's trying to get on my good side. Mom doesn't elaborate as she pulls onto the highway that leads to our house. But as she turns into our development, she clicks off the stereo, just as Charlie Pride hits a high note. Huh? Mom never turns off Charlie Pride. She thinks that's un-American. "Uh, Sabrina, honey, remember how I wanted to make sure of things before telling you who sent me those flowers?"

A feeling of dread brews in my stomach.

Mom brakes at a stop sign and puts a sympathetic hand on

my arm. "I know it's been hard on you with your father not around."

Oh, no.

"I didn't want to say anything, in case you got your hopes up, but . . ." Mom leans forward to look both ways and then drives onto our street. "What I'm trying to tell you is that I've found you a new daddy."

What the—a new daddy? "Mom, what are you talking about? And don't even try to keep me from seeing my father tomorrow because it's our—"

"Honey, he already canceled, remember? And I know this will be a big surprise and maybe I should have told you sooner, but, baby, I've never been happier in my life and I pray you'll be supportive."

Supportive? Supportive of what?

Is Mom getting *married*?

Before I can even begin to comprehend what is happening, she pulls into our driveway where another car is already parked and a man is leaning against the back fender.

Oh my gosh, no, is this some kind of a joke?

Mom smiles like she's just won the lottery. "Look at your face, sweetheart, I knew you'd be excited!"

Welcome to the Barton Family Campground's
GO GOLFING WEEKEND!

Friday, July 9:   7 pm   Swingin' Bluegrass with
                              Butch and the Boys

                     8 pm   Tonight's movie:
                              THE GREATEST GAME
                              EVER PLAYED

Saturday, July 10:   10 am   Kids' Crafts:
                                   Craft foam sun visors

                          3 pm   Mini-Golf Tournament

                          5 pm   Hole-in-one Hayride

                          7 pm   Karaoke

                          8 pm   Tonight's movie:
                                   THE LEGEND OF
                                   BAGGER VANCE

                         10 pm   S'mores & cocoa by the
                                   community fire

Sunday, July 11:   9 am   Nondenominational
                                church service

19 ~ Dee

I should be loving this moment. Going down the highway on a Saturday morning in a Ford truck with the windows open and country music blaring while Jake's trailer rattles behind us should make me feel powerful and ruggedly cool, like we're in a music video. Like I'm part of something big, something special. Isn't that what summer is for?

But no. I can't enjoy this.

I don't feel allowed to enjoy *anything*, just like in those months following Dad's death when I would feel guilty for laughing. And it doesn't help that Roxanne is sitting in the front seat beside Jake, savoring their easy camaraderie as they discuss track conditions and the current standings of racers on the circuit, talk I can't contribute to.

I would have stayed home, but Mom vetoed that notion when we had our coffee earlier this morning on the porch. "No, go to the race and have fun, sweetie," she had said. "You should get away from all this for a while."

"But what about the lawsuit? Shouldn't we do something?"

Mom walked to the railing, staring down at the campsites as though they might disappear if she blinked too hard. And because of me, now there's a chance they could. "Honey, there's nothing we can do until the trial date is set, so you should enjoy the summer." She reached up to touch a dried geranium. "And why do I bother with these plants? I always manage to kill them by August."

Mom may not have said it, but I knew what she was really thinking—that she should have sold the campground to begin with. She broke off a crunchy red petal, reminding me of the bouquet she got weeks ago. "Mom." The words tumbled out before I could stop them. "Who sent you those gerber daisies?"

Dried leaves fluttered down onto the railing. She brushed them away and then looked at Dad's empty rocking chair. "It doesn't matter, sweetie."

Mom grabbed a watering can from the steps and stood on tiptoe to water the geranium. When overflow streamed out of the bottom and splashed on her shirt, she flung the can into the yard and gripped the railing with both hands. "It wasn't right for me to be getting flowers in the first place, so it doesn't matter one damn bit."

I wanted to say something—*anything*—but she apologized and went back inside, shutting the door behind her. So I should have stayed home, despite Natalie's offer to watch the store, and Madeline volunteering to take care of the activities for this weekend's golf theme. It was her boring idea, anyway, but to her credit, she has been helping a lot. And after yesterday's meeting, Madeline even consoled Mom with a brisk hug, which proves there is a bright side to everything.

Or that I'm desperate for any kind of brightness.

As we enter historic downtown Charles Town, West Virginia, forty minutes later, I pretend to study the gorgeous churches and beautifully maintained houses. Jake turns off Main Street and onto a winding road lined with blue chicory weeds growing rampant along a cornfield. "Hey, you okay back there, Dee?" he asks. "You're being awfully quiet."

"I have a lot on my mind."

And you two are doing enough talking for all of us.

"Yeah, that sucks about Mona taking you guys to trial." Jake props his elbow on the door. "Why do you think she changed her mind?"

Roxanne shifts in her seat to face him. "Ivy thinks it's because she found out about Rex buying those lots from Dee's mother. Mona probably believes more lots could be sold so she's playing with us."

Something inside me breaks.

"*Us?* There is no us, Roxanne. The lawsuit is between me, my mom, and Ivy, so there is no *us*, okay? And it's pretty funny how you somehow managed to weasel your way into our private affairs after blowing me off all summer."

Jake gives me his oh so familiar judgmental look. "Dee, come on, be fair."

"Be fair, are you kidding me? I'm the bad guy? Sure, maybe I am a little stressed, but it's hard not to be when my entire world is falling apart, okay?"

"I know, but you're being a bitch and that isn't like you."

It feels as though someone shot me in the chest. I slump back in my seat, glaring out the window with my mouth in a tight line. "Well, fine, maybe you should be going to the race with just *Roxanne* or whoever *else* you've been texting."

"For your *information*, I haven't been texting anyone," Jake says, throwing on his left blinker as we come upon a steel fence leading to the track entrance. "And maybe I never should have offered to make that moron Blaine jealous by dancing with you because he's clearly the kind of guy you like."

Roxanne's mouth drops. "What? It was *your* idea?"

I'm too upset to even wonder why she's so shocked.

Jake drives into Summit Point Speedway where the sound of roaring engines matches the roaring in my head. He pays the gate fee, saying nothing while we get our pit passes. But as he pulls into a crowded parking lot full of trucks, utility trailers, and kids on dusty bikes, his bad mood visibly lifts. Jake steps out, pausing with a contented smile before greeting nearby racers who clap him heartily on the back. Only one person seems more enchanted than him, if that's possible. Roxanne. She takes in everything—the drivers, the karts propped up on metal stands, the fiery red tool chests. Her face seems to glow with happiness, making her look so . . . pretty.

"What?" she asks, after noticing me watching her.

I grab the door handle. "Nothing."

Jake kicks it into high gear, unlocking the trailer and barking commands for Roxanne and me to start unloading while he goes to buy tires and a new drive belt. I do *not* want to be alone with her, but Jake takes off, leaving us no choice but to work without speaking, setting up the canopy and folding chairs. Sweat beads on my forehead as we line up Jake's fire suit, helmet, gloves, driving shoes, and the wood sawhorses that look amateurish compared to the fancy metal stands other drivers use.

"Should we get his"—*don't say "thingy"*—"kart out of the trailer?"

Roxanne shakes her head. "No, it weighs over two hundred pounds."

What, does she think I'm some feeble powder puff? "I've been chopping firewood since I was nine, Roxanne. I can handle it."

"Fine." Roxanne loosens the ties that hold the kart in place and puts one hand on the frame and the other on the steering wheel. We start pushing, but as the rear tire pokes out of the trailer and starts to roll down the ramp, my foot slips.

"Hit the brake, Dee, hit the brake!"

It's too late. The kart gets away from us and crashes into the sawhorses, sending them flying into Jake's tall tool chest.

Oh my gosh, Jake's kart!

I crashed Jake's kart.

A sickening feeling rises in my chest as I crouch by the front tire. There's a dent on the frame and some scratches. I lick my fingers and try to rub them out. It doesn't work. I wasn't strong enough to handle it. I can't handle *anything*. "Crap, crap, *crap*, how could I be so stupid?"

Someone kneels beside me.

Roxanne. She inspects the frame before turning to me with a softness in her eyes that I've never seen before. "Hey," she says. "It's okay, those scratches have been there for a long time, so don't worry—you didn't ruin anything."

I'm not sure if she's telling the truth.

But it is nice, her trying to make me feel better. And she's not wearing her usual cargos today. Instead, she has on red cuffed shorts and a slim-fitting shirt that makes my Bermuda shorts and top seem conservative in comparison. Did her mother convince her to go shopping? Roxanne stands and reaches for a sawhorse. "Come on, help me hide the evidence so Jake doesn't find out."

"What won't Jake find out?" someone asks.

Danny Reynolds walks toward us carrying some kind of engine part, his skin tanned and his hair highlighted to a summery strawberry blond. He grins at Roxanne. She blushes and awkwardly tucks back her own red hair as he hands her the part. "Hey, here's one of my spare drive belts. Tell Jake he owes me a soda for it. And you're Roxanne, right? I'm Danny, it's nice to meet you."

I don't know why Roxanne was being so nice to me minutes ago. But I do know two things: She is *not* romantically interested in Jake.

And maybe Danny isn't so awful after all.

The next thirty minutes pass in a frenzy. After Danny leaves, Jake returns with his new tires. Roxanne puts them on the kart and uses the air compressor to fill them while Jake installs the drive belt and changes the spark plugs. Roxanne then starts to mix gas and oil together. "Why are you doing that?" I ask.

She hesitates before saying, "Um, a two-stroke engine doesn't have an oil pan, so to get lubrication, you have to mix the oil and gas together."

Oh. Right.

When the announcer calls for the first heat of Jake's division, he and the other drivers weigh in their karts before pushing them to the pits. Jake shakes hands with his competitors and then steps down onto the narrow seat, Roxanne kneeling beside him with an electric starter. I hold my ears as the engines rev in unison, my adrenaline pounding as Jake shoots off after the starting flag drops, at first sitting up straight and then scooting down to an almost flat position as he speeds past everyone to take the lead. *Okay, that was cool.*

Roxanne claps her hands as he disappears from sight. "Yes! It's awesome if you can take the lead before hitting the first turn."

Other crew members cross the pit lane to watch the heat from a wall by the track. We follow them, hoisting ourselves up to sit. The rough concrete digs into my thighs and cigar smoke drifts over us until the roar of engines comes from the east side of the four-mile track. The first driver takes the turn and fires down the straightaway. "Is that Jake?" I ask.

My heart pumps with excitement. Roxanne stands and yells, "Yeah, a good fifteen yards ahead of everyone!" She leans forward and holds her arms out in a broad sideways V as Jake thunders past us. "That's, uh, to let him know how much he's leading."

"Hey, you know your stuff," Danny says, lifting himself up onto the wall to join us since his heat is later. "How long have you been into racing?"

Roxanne sits again, biting her lip as though she's unsure at first how to answer. "Oh, ever since I used my Barbies as speed bumps for Tonka Trucks. I, uh, want to follow in Cindy

Woosley's footsteps. She was the first female pit crew chief in NASCAR history."

She holds her breath, dreading his reply. So am I, because he's friends with Blaine and Blaine would most likely think a girl is gay or backward if she liked racing. But Danny nods. "Cool! That'd be a sweet job, wouldn't it?"

The sun shines on Roxanne's red highlights. For some reason, I think of FLIRT RULE #1 as she gives him a quick smile.

It's a very nice smile.

Someone clears his throat behind us. We turn to see Rex taking off his cap. "Hello, Roxanne, it's nice to see you again," he says before turning to me. "And you're Dee, Jane's daughter, right?"

Are you kidding me? Maybe Danny isn't that bad after all, but the last person I want to chat with is Rex, who must be thrilled about the possibility of Mom having to sell more land if Mona wins the lawsuit. My temper seethes as Rex says, "We've never formally met, but I heard about the case going to trial, so I wanted to see how your mother is doing."

"We're fine," I reply with as much anger as two words can convey.

Rex nods uncomfortably. He looks different today, with his dirty shirt and oil stains on his knees. He wipes his forehead with a rag before pulling his cap back on. "Well, um, tell your mother I said to hang in there, okay?"

Yeah, Rex is sadly mistaken if he thinks I'm going to forward his message. His cell rings, cutting off any further conversation. He frowns as he reads his text message. "Oops, I forgot to RSVP for a party tonight. Guess that puts me on Miss Manners' hit list, doesn't—" Rex stops when he sees my *I seriously do not care* expression. "Right. Uh, Danny, we should get ready for your heat," he awkwardly says. But after they leave, I realize something.

The meeting with Mona's lawyers was only yesterday afternoon.

So how does Rex know about the trial?

Jake wins his heat with a finesse that would have had me mesmerized if it weren't for Rex. Even Roxanne seems distracted. She hops off the wall just as the checkered flag waves and heads in the direction of Rex's monster-sized trailer—I guess to see Danny's kart. Jake climbs out of his kart and takes off his helmet, sweat pouring down his face and his hair a tousle of wet curls. As he unzips his fire suit and ties the sleeves low around his waist with his damp shirt sticking to his muscular chest, I can't help but think of Natalie's blog entry about how sexy guys are in uniforms.

Good grief. Sexy doesn't even begin to describe Jake right now.

"What's that look for?" Jake asks after he attaches a long handle to the steering wheel and uses it to start pushing the kart to the parking lot.

Look? Did I make a look?

"Nothing. You're just hot—I mean, overheated. Want some of my water?"

"Sure, thanks." Jake takes a long drink from my bottle. We pass Danny's trailer and see him showing his engine to Roxanne as Rex talks on his cell phone. Wow, maybe she isn't as shy as I thought. But what about Torrance, is Danny still going out with her? And does he have any clue that she's seeing Blaine behind his back? I watch as he steps into his fire suit, his arms not nearly as muscular as Jake's.

"Nice, real nice, Dee, just go jump on him, why don't you."

Huh? "Whoa, hold on, Jake, I wasn't—"

Jake angrily hands back my water. "It's fine. Ogle all you want. And hey, he's single now, so there's another flirt victim for you."

That answers my Torrance question. But does Jake truly think I'd have any interest in Danny, his biggest competition? Is that the kind of person he thinks I am? Maybe he was right about me being rude to Roxanne, but to assume I'd sink that low . . . that hurts. That really hurts. So I run to the opposite side of a hot dog stand and pull out my phone.

"Hey, Natalie . . . can you borrow your grandmother's minivan long enough to come get me? I want to go home."

20 ∽ Dee

My mood hasn't improved by the evening, especially after Natalie and I finish what has to be the rowdiest hayride in all of history. Natalie takes a weary bite of her Skinny Cow. "How *did* that kid stick an entire Goldfish cracker up his nose?"

I cringe at the memory of having to pull it out while twenty kids cheered. "No, the better question is why he thought it was hilarious to eat it afterward."

Natalie almost dry-heaves. "Please, let's never discuss that again!"

"Deal," I say, just as Jake pulls into the campground, his tanned arm resting out the open window and Roxanne beside him. I expect them to start unloading the trailer, but as soon as Jake parks, Roxanne is out the door and running straight for . . . me?

"What in the *world* is wrong with your phone?" Roxanne asks when she reaches the porch, panting hard.

Huh? Yeah, my phone is dead—again—but why would she call me? Roxanne takes a shaky breath, her hair windblown and her nose a dull red. "I couldn't find you after Jake's heat, so he gave me your number. Oh, and Jake won his race, in case you're interested."

Seriously? *In case you're interested*, is that some kind of a dig to make me feel bad for leaving? And here I was stupid enough to think we were starting to get along at the racetrack. "Is that why you ran over here?" I stand to face her, my self-control washing away like mud from the riverbank. "To tell me how rude I was to Jake, a guy who judges me even more than you do, if that's possible?"

Roxanne steps back, pulling at her stained shorts. "No, that's not—"

"Go ahead, tell me how pathetic I am, Roxanne, and how the lawsuit was my fault. It doesn't matter what you think because I'm already quite aware of my flaws and how I screw up *everything*."

Natalie shakes her head, her lips in a fierce, determined line. "Dee, stop saying that, okay, because if anything, it was my fault."

Roxanne lets out a massive groan of frustration and stomps her foot. "Enough, already! It's neither one of your faults because *I'm* the one who told Sabrina that Dee was upstairs with Blaine, and I swear, I'm so sorry about that, but it's not—"

"What?" Natalie jumps to her feet. "Why did you do that?"

"Because I thought Dee was only using Jake, okay? I didn't know they had—"

"That's not true!" I say. "It was Jake's idea—"

Roxanne grabs the sides of her head and shouts, "I know that now, okay? So will the both of you *please* shut up for one freaking second so I can tell you something!"

Her words seem to ricochet off the porch soffit.

The throbbing rumble of a passing diesel truck surrounds us as Roxanne holds her hands out in front of her. "Please. Let me talk, okay?"

There it is again, the softness in her eyes, the same one I saw at the racetrack after crashing Jake's kart. She takes a deep breath. "Okay, it's true, I told Sabrina. I'm sorry about that and I'm sorry for being so mean to you all those times. But, Dee, before you left the racetrack, I heard something, something you *have* to know about!"

Now it's my turn to feel breathless. "Is it about the lawsuit?"

"Duh. Only if you think Rex Reynolds dating Mona Owens has anything to do with it."

Surely I did not hear her correctly.

"Mona and Rex?" Natalie shrieks. "Why didn't you just say so, Roxanne!"

"What do you think I've been trying to do? And yeah, after Jake's heat, I wanted to talk to Rex because I thought it was odd the way he knew about the trial already, right?"

"Uh, heck yeah," I say, ignoring Natalie's confused look.

"So, anyway," Roxanne continues. "While Danny was getting ready for his heat, Rex was talking on his cell, right? And I heard him say 'It's going to be great seeing you again tonight, too, Mona.' It had to be Mona Owens!"

Rex . . . with Mona?

Little clues start to funnel down my jumbled brain. How Rex paid Mom that visit at the beginning of June, how he "generously offered" to buy those lots and give Mom a usable deposit, and how he must have then sweet-talked Mona into going for the full two million so he can get his hands on more if Mom loses the trial.

A rustling comes from the bushes by the porch. The Cutsons are crouching in the mulch, wearing Spy Gear headsets and fake rubber snakes tied around their scrawny waists. Lyle drops his shoulders in defeat when he sees me staring at him over the railing. "Dang! Our cover is blown."

"Hey, why'd ya stop fighting?" Tanner asks us. "On Jerry Springer they never stop fighting until someone gets walloped in the mouth."

Natalie marches down the steps and yanks off their headsets. "What did I tell you two about spying and watching Jerry Springer? Just go back to your parents, okay?"

"Can't," Tanner protests, pulling out a stick sword that was wedged under his snake belt and then jumping into a warrior's pose. He jabs the air a few times. "Mom and Pop are fighting about that big-boobied woman you were just talking about."

Roxanne moves closer, nearly tripping on one of the potted azaleas lining the stairs. "Who, Mona Owens?"

"Yeah," Lyle says, reaching for his own stick and challenging his brother to a duel. "Mom was mad at Pop for talking to Big-Booby at the Budweiser store."

"Budweiser store?" Natalie asks. "Oh, do you mean a liquor store?"

"That, too." Lyle strikes Tanner with a *thwack, thwack, thwack.* "She told Pop she was buying stuff for some party tonight."

Okay, really, their parents need a talking-to if they let them watch Jerry Springer and go into liquor stores, but something Lyle said now has Roxanne trotting toward him like a hound on the scent. She grabs their sticks. "Enough with the swordfight. Focus, Lyle, what did she buy?"

He shrugs. "I don't know, a bottle of something red."

"Wine!" Roxanne turns to me. "Larson Walker's wine tasting party. My parents are there now—Larson invited nearly everyone in the development so of course he'd invite Rex!"

Natalie runs up the steps and grabs her backpack. "What are we waiting for, then? Let's go see for ourselves. You think Jake will let us use his truck, Dee?"

Uh, no, I'm not about to ask after what happened between us today, and Nat's grandmother took back her minivan for bingo. Mom's truck is gone, as well, and I'm too exhausted—both mentally and physically—to bike or walk, so that leaves us only one option. I dart into the store, grabbing the set of keys hanging from a deer antler before striding back out with determined steps.

"Let's go," I say as the screen door slams shut behind me.

Natalie follows me to the golf cart. She jumps in, sliding to the middle of the seat with me behind the wheel. We both look at Roxanne who is still by the bushes, shifting her weight as though she isn't sure if she should join us.

I raise an eyebrow at her. "Are you coming or what?"

"Do you see Rex's car?" Natalie asks.

Roxanne stands on the seat, holding on to the roll bar for balance as she scans the vehicles parked along the street. "He has a black Prius, but I don't see it anywhere. Maybe they're running late, because Danny raced today."

"Prius," Natalie says. "And here I'd pegged him as more of

a gas-guzzling Hummer kind of guy. Pull up closer, Dee, we can't see anything from here."

I wait until Roxanne is seated and start the golf cart again, creeping forward to hide behind a Chevy Suburban. It's better, but we have to stand to see. On Larson's back deck, couples in sports coats and dresses sip wine and accept hors d'oeuvres from passing waiters. As much as I despise the Listerine taste of wine, the party looks so elegant. Roxanne's parents are with another couple, although after closer inspection I notice how Dr. Swain is doing all the talking whereas her mother seems . . . sad.

"There's Sabrina," Natalie says. Yep, there she is, lounging with her glam friends on cushioned wicker furniture at the basement patio. Blaine stands by the French doors, animatedly talking as though he's relaying anecdotes from the golf course. Natalie pretends to gag. "Yuck, look at the way Torrance Jones is fawning over Blaine as though he's *so* fascinating. I swear, she gives new meaning to the helpless card."

"Helpless card?" Roxanne asks. "Oh, yeah, from one of your blog posts! What you said was so dead-on, how there are times when it's acceptable to play the helpless female card, like when you're pulled over for a speeding ticket."

A passing car douses us with light, showing the flattered glow on Natalie's face. "Right! 'But to do so in any other situation does nothing but weaken all of womankind. *Weak—bad. Strong— good.*' Cool, you read my entries? Then you'll love this—remember Meghan, the divorced woman with the bratty daughters? Well, she sent me a message about this hunky pharmacist who asked her out. So far they've been on two fabulous dates and—"

I cut her off by raising my hand. "Oh my gosh, look!"

Mona steps out onto the deck in a billowing floral dress and strappy sandals. She isn't alone. A man wraps an arm around her waist, but it's not Rex. It's someone *else*, even though we had it all figured out—why Rex visited the campground, why he was so polite at the racetrack when he asked me to tell Mom to hang in there—

A flash of recognition overwhelms me.

Hang in there.

That's what was written on Mom's bouquet card.

Rex is Mom's *not exactly*.

And the man with Mona is Larson Walker.

I can't believe it. No, I don't *want* to believe it.

Mom with Rex Reynolds?

And Mona with *Larson*, of all people, who is now taking a canapé off a serving tray without thanking the waiter. He licks food off his manicured fingers and kisses Mona on the forehead, reminding me of the day Blaine first introduced me to him. Larson had kissed my hand in the same debonair fashion, so either he's just a naturally charismatic person like Blaine . . . or he's completely full of it.

"What do you know about Larson?" Roxanne asks.

"Not much, other than that he moved here from somewhere in Pennsylvania four years ago and bought the Riverside Inn. Oh, and his wife left him when Blaine was younger," I add, leaving out how Blaine hates her for it, which explains his attitude toward women.

Still doesn't explain why I used to put up with him, though.

"Well," Natalie says, as she sits and pulls her laptop from

236

her backpack. "If someone in this neighborhood has an unsecured wireless network, then we can see what else ole Google has to say about him!"

As Natalie's computer boots up, Roxanne watches her mother nod politely as her father talks with another couple. From the way Victoria's hands fidget, I can tell she's bored out of her mind. That's odd—you would think she'd be a pro at social events.

"Yes! We have Internet!" Natalie says.

Her fingers fly over the keyboard. She surveys the list of Web sites the search engine brought up and says, "Let's see, we have a Calvin Larson Walker, a Cody Larson Walker, and a Leigh Larson Walker—wait, here's a Facebook page for Larson Walker." She clicks on it, but the profile picture of a brunette wearing a sexy nurse costume is definitely not him. Natalie keeps searching long enough for the waiters to make another round. She then stops and taps her nails against the keyboard, staring at the bumper of a Cadillac convertible.

"Huh. Don't you think this is weird?" she asks.

I motion to the party. "What, Larson being with Mona?"

This seems to set off a trigger in Roxanne. "Why would that be weird, because Mona isn't worthy? Because she's different?" she asks, her face turning red. "Who are you to say a man like Larson couldn't love a woman like her?"

Something tells me she's not talking about Mona.

Natalie holds her hands out, coming to my defense by saying, "Whoa, Dee didn't mean it that way, but come on, Larson looks like a total player, so his hooking up with Mona is like George Clooney hooking up with a waitress his own age."

"How do *you* know? Maybe George woke up one morning and said, hey, I want a woman who can serve me a damn good piece of pie. Maybe George is—"

"Maybe George is *broke*," Natalie says, pointing to her computer screen. "What I was *going* to say is how it's weird that Larson's inn reviews for the past six months have been terrible. Poor service from a short staff. The rooms aren't kept clean. And one of the bands from the pub is suing him for back payment! This can only mean—"

"Shh!" I wave my hand frantically in front of her.

"Did you just shush me?" Natalie asks.

"Would you please just be quiet?"

They follow my gaze. Larson is now walking toward us, pulling a cell phone from his trouser pocket. We duck lower, my stomach clenching when he nears the Suburban. He stops, glancing around to make sure he's alone before dialing. *Holy crap*, Natalie mouths as Larson holds his cell to his ear and drains the rest of his wine.

"Hello, Henry, it's Larson, how are you? Yes, I know . . . I'm a couple months behind with my payment, but if you can be patient a little while longer, I can assure you I'll get caught up soon. Yes, I know. Thanks, Henry."

We don't move a muscle until Larson hangs up and saunters back to his party.

Couple months behind? Holy crap is right.

Natalie turns to Roxanne. "Hmm, still think all George wants is pie?"

"Yeah. Two million dollars' worth of pie," she says, slumping back against the roll bar. "But if he's using Mona, what can we do, try to prove it? There's no chance of that happening un-less we can find someone to dig up dirt about him, someone who can . . ."

Roxanne stares at her mother.

She opens her mouth, and then closes it quickly, as though she changed her mind. But when Roxanne sees Mona cleaning up a wine spill like a servant she says, "I have an idea," while hopping out of the cart with a burst of confidence and opening her cell. She dials, and seconds later Victoria Swain steps away from the crowd, answering her own phone as she walks down the deck steps.

Roxanne's determination fades as Victoria steps onto the curb.

"Uh, hey, Mom, it's me. Please don't be mad, but—"

Victoria Swain's free arm drops to her side in a clenched fist as she responds to Roxanne's *please don't be mad* line, not knowing that we can see her. It reminds me of the time when I saw Blaine walk past me at the mall while I was in line for a smoothie. I called his cell, but he ignored it after seeing my name on the screen. That really sucked, but this sucks more.

Blaine was just a bad boyfriend.

Mrs. Swain is Roxanne's *mother.*

"Mom, stop, I didn't do anything. It's just that I'm at—" Her mother keeps talking as she walks, until Roxanne finally says, "Look to your right, Mom."

Victoria jerks her head up, searching until she sees Roxanne on the sidewalk, who gives her a weak wave. Victoria tiptoes across the yard in her heels. "Young lady, what's wrong, are you okay? And why, exactly, am I not supposed to be mad?"

"I'm fine, Mom, it's just that . . . I need . . ."

"And how in the world did you get here?"

Roxanne has no choice but to nudge her head toward where Natalie and I are trying to look inconspicuous. "I sort of drove over here with them. But there's a very good reason why we—"

When Victoria leans over and sees the golf cart, it is clear that she's *not* happy with our mode of transportation. "Roxanne Swain, you came here in a vehicle that's not legal! You knew I wouldn't approve of that! And look at your new shorts, they're covered with motor oil. Here I was so excited when you finally agreed to go shopping the other day, and now they're ruined!"

"Mom, I'm sorry, but I told you people don't wear stuff like this to races—"

Victoria holds her hands up, ducking her chin to her shoulder. "You don't have to explain. I should have known better. You're like your father, who acts as though everything I do for the family is a complete joke."

As a stylish couple carrying a bottle of wine strolls past them, traces of Roxanne's hostility return, the same anger that caused her to slam doors and pee ice cubes. But instead of yelling, Roxanne takes a deep, calming breath and says, "No, Mom, I never . . . Can we please just start over? I'm sorry for riding here in the golf cart, but we had a good reason why. And I need your help. It's important."

Victoria narrows her eyes. "A favor? You're asking me for a favor?"

Roxanne nods. "Yes, I need you to find out all you can about Larson Walker, both business-wise and personal."

"Are you crazy, Roxanne? I will not snoop into Larson's

private affairs when he's been nothing but kind to us. He's going to be our next-door neighbor, for heaven's sake."

"The guy's a jerk, Mom! He's only using—" Roxanne stops, as though she's leery about saying more, which is smart. What if Mrs. Swain blabs about our suspicions to Larson? "I can't tell you why, but it's important, so can you please do it? Can you please take my side for once?"

Victoria's clenched hand starts to slowly open like she wants to say yes—needs to say yes—but her bitterness drowns out the notion. "Yeah, as if you've *ever* taken my side. And maybe I don't want you involved with Dee right now."

Whoa, hold on, what does she have against *me*? A sudden resentment floods my veins, but it's nothing compared to Roxanne's reaction. "Are you serious, Mom? You're the one who wanted me to be friends with Dee, remember? You wanted me to dress like Dee. You wish I could *be* Dee, someone who is pretty and thin."

Victoria steps back, complete surprise on her face. "No, that's not true, Roxanne. I just want you to not push me away so much!"

"Yes, you do think that and you know it," Roxanne says, tears brimming. "You wish for a normal daughter, not one who wants to go to Lincoln Tech and has grease under her nails."

Oh God. No wonder she hated me.

"Roxanne, I—"

"And you're right, Mom, it's crazy to ask you for a favor. I was crazy to think you'd trust me enough to do something that doesn't make sense when you don't even trust me to look underneath the hood of your precious car. Look at us! We can't even have a conversation. And yeah, maybe I do push people away. But so do you, Mom. *So do you.*"

Jazz music drifts out from the party as they lock eyes.

I hold my breath, feeling horrible for witnessing their raw emotions and wishing that Mrs. Swain would say something, *anything*. She doesn't. Instead, she goes back to the party, leaving Roxanne with no other choice but to slowly walk back to us. We drive to the campground in silence, pulling off the road whenever a vehicle approaches. But after I park the cart in the shed, I say to Roxanne, "There's something we need to introduce you to."

Natalie picks right up on it. "Yep. Skinny Cow Fudge Bars. Want one?"

Roxanne nods. "Yeah. Yeah, I do."

But as we open the store's freezer, her cell phone begins to buzz. She reads a series of texts that flash on the screen. "They're all from my mother!"

Larson is a UCLA grad, used to sell real estate before opening a restaurant, loves French cuisine so much that . . .

. . . he has lunch plans at a French restaurant in Fairfield tomorrow at 1:00, which is odd. Earlier on, Mona told me she works Sunday afternoons at the VFW . . .

. . . Roxanne—please be careful. And my car is making this funny ticking noise. Think you can check it out?

21 ∽ Sabrina

If I hear Blaine say the word "bogie" one more time, I may vomit.

Bogie, wedge, divot, birdie, mulligan—I have no clue what those words mean. And I'm sure Torrance and Bridget don't know either, but they listen raptly to Blaine's boring recounting of his *amazing* golf game with unwavering attention.

Please.

"We were behind these old women," Blaine says, acting as though we didn't just break up *yesterday*. "And Prescott, here, decides he's tired of following them. So he uses his five wood to hit up behind them. You should have seen them jump!"

Prescott laughs and affectionately rubs Vanessa's neck like he's such a good boyfriend who never cheats on his lady, oh, no! "It worked, didn't it? We played through and saved at least forty minutes in our game. Too bad Danny wasn't there."

Of course Danny wasn't there. He had a race, but something tells me he wouldn't have thought so highly of Prescott's stunt. Blaine, however, claps him on the back and Torrance giggles, even though—hello—Prescott could have hurt one of the older women.

Jerks.

Did I always know they were jerks? Yes, I did, so either I've overlooked it for so long or I'm a jerk, too. But leaving this crowd now with senior year right around the corner would be socially disastrous. And besides, I was here long before the charming duo of Larson and Blaine Walker breezed into town. I am not about to be shoved out of my own territory, even though my territory sometimes feels like a war zone—and Blaine will probably soon start bringing around whichever skank he was cheating on me with. Is that why Danny isn't here tonight, because he broke up with Torrance and now he doesn't feel welcome?

Oh, no. That's *not* going to be me.

Of course, Torrance claimed to be relieved because Danny always smells horrible after working in his garage. Yeah, right.

I check my cell for the time. Two more hours of torture to go, since my stupid car is still in the shop and Mom is my only way home. No, make that a *lifetime* of torture, if Mom is actually serious about her engagement and Blaine becomes my *stepbrother* and Larson my *stepfather*. No wonder Blaine agreed to the breakup because things were too "weird." This is more than weird.

This is nauseating.

Once again, my head throbs at the memory of seeing Larson waiting in our driveway after the settlement meeting. The way he smiled and leaned against his car like a dog that has just marked his territory brought my own hackles up. But Mom was ecstatic to see him, even more so than the day she won front-row Reba McEntire tickets. So although the thought of her with my ex-boyfriend's *father* makes me ill, I have to admit it's nice to see her happy.

I still can't help but ask myself: Why did he pick her?

At least I do know the when. Mom confessed how it was Larson who sent her the tiger lilies, which was most likely the real reason she offered to drive me to Blaine's after my car wouldn't start. So I'm betting Larson asked her out sometime after Rex gave her a tour of the Swains' house.

From the upstairs deck, I hear Mom's nervous laughter. This morning she threw open my bedroom door at eight, wearing a jogging suit and hardly any makeup. "Wake up, sugar," she said, "the mall opens at nine. I have to find the perfect, PERFECT outfit for tonight's party, so will you *please* help me? I made you coffee. And I heated up one of those yummy Toaster Strudels you love so much."

For some reason, I thought of Meghan from the blog, and how her daughters didn't help her shop for new clothes. So I said yes.

"Camera!" Mom exclaimed as I crawled out of bed. "Don't let me forget the camera tonight. I need plenty of photos of our first family event. Can I borrow yours? Mine is so big and clumsy. Just think, a wine tasting party! Doesn't that sound classy?"

Mom rattled off more things from her shopping list, like extra panty hose in case hers got a run and wine from the liquor store, while she shoved dirty clothes in my hamper and shooed dust off my bureau with her palm. I was about to tell her that no one wears panty hose in the summer when she slowly picked up the framed photos of Dad and Blaine. "Sweetheart . . . I'm sorry your father canceled on you again this weekend. And

I'm truly sorry about you and Blaine breaking up. I feel like that's all my fault, but, Sabrina, I couldn't help but fall in love with Larson, so *please* be happy for me."

But nagging doubts make that impossible.

Especially when it took us nearly four hours to find a summer dress that wasn't too young and wasn't too old—something that's harder to do than I thought.

And especially when we had to spend the rest of the day running errands for Larson, picking up napkins, getting his dry cleaning, *and* calling people like Rex who forgot to RSVP for the party. And Larson even dissed the wine she gave him as a gift. "Aw, you're too sweet—you bought this cheap wine as a joke, right, darling?"

It wasn't a joke. She loves that wine, regardless of the price, but instead of standing up for herself, Mom tittered out a self-conscious "Yeah, ha, ha, ha!"

Like father like son, I think, while Blaine demonstrates the putt that won his game.

No. *Like mother like daughter.*

She's putting up with Larson's tricks just like I put up with Blaine's because I was so afraid he'd break up with me if I didn't. She's hanging out with people she really doesn't like, just like I do, because I'm terrified to lose the security of popularity. And I put up with all of my father's canceled plans and excuses because I don't want him to leave me.

Just like he left Mom.

But the funny thing is, it feels good to stand on my own without Blaine. It feels good to not be afraid or weak anymore. What did Superflirt—whoever she is—say? *Weak—bad.*

Strong—good. And aren't I the one who always said that weakness will get you nowhere?

It's time for me to follow my own policy.

And I know just where to start.

I leave the patio without bothering to excuse myself and walk into the basement that is crowded with men playing pool, smoking cigars, and chiding each other in that manly *just kidding, dude* way. Upstairs, the rest of the house is also crowded, so I duck into Larson's office that could pass as a *GQ* photo set, with his executive-style chair, mahogany desk, and leather sofa with flanking dracaena plants.

The leather feels icy against my thighs as I pull out my cell. Dad answers on the fourth ring, echoes of high spirits, shrieks, and music coming from the background. "Sabrina, is that you, can you hear me?"

"Yeah, but the better question is, can you hear me?"

Because he's going to hear a lot.

"Sorry, hon, we're at Hersheypark in line again for the Storm Runner roller coaster," he says. "It's awesome! Zero to seventy-two in two seconds flat."

Huh, Hersheypark, so that's why he bailed on me—again—because he wanted to take his happy new family out for a happy Hershey day without me around. And now that I think about it, the weekend of Angela's birthday party, was that why he didn't protest when Mom made me stay home, to keep things less awkward? Sure, maybe Belinda and Angela didn't want me there, but can I blame them? It's not as though I was the sweetest person, so of course they wouldn't want me around. Why didn't my own father?

It's time to find out.

"Hey, Dad, why didn't you invite me along? This *was* our weekend, remember?"

The clicking sound of an approaching coaster and the whoosh of brakes tell me they must be near the front of the line. Dad waits for a safety announcement to end and says, "I didn't think your mother would allow it, Sabrina. You know how Mona gets sometimes."

Tears gather in my eyes. I look up to Larson's ceiling, trying to blink them away before my mascara is ruined. Maybe he's right, maybe Mom would never let me go because of the shopping and Larson's party. But maybe she wouldn't let me go simply because she *wants* me in her life. She needs me.

She'll even fight for me.

That's what I want, for Dad to fight for me, to do whatever it takes to make me a part of his life. My lips quiver and my throat feels as though it's wrapped with cable as I say, "Yeah, I know how Mom is, Dad. But guess what? She's here. She's *here*, with all her flaws and faults, she's here, she never left me, not like you did."

From his end of the line, I can hear Belinda announce that it's their turn next. "Oh, okay," he tells her before saying to me, "Sabrina, look, I'm sorry things never worked out between your mom and—"

"No, this has nothing to do with the divorce. If you're happy with Belinda, then I'm happy for you and I'll try to get along better with her, but what did you tell me the night you left? You said things between us would never change, didn't you?"

"Yes, but—"

"You broke that promise, Dad. You never fought for me. Instead, I always have to fight for you. So go ahead, have fun on the roller coaster, but you need to realize that before you know it, the ride will be over and it will be too late for us to have any kind of relationship because I'll no longer be waiting in line for you."

"Sabrina, I—"

"Goodbye, Dad."

By the time I get back down to the patio, my headache has tripled and the boring conversation has turned from golf to clothes. "So, Sabrina, you didn't tell me where you bought that *fabulous* dress," Bridget says, biting into a chunk of Brie cheese that she'll probably chunk up later in order to keep her emaciated figure. "Did you, like, get it at Lord & Taylor? Torr and I went shopping there yesterday. We got the cutest outfits. Mine is just like the one Miley Cyrus wore in her latest video."

I hate that video. And slimy Brie cheese. And how would they react if they knew where I got my dress? Probably the same way Larson reacted to Mom's cheap wine.

Huh. Let's find out.

"Thanks, Bridget, you really like my outfit?" I ask her, smoothing down the bodice and making the skirt twirl by twisting back and forth like an agitating washing machine. "I got it for ten dollars."

"Seriously?" she asks.

"*Seriously,*" I repeat in a shrill, girlie voice. "From *eBay.*"

Torrance drops her mouth and Bridget almost chokes on the Brie. "You actually shopped on eBay? Was it, like, *used*? That's so gross."

I cock my head to the side, as though deep in thought. "Hmm, no, not this one, but that skirt you borrowed from me, Torrance? That was totally used. Oh, and my Kate Spade bag? The one you *love so much*? It's, like, a total knockoff."

Chunk on that, ladies.

Welcome to the **Barton Family Campground's**
GO GOLFING WEEKEND!

Congratulations to Madeline Barton for winning yesterday's
mini-golf tournament with an outstanding score of eight
below par! Way to go, Madeline.

22 ~ Dee

Saturday's events don't really sink in until I wake up Sunday morning. Fighting with Jake, which bothers me more than I care to admit. Hanging out with Roxanne, who is, well, *nice*. And Danny—Jake was right, he's actually pretty cool, once he's away from Blaine and his conceited bunch. *But Rex Reynolds with my mom?* No, that part is NOT cool. I mean, he's the guy who destroyed all our beautiful land. He's the one making a killing from the swanky houses he built, and he's the one who will benefit from the lawsuit after he gets his hands on those four acres. A nagging thought keeps haunting me, though.

If my mother likes him, how bad can he be?

And she did say that he offered her more than a fair price, as well as a large deposit she could use to pay off Mona. Was he being helpful . . . or crafty? No, this is a subject I can't deal with right now. That's tomorrow's worry, but today?

Today is for spying.

"So, how exactly are we going to get to Larson's?" Natalie

asks me as she peers into the bag of snacks we bought from the store.

"Shh, not so loud!"

I motion to where Madeline is writing an announcement on the message board with pinpoint precision. When she starts to watch us suspiciously, Natalie leans back into the porch swing and calls to her, "Well, I hear that congratulations are in order, Mrs. Barton, after your mighty victory in yesterday's golf tournament."

Madeline reads her announcement with what she must think is a humble smile. "Oh, it was nothing."

Natalie gives her a double thumbs-up. "Well, ya did all right, Dee's grandmother. And good news—the little girl you beat finally stopped crying at midnight."

Madeline's pride over her big win trumps any suspicions of us, but I still have no clue how we are supposed to get to Larson's. Roxanne is taking care of that part and after a few more minutes, we hear gravel crunching beneath tires. A familiar red truck appears. The driver brakes, pulling his sunglasses down to the bridge of his nose before saying, "I hear you ladies need a ride."

Jake.

Jake *and* Danny, who opens the passenger door and moves to the backseat. Roxanne appears out of nowhere, carrying a stuffed backpack. "Well, what are you waiting for?" she asks, taking Natalie by the sleeve and pulling her to the back with Danny, leaving the front seat open. *What?* I thought Jake was still mad at me. Did Roxanne talk to him? And why, exactly, does she find it necessary for me to sit beside him?

Honestly. If we didn't just start getting along, I'd totally kill her.

I've often wondered what a stakeout would be like. They seem so fascinating on TV, what with the binoculars, coffee, and junk food—can't have a proper stakeout without junk food. But what happens if you have to pee? Poor Natalie is finding out the hard way. She fidgets and squirms in the backseat. "Why did we have to get here so *early*? And why can't I go to the bathroom?"

We are parked in the Swains' new driveway behind the construction dumpster, with Roxanne's eyes focused on Larson's closed garage doors. "Because," she says, clutching the backpack on her lap. "You can't blow a stakeout by arriving too late. Larson's lunch is at one o'clock and it takes about forty-five minutes to get to Fairfield, plus we had to factor in the chance that he could leave earlier to run errands."

"But that doesn't tell me why I can't pee," Natalie says, her legs tightly crossed. "There's a port-o-pot right there."

"Nope, too risky," Roxanne says. "It's already twelve-thirty. Larson *should have* already left."

I prop my bare feet on Jake's dashboard and adjust my favorite pink skirt that I broke down and wore because refusing to flirt doesn't *really* mean you can't dress flirty, right? "Oh, please. Blaine was always late so if Larson is anything like him, she has plenty of time."

With that, Natalie opens the door and runs to the portable clutching her stomach. Danny digs into a bag of Cheetos and says, "You know, I never liked Larson much. Neither did my dad—Larson kept trying to get extra work done for free, and I'm pretty sure he still owes Dad some money."

Rex doesn't like Larson? Well, I suppose that's a mark in Rex's favor. But I'm just now realizing there's a remote possibility that Danny could one day be my brother.

Oh, no, do NOT think about that now.

"And man, a real stakeout," Danny says. "Just like in Splinter Cell."

Roxanne's mouth drops. "Get out, I love that game! Last week, I got through Conviction's final mission with no cheat code help."

"Mission eleven? How did you get by the agents near the turret?"

As they talk about Black Arrow guards and assassinations, Jake tilts his head to scratch his ear and glances toward my bare legs. Is he checking them out? Or is he only annoyed that my feet are leaving marks on his freshly polished dash? He jerks his gaze away and says, "So, why are we tailing Larson? What if he just has a business meeting today?"

I kick my legs down and cover my thighs with my purse. "I guess that could be true, but how many people do you know who have Sunday business meetings at French restaurants? They're more for romantic rendezvous."

Jake drums his fingers on his knee. I'm about to thank him for driving us—especially if there is someone *else* he'd rather spend the day with—when Danny notices Larson's garage door rising and a silver Audi creeping out. "It's him. Get down!"

Jake and I duck at the same time, crouching on the seat with our faces inches apart. The smell of his citrusy shampoo and the warmth from his skin make my heart pound. Jake blinks, his green eyes holding me captive until Danny taps the seat. "He passed us. Hurry up, Jake, before we lose him."

Moment gone.

Jake starts the engine as Natalie dashes back into the truck. "Ugh, remind me to *never* go into a port-o-pot that's been used by construction dudes," she says. "Man. They must eat tons of fiber."

Moment definitely gone.

We follow Larson for nearly an hour, with Danny and Roxanne barking orders from the backseat. *Change lanes. Slow down. Stay four car lengths behind. Dee, look away, act natural.* Does being good at spy-themed video games make you good at tailing people? It must. We follow Larson all the way to Fairfield. He parks at a swanky restaurant and steps out of his Audi, wiping dust off the hood with his sleeve before going inside. "What now?" I ask. "We haven't thought this out and Larson knows everyone here except for maybe Natalie—"

"I'm going in," Roxanne announces.

No, that's impossible. Larson will surely recognize her.

I turn to see her clutching her backpack, letting out a breath of air with her cheeks puffed like a diver getting up the nerve to jump. She grits her teeth and says, "Just let me out, okay?"

We watch as she disappears behind a thick cluster of the pine trees that surround the parking lot. Minutes later, I have to do a double take when she steps out in a cotton summer dress and cute strappy sandals, her hair pushed back with a wide headband and pink gloss on her lips.

Oh my gosh.

Roxanne tosses her backpack through the open window. "Don't say it, okay?"

"Say what, that you look beautiful?" Danny asks.

The minutes drag after Roxanne steps into the restaurant. Jake eats Twizzlers and Natalie discusses Disney fast passes with Danny, seeing as how he's been there twice, until we notice Roxanne waving from the front door. When she makes frantic camera motions with her hands, I grab my purse and jump out without thinking twice.

Inside, a stylish hostess tries to block me but Roxanne grabs my arm. "There you are, Priscilla! Tsk, tsk, late again. Mother and Father are so disgruntled!"

Disgruntled? And *Priscilla?* "Hey, do I look like a Priscilla to—"

Roxanne shushes me and heads down the hallway past several small dining rooms before pulling me behind a large palm plant. She points to a table next to the fireplace where Larson is holding hands with an attractive woman in—I'm guessing—her late forties wearing a blue wrap dress and diamond studs the size of grapes in her ears. "Now there's your *Gotcha*, Priscilla," Roxanne whispers as a waiter serves Larson a plate of food. "He's cheating on Mona."

Son of a scum-sucking toad!

Of course Larson is cheating on her, just like George Clooney will always prefer models to pie-serving waitresses his own age. My face burns as the waiter makes small talk with Larson and his date. But then it hits me. "No. He's cheating on *her*, the one at the table."

"What? How do you know?"

"Simple. Because his food was served when he arrived, meaning she pre-ordered it for him. People who haven't been dating long don't have that level of intimacy yet. And," I say, just as his date shoves a healthy amount of cheese soufflé into her mouth, "most women eat salad when they're first dating, because Lord forbid she dare have an appetite."

Roxanne nods. "Good point. Got the camera? This would make an interesting photo."

Oh, yes. Yes, it would.

I fish my digital from my purse and hand it to Roxanne. She leans out to take their picture, but when the flash fills the hallway with light, she pins her back against the wall with her stomach sucked in. "Man, maybe I should have been eating more salads."

"Are you kidding? You look great."

"Yeah, right. You're just saying that."

"Roxanne, I swear, you are not—"

A couple walks by and stares at us. Okay, no time for chit-chat, we need to bolt. Now. Outside, Nat is lingering near an empty bench. She quickly leads us to where Jake is now parked in a less conspicuous spot, but before we make it to his truck the restaurant's back screen door opens. A waiter steps out with an unlit cigarette dangling from his lips. As he bends his head to light it, Roxanne yanks Natalie and me down until we are crouching beside a Volvo. "Isn't that the guy who served Larson?" she whispers. "It seemed as though he knew Larson and his date personally."

We lift our heads over the Volvo's hood to see the waiter

inhale deeply as though his life depended on nicotine. "Huh. He *could* be quite helpful," Natalie says.

"Indeed." Roxanne grins. "What do you think, Natalie, the helpless card?"

Natalie ducks back down, turning to me with her head cocked to the side and a challenging gleam in her eye. "Well, playing the helpless card *is* perfectly acceptable in emergency situations such as these."

As a busboy opens the screen door and flings dirty water out onto the parking lot, I wipe away their ridiculous notion with a flick of my wrist. "Oh, no, I'm retired from flirting, re-member?"

"Are you serious?" Roxanne asks, picking up the sides of her new dress and giving it a shake. "I'm wearing a dress my *mother* picked out so the *least* you can do is whip out the Superflirt, okay?"

I look over to where Jake and Danny are waiting in the truck. No, for some weird reason, I don't want Jake to see me flirting anymore. But what if the waiter does know something that can help us with the lawsuit? And I'm losing time, now that he's halfway through his cigarette.

Well, fine, a flirt's got to do what a flirt's got to do.

While the waiter's back is turned, I fluff my hair and creep out from behind the Volvo, easing my way onto the sidewalk, and making it appear as though I'm just going for a stroll. "Beautiful day, isn't it?" I ask, catching his attention while walking toward him in full flirt mode with my hips swaying.

The guy tries to hide his cigarette by cupping it in his palm. He's about nineteen, with streaks of acne and heavy jewelry peeking out from underneath his uniform. "Can I help you with something? The, ah, main entrance is around front."

I thrust my lips out in a pretty pout. "Oh, I know. I'm having lunch with my parents, but it's *boring* so I went for a walk. Who are you, the head waiter or something?"

The guy nervously stomps out his cigarette and brushes the smoke away with his hands. "Well, no, I'm not really the head waiter."

"Stop," I tease, swatting his arm. "You're being way too modest."

Someone snorts from around the corner. Natalie and Roxanne must have crept up to eavesdrop. The waiter looks over my shoulder so I block his view and twirl a lock of hair around my finger. "I saw how you carried those heavy trays, and wow—I could never remember the names of all those wines!"

Argh! I'm teetering way too close to fake flattery territory, but the waiter smiles, proving that I struck a chord by complimenting what some could see as a mundane career. "Well, yeah, my parents hate my job, so thanks . . . um, what's your name?"

I think for a second, and then drawl out a coy "Priscilla."

Another snort.

"Cool. And, hey, Priscilla, I bet you'd be a good waitress, too."

"Really?" I press a hand against my chest and give a little hop, like a beauty pageant contestant who just won the crown. "That would be so incredible."

I look deep into his eyes. *One . . . two . . . three.*

Gotcha.

Time to go for the kill.

"But something's bugging me." I rest my hand on his fore-arm. "That couple you served by the fireplace—the tall man and the woman in the blue dress—they were so familiar!"

I toss my hair back, just as the wind picks up. Oh, the sweet timing. The waiter watches my hair tumble across my shoulder and says, "Yeah, uh, Kathleen Myers? She's a real nice lady. Her husband was nice as well—he used to leave me these huge tips before he died last winter. That was, like, a total bummer, man."

What? That Kathleen lady is a *widow?* And a wealthy widow at that, judging from the huge tips and her diamond jewelry. *What exactly is Larson doing with a rich widow while he's also dating Mona, a woman who's trying to win a large lawsuit?*

The answer is clearer than the pimple on the waiter's nose.

On the way back to the campground, Roxanne and Natalie have themselves a jolly time mocking me from the backseat. *Me? A waitress? You think so, big strong waiter guy who can carry those awfully heavy trays?*

"Ha ha," I say to them, just as Jake gives me one of his dis-approving scowls. "And yeah, I know, Jake, so you can stop looking at me like I'm a complete idiot."

He grips the steering wheel, watching the road with steely determination before saying, "I never once thought that, Dee."

I turn to face him. "Oh, please, you love making me feel like a total bimbo!"

"No, I never once thought you were an idiot or a bimbo, Dee. But yeah, I've always hated the way you flirt."

"Yeah, the truth comes out."

"But—not for the reason you think," Jake says, before

putting on the blinker and turning onto the road that takes us home.

After much deliberation, we decide that showing Ivy the picture of Larson is not a good idea. Not only would she say that if Larson is, indeed, a conniving dirtbag, it has absolutely nothing to do with the case, but she'd also be furious about us following him. And there's the restraining order, the "very real, very serious restraining order," she's warned me not to violate a thousand times. If she knew I was anywhere near Blaine's house, she'd flip her lid.

Besides.

Ivy doesn't look all that good when we get back.

Her sophisticated makeover from a couple of weeks ago has morphed into a disheveled mess, with her tailored clothing replaced by frumpy sweats and her hair a battlefield of frizz as she pores over paperwork. After the disastrous settlement meeting, she blamed herself, saying that maybe those Wyatt, Hyatt & Smith farts were right to push her out if she's the kind of lawyer who allows her clients to be destroyed.

But nobody is going to destroy us, not if I have anything to do with it.

I have a plan . . . one that requires a little help.

The Cutson brothers, wearing Spy Gear headphones, are giggling behind an evergreen, listening to two girls on playground swings gripe about cramps and uncomfortable tampons. I sneak up behind them and grab their scrawny arms.

"Hey," they yell. "Let go!"

"Absolutely," I say in a super-sweet voice. "I just wanted to compliment your stellar spying skills. Those girls had no idea you were watching them. I bet you two are the best spies in the whole town. No, the whole state!"

Lyle takes off his headset. "We're not stupid, Miss Dee."

"Yeah," Tanner says. "What do you want?"

Well, well, well, charm doesn't get you far with these guys, so I drop my smile. "Fine. I have an assignment for the both of you next Friday night. A secret mission, one that you will accept or I'll be forced to tell your momma about that little incident involving water balloons and Miss Ivy's camper, deal?"

"You ain't got no proof!" Tanner protests. I stand tall over them with my arms crossed, causing the two dirty mongrels to whisper in each other's ears.

"Deal," Lyle says. "But for five bucks each."

"And," Tanner adds, "we want the money first."

Good. In exactly five days, it will be time to *really* break the restraining order.

23 ～ Sabrina

Hey, hey, hey, is everybody having fun?"

Chuck Lambert stands at the mike on Friday night, ruddy cheeks glistening and husky voice booming over the speakers. His hair is brushed back pompadour-style off his forehead and is anchored with enough hairspray to survive a tornado.

"Yeah!" a few kids yell from the pool.

"Of course you are. Everyone has fun here," Chuck bellows. He leans back and laughs, his lifted shirt exposing a flabby white stomach. So gross. But I should be grateful. Mom could have ended up with him. Larson is bad enough.

"But, folks, before we get on with the karaoke, I have some bad news." Chuck hangs his head with remorse, like a bad actor in a car dealership commercial. He walks over to loop a beefy arm around Mom's shoulders. "Unless I can talk her out of it, this will be Mona's last appearance, now that she's chosen to retire."

A few polite groans of protest come from the crowd.

"So, let's make her last night a good one," Chuck says, handing Mom the mike. She thanks him and steps to the front of the stage, wearing subdued shorts and a crisp blouse. Even her nails, her trademark, are cut to a more modest length, and she doesn't bother to name them anymore even though she's *always* named her nails. No more Billy Joels or Jungle Fevers or Girl's Best Friends—the ones with little faux diamonds glued on.

I never in my life thought I'd say this but . . .

I want the old Mona back.

"Well, I sure am going to miss this," Mom says without her usual showgirl bravado. "But it's onward and upward, right? So let's get this gentleman up here who's gonna sing a Willie Nelson song, ain't that right, honey?"

The camper nods, his crooked teeth clenched as the starting beats of "Mamas Don't Let Your Babies Grow Up to Be Cowboys" play. I still can't believe she's quitting. She loves karaoke more than her miniskirts, but even they are in bags waiting to go to Goodwill.

"You okay?" I ask as she sits down beside me.

Mom nods, her smile fake as she hands a pink songbook to a young mother with a toddler on her hip. "Of course, couldn't be better. And you?"

"Fine, just fine," I lie in return, even though Torrance and Bridget haven't texted or called since Larson's party, meaning that come next school year I'll be lucky to make it into Spanish club, let alone the homecoming court. The only person who has tried to contact me is my father, but I just can't deal with anything he has to say right now. Not yet.

Junk food.

Tonight I need junk food and something tells me Mom does, too. "Hey, want anything from Chuck's coffee café? I can get you a mocha frappe, remember, with tons of whipped cream and cocoa sprinkles, yum-yum!"

For a second, she seems tempted. "Well, no, maybe just a hot tea. And when you get back, sweetie, can you help me come up with ideas for the wedding?"

Ugh. Hearing her say "wedding" makes my stomach turn.

And tea? Since when does she drink boring tea instead of the yummy mocha frappes that follow her *life's too short for light* policy? What, does being "classier" for Larson also apply to beverages? Oh, no, I'm getting her a mocha frappe. But as I start walking toward the café on a paved pathway, two skinny twin boys run up to me with tears streaming down their faces.

"Lady, oh, lady! We need your help," one of them says.

"What's wrong?" I ask. "Are you hurt?"

The one kid shakes his head and churns out a huge wail, his shoulders heaving up and down with each sob as though he's having a seizure. "We l-l-lost our puppy, she's gone, *goooone*, I tell you, gone!"

The other one sniffs hard enough to siphon gas from an automobile and then wipes his nose with the back of his hand. "Yeah, she's in those woods back there with all those coyotes and wolves."

"Seriously, guys? Coyotes and wolves?"

"R-right," they both repeat, now looking kind of familiar.

Oh, whatever, guess I should help them. "Fine," I say, leading them toward the office. "Let's get your parents and they can help ward off all those nasty beasts, okay?"

The boys both rear back. "No!" one of them yells, "we're, um, not staying at this campground. We're staying at the other one."

Huh? The *other* campground? "You mean Barton's, that's, like, two miles away? What in the world are you doing way out here?"

The two kids glance at each other, and I suddenly remember seeing them at Barton's playing kickball. "We were chasing our puppy," one says. "Remember? He's still by himself in the woods, so you've just got to help us, lady, you've got to!"

"Yeah, don't let him die, lady, *don't let him die!*" The other boy starts to cry again, large, round teardrops falling down his face as he grabs my arm and pulls me to where a small path crosses over a bridge and into the woods.

Wait a minute. "Hey! Before you said the puppy was a *she.*"

They stop, the dirtier one shuffling his feet. "Uh, yeah, at first, but then she turned into a he. Darnest thing we ever saw! Animal Planet is thinking 'bout doing a special on it."

The lying monster.

"That's it." I pull out my cell while holding on to one kid. "Give me your parents' number."

He struggles out of my grasp and the other twin snatches my phone and they both sprint over the bridge. "Hey, come back here!" I yell, taking off after them and wishing I wasn't wearing sandals. They run up the path into a large open clearing with benches made of cut logs and shadows from the towering oak trees covering the mossy ground. I skid to a stop when I see who is waiting there. Dee Barton.

It was nothing but a hoax, just a big fat joke.

And I am not amused.

"Do you realize I could have you *arrested* for being near me?" I ask.

Dee shrugs, her posture steadfast and weary, as though she

is both exhausted and determined at the same time. "Go ahead, I don't care, but you won't get far without any proof or witnesses."

"Oh, yeah?" I motion toward the twins who are now sitting on a log. But one of them snaps his fingers in the air and says, "We ain't seen nothing, puppy hater."

Dee walks closer. "Sabrina, I'm sorry to trick you—I know you work at Chuck's on Friday nights, so this was the only way I could think of to get near you. But it's important that we talk about something."

What, talk to her, the person who ruined everything for me? Since that night at her campground, I've lost my boyfriend, my friends, *and* my mother. And so what, maybe parts of my life did suck before, but there were times when it was incredible to be Blaine's girlfriend and everybody knows that popularity is a lot better than the alternative.

As a cloud passes in the darkened sky, rage floods my body, making me shake. "Yeah, you're good at tricks. Just like when you wrote Blaine that letter last September, hoping he'd dump me as a result. Well, congratulations, you got your wish because we're no longer together. So *hand over my phone*, Dee."

The boys pull M&M's packs from their pockets and tear them open as though they are enjoying the show. Dee shoots them a reprimanding look before saying, "Give me four minutes, okay? That's the least you can do considering how *you* completely destroyed me at school. And what else? Oh, yeah, you're trying to completely destroy my home as well."

She's right about both things, but it still doesn't keep me from holding out my palm. "The phone, Dee. Now."

Her hand trembles as she places it in my outstretched hand,

our fingers briefly touching. I turn and stride away, hearing leaves crunch underneath my feet as she says, "Yeah, I did write that letter because I wanted him back. Why, I have no idea, but check your facts, Sabrina. It was dated September 21, three days after he broke up with me and *one week* before you two started going out on the twenty-eighth, my birthday—happy freaking birthday to me."

My stride slows.

Blaine asked me out on September 12. Meaning, he was still seeing Dee when we first started dating. She wasn't the other woman.

I was.

"And yes," Dee continues, "maybe I did briefly flirt with Blaine in the store because I was mad at him for coming to my campground with you. But he followed me *after* I told him to leave me alone. Look me in the eyes and tell me you don't believe that."

I want so badly to turn around and say without a shred of doubt that no, Blaine would never do that to me. But I can't.

The buzz of cicadas surrounds us. Pungent smoke from a nearby campfire blows our way, bringing with it the faint sound of Mom announcing another singer. From behind me, Dee takes a long, hard breath. "But I didn't come here to talk about Blaine. I came to talk about Larson. When did he start dating your mother, before or *after* she filed the lawsuit?"

My body stiffens.

"What? Why are you asking me this?"

Dee presses on. "You know why, Sabrina."

I whip around and hiss, "Leave my mother out of this. What are you trying to say, that he's only after her money, that she's not good enough for him? My mother is happy. For the first time since her divorce, she's happy, and you better not do anything to stop it."

Dee hesitates, then reaches into her back pocket. "Larson is the one who will be happy, Sabrina, if your mother wins the lawsuit. Here, I printed a copy of the picture we took last Sunday of Larson with another woman, named Kathleen Myers."

I snatch the paper from her.

The cicadas' echoing chirp turns into a dull roar as I study the image of Larson staring adoringly at the other woman, his hands linked in hers, just like he's done with my mother. My mind swirls.

What is going on?

Dee takes advantage of my silence. "She's a widow, Sabrina. A wealthy widow. And Larson is broke. We don't have any concrete proof other than a phone conversation we overheard, but doesn't this make you suspicious?"

Yes.

Yes, it does make me suspicious, but this isn't possible. Sure, Larson was always seeing someone new when Blaine and I dated. And, fine—Larson did ask Mom out *after* the lawsuit was served, but using women for money? No, I refuse to believe this. "You're lying, Dee. This could be an old picture."

She shakes her head slowly, her voice soft when she says, "Check the time stamp. And I'm not a liar. But I think Larson is lying to your mother . . . just like Blaine lied to you about Torrance."

Torrance and Blaine?

No, Torrance might be a terrible friend, but even she wouldn't stoop that low. But the lipstick-stained cup at the coffee shop was so similar to her favorite shade . . .

Oh my God.

I want to punch Torrance. I want to punch Dee, but instead, I throw the paper down and thrust a finger in her face. "You're sick, do you know that? Sick. So enjoy getting arrested tomorrow once the sheriff hears about this."

I turn to leave, my pulse pounding as Dee says, "Go ahead, call him. Do what you gotta do to make my life hell. You always have, haven't you?"

Keep walking, keep walking.

"Are you afraid I'm right?" Dee yells. "Then prove me wrong, Sabrina. Show your mother the picture. Or go ahead, win two million dollars at my family's expense. But what happens if Larson cons it away from your mother? Just how happy will you both be then?"

I stop. Turn around.

Retrace my steps and snatch the picture from the ground.

Whenever one of those *tales of women's betrayal* shows comes on TV—the ones where a disgruntled wife cries about how she had no clue about her husband's two other wives or that her spouse was an enemy spy—I shake my head and think, "What a stupid moron." But now, I can understand how women can be so naïvely trusting, how they can turn a blind eye to what's right in front of them. Because they, like all of us, need to be loved and to believe that the person who loves them is good and decent. If not, it would only mean that *they* aren't worthy of good and decent.

That's how Mom feels with Larson. That's how I felt with Blaine. And I suspect that's how Dee felt with Blaine as well.

In the morning, sounds of crashing pans come from the kitchen. I run in to find Mom by the stove, wearing an apron that's trimmed with red strawberry prints. She greets me with a warm smile, traces of flour on her cheek. "Hey there, sweetie, I'm making cookies! Poor Larson has been so busy, what with his emergency business trip this weekend. So I'm planning a nice family dinner for when he gets home Sunday night. Try this recipe and tell me what you think. Be honest!"

The last time Mom made cookies they burned while she watched her soaps, but I say, "Yeah, sure," and grab one before sitting on a bar stool. They have *way* too much vanilla in them, but I nod and tell her, "They're good, Mom."

"Really?"

"Really."

"You know," Mom says, "I had such a lovely time at the party last weekend. It was nice, being with you and Larson, like we were family, you know? I miss that."

Show her the photograph.

Mom hesitates, staring at the black-and-white-checked tile before brushing the crumbs on the counter into a neat pile. "And who knows, maybe it's my fault your father cheated on me. Maybe it was me who drove him away and then I only made it worse by dragging him through court. I just wanted..."

"You were angry. You wanted him to hurt as much as you did, and he did hurt you, Mom, he hurt you very badly."

"Yeah," Mom whispers. "He did."

A revelation hits me. "Mom, did you sue Jane because you were angry?"

She busies herself by sprinkling Comet into the porcelain sink and cleaning it with a damp sponge. "Heavens no, Sabrina! What could possibly make you think that?"

"Because it's the truth."

Mom attacks a black mark on the porcelain, her body shaking as she scrubs it again and again until she finally confesses, "Fine. Maybe I was furious over her judging me, the way I dress, the way I act, just like all women judge me. And I was mad at how she refused to give me a second chance, just like your dad refused to give our marriage a second chance. I would have toned it down. I know I can get a little carried away every now and then."

A little?

"Okay, a lot." Mom stops scrubbing and traces a nail along the countertop. "But she fired me."

"You sued her because she *fired* you?"

"Yes, Sabrina!" Mom yells, throwing the sponge in the sink and wiping her hands on her apron, getting Comet powder on the strawberry prints. "You don't understand. It's one thing to be fired by a man . . . but by a woman, especially a single mother like me? No. It's just that . . . you would think a woman would never do that to another woman."

She's wrong. I do understand.

But I still have one more question. "Did Larson convince you not to settle?"

She doesn't answer. The expression on her face says it all.

I reach into my pocket for the picture. "Mom, we have to talk. Now."

Welcome to the **Barton Family Campground's**
DO YOU BELIEVE IN MAGIC WEEKEND!

Friday, July 16: 7 pm Magic show with Tyson Ruff and friends

8 pm Tonight's movie: HARRY POTTER AND THE SORCERER'S STONE

Saturday, July 17: 10 am Magic class with Tyson Ruff, pre-registration required

3 pm Horseshoe Tournament

5 pm Mystical Hayride

7 pm Abracadabra Karaoke with DJ Drake

8 pm Tonight's movie: HARRY POTTER AND THE CHAMBER OF SECRETS

10 pm S'mores & cocoa by the community fire

Sunday, July 18: 9 am Nondenominational church service

Did you shave, Dee?" Natalie asks.

A young boy with a magician's cape tied around his neck runs screaming in front of the lodge window and leaps from the top step, his cape billowing out like Superman's. "Yep, everywhere that requires shaving."

Natalie leans back against the counter, punching numbers into the cash register so the drawer opens and then slamming it shut. At the pavilion, the town's fire chief, Tyson Ruff, is teaching some kids a card trick while two sisters try to make each other disappear with fake wands. That's what I want. To just disappear.

"And we're sure about this outfit?" Natalie pokes her own twisted tissue wand at the plaid shorts, yellow T-shirt, and matching cardigan I'm wearing. "After all, it's an important decision. Remember all those horrible, ratty celebrity mug shots we saw online?"

Mug shot.

If Sabrina goes through with her threat, I'll go from Super-flirt to criminal. What *was* I thinking last night, did I expect her to say, golly, thanks for the info, you're a life saver? And what would Ivy say if she knew I broke the restraining order? She'd freak out, which is why I didn't tell her. Instead, I made sure to wash my hair early this morning and put on extra de-odorant in case I get interrogated or have to share a cell with a woman named Hildegard Hairpuller or Bertha Buttkicker. Good thing we have a magic class instead of our usual Saturday craft hour. I can hide out in the store with Natalie and watch for the sheriff, who I hope will be compassionate enough not to put me in handcuffs.

Oh my poor mother.

Now I understand why people drink to settle their nerves. As a camper who is dressed up as Dumbledore rolls by on a skateboard, I reach for a Snickers bar, my drug of choice for the day. "Isn't that your second one?" Natalie asks, watching me rip it open and take a huge bite. "The last thing we need is for you to throw up in the squad car and be covered in vomit when they're taking your fingerprints."

"Relax, Dee," Roxanne says as she opens the screen door and two junior wizards push past her. She notices my empty wrap-pers and then glares at the little girl who is trying to confiscate her Snapple using a Harry Potter *Accio* summoning spell. "No one's getting arrested, except for *annoying brats who try to take my green tea!*"

The girl shrieks and runs out of the store.

"How do you know, Roxanne?" I ask, spewing a bit of choco-late on my shorts. Great. Now I'll have barf *and* pooplike stains on my clothes. "Sabrina probably told Mona all about how demon-girl Dee tracked her down."

Roxanne sits beside us on an empty stool, making me stop thinking about myself long enough to realize that she's wearing a tank top—a tight, figure-showing tank top—along with her cargo shorts. She looks good. Sexy tomboy good. "Dee, it's ten-thirty," Roxanne says. "If Sabrina did tattle, the sheriff would have been here by now, so ease up on the chocolate, there, Piggly-Wiggly."

I choke on a peanut. Did she call me Piggly-Wiggly? The peanut starts to feel more like a coconut in my throat, making me cough. As Natalie pounds on my back, I laugh and choke at the same time, all of the mounting stress from the lawsuit and a Snickers sugar rush turning me into a delirious, suffocating mess. "Piggly-Wiggly. Oh my gosh, that cracks me up!"

Natalie turns to Roxanne. "Oh, man, she's lost it."

Roxanne starts to smile, but something outside the window catches her eye. She blinks, pointing at what could only be a state trooper coming to arrest me. "Ah, Dee?"

It's a Trooper, all right.

A bright yellow one with Mardi Gras beads hanging on the rearview mirror.

At first I think it's Mona, but it's *Sabrina* who parks and then heads toward us in the store. The screen door creaks extra loud when she enters with her chin tilted up in defiance. "Okay, here's the thing," Sabrina says when she sees us. "Just because I came here does *not mean* we're friends or anything."

My sugar rush turns to panic.

Is this a trap? Her way of getting back at me? I'm about to

277

make a break for it when Sabrina says, "And, Dee, I didn't call the sheriff."

Natalie's face hardens. "Then why are you here, huh? Need more evidence for your case? Or—hey, want to take another picture of me, maybe while I'm scratching my butt cheek this time, something to give all your friends a good chuckle."

I can't believe it when an embarrassed flush darkens Sabrina's face. "Look, I don't blame any of you for hating my guts. So if you want me to leave, just say the word and I'll take care of Larson myself."

Here's my big chance.

I can throw *her* out and let *her* know how it feels to be an outsider, but something she said stops me. *I'll take care of Larson myself.*

She believes us.

"You showed your mother the picture, didn't you?" I ask.

Sabrina nods, her lower lip giving the slightest twitch.

"And I take it that it didn't go well?" Roxanne asks.

Sabrina nods again, more briskly this time, with tears glistening. Wow. Seeing the ice queen breaking down should be satisfying . . . but it's not. So when she notices the Snickers bar still in my hand, I can't help but take one from the display and slide it toward her. "Tell us. How bad is it?"

Sabrina sits with perfect posture as she rips off the wrapper. But then she slouches, her composure crushed as she says, "Bad, real bad! Mom was furious and said the woman in the photo could be his *cousin* or something. And then she called Larson and asked if he would sign a prenup—just to prove me wrong—and he said that true love like theirs will last forever, so there's no need for a prenup."

"Oh, gag," Natalie says. "And she fell for it?"

"Hook, line, and scumbag. She refused to even talk about it, and—huh? Is that guy out there by the pool dressed like Dumbledore?"

Yeah, that's Mr. Clark from Dundalk, but I'm not about to casually discuss his obsession with Hogwarts. She's not getting off that easy. "Look, Sabrina, let's stop the tap-dancing, okay? You know *perfectly well* I never pushed you and that Blaine lied about what happened, so why don't you just tell the truth and have the lawsuit dropped? Then maybe my nightmare of a summer would go back to normal *and* Larson would leave."

Everything would be over.

"I'm sorry, but I can't," Sabrina says softly. "Mom refuses to believe he's conning her, even though he's the one who convinced her to go to trial." She pauses, taking a huge bite of her candy bar like she hasn't had chocolate in months. "And she said that if I change my statement, she'd tell the judge I'm lying because she's marrying Larson and that . . ."

She stops. "And what?" Natalie asks.

Sabrina takes a deep breath and looks at me. "And that she'll have you arrested."

It takes a second for the words to sink in.

Sabrina is *protecting me*? Why?

"Larson also convinced her to go to *Vegas* next weekend to get married." She crumples the candy wrapper and banks it into the trash with impressive accuracy. "And we all know that I can't stop him without your help, and you can't stop him with-out me. If we want this to end, then we need to work together and find more proof that Larson is a gold digger—even if it means breaking a few rules. So *my* question, ladies, is this: Are you in?"

Duh.

Did she seriously have to ask?

Two hours later, Natalie, Roxanne, and I are ringing Sabrina's doorbell. She opens the door and lets us in. "Good timing, Mom just left for the grocery store."

It's amazing how much her house screams of Mona, with its cool '50s vibe, antique jukebox, and a glass cake stand holding a plate of cookies beside a vintage television. Roxanne leans over to read the titles of about fifty Harlequin novels stacked on the kitchen counter while Natalie helps herself to a cookie. "Ew," she says. "Too much vanilla."

"Tell me about it." Sabrina takes one anyway and then leads us down the hallway to her bedroom while saying, "Okay, step one, we need to sneak into Larson's house without tripping the alarm."

Earlier, at the campground, we agreed that the best place to find any kind of evidence would be Larson's home office, seeing as how there are too many employees roaming around the inn. And now, being in Sabrina's bedroom—what I would have called the Devil's Lair only yesterday—is both disconcerting and oddly exhilarating. Especially when I see the photo of Blaine on her dresser, smiling with all his charm.

Ha. He doesn't know yet that he's part of our plan.

"Wait, don't tell me," I say. "Blaine made you turn around when he entered the alarm code, too, right?"

"Every time," Sabrina says, flicking his photo with her finger hard enough to knock it backward. She then grabs her cell and dials. "So watch and learn, ladies, watch and learn."

We watch.

And we learn as she brushes her dark hair back and holds the phone against her ear, giving us a wicked grin before saying, "Torrance, *heeey*, it's been, like, a whole week since we've talked!" *Nod, nod, nod.* "What I said? Honey, I was just kidding about buying my clothes off eBay. Oh, you knew all along? Right, of course you did!"

Sabrina breathes out a gloomy moan. "How am I doing? Well, it's been rough. I'm so depressed over Blaine. What's that ... Yes, being dumped really does hurt—thanks for the reminder, Torrance."

She covers the phone long enough to whisper to us, "Hello, I dumped him," before saying, "I just don't know what happened, Torr. I wish I could *beg* him for an answer, but I don't know where he's going to be today." She nods and interjects a few *uh-huhs*. "He has a lesson at the driving range at three? And you know this specifically because ... Right, because Prescott told you, sure. And, um, what are you doing today? Oh, yay, that sounds just *fabulous*. Well, thanks, Torr, you've been a *great friend*. Love ya!"

Sabrina clicks the phone shut. "Game on."

"Aren't you afraid Torrance will show up?" Roxanne asks her.

"Nope. She told me she's having a spa day with her mother. Not even the chance to see me beg would keep her from a mani-pedi." Sabrina turns to where Natalie is snooping through her cosmetics bag and looks at her like a cobra stalking a field mouse. "And now for step two."

Natalie drops the puffy brush she was dabbing her cheeks with, her body tense and nose twitching like this mouse is about to bolt. "Uh, maybe this isn't the best idea. What if Blaine recognizes me? And what if Larson shows up?"

I push down on her shoulders before she can escape. "Blaine won't. You and I didn't become close until *after* we broke up and besides—he probably wouldn't recognize the woman who cleans his house twice a week, so you'll be fine."

"And my mother said Larson is out of town for the weekend," Sabrina says, flipping through the clothes in her closet. "And trust me, once I'm done with you, your own momma won't recognize you. And if Blaine does, well, it won't matter as long as you show enough leg."

Natalie leans her head against the back of the chair and swallows hard. I kneel down beside her and say, "Nat, come on, *you're* the real Superflirt. You're the one who's been writing the blog everyone loves. You're the brave one, Natalie, not me."

She twirls a finger with a sarcastic frown. "Yeah, it takes a lot of courage to write an anonymous blog, big whoop."

"It is a big whoop," Sabrina says, taking a black miniskirt and then dismissing it by throwing it on her bed. "Your writing is fantastic."

The worry lines on Natalie's face soften. Roxanne drapes a towel around Natalie's neck and leans down to say, "She's right— your blog rocks. So shut up. This should be a piece of cake for you."

"I hate cake," Natalie whines, her eyes widening when Sabrina pulls out an adorable pink minidress. "Oh, no. I'm not wearing that."

"Natalie, stop! You'd look fabulous in this—" I take the dress from Sabrina and check the label. "Hollister, are you kidding me? You got a Hollister dress off of eBay?"

Sabrina picks up her scissors and taps them against her palm as though uncertain how to answer. Finally, she says, "Yeah. I did."

"Cool. You totally have to show me how."

25 ∼ Sabrina

Maybe tomorrow I'll be able to comprehend the fact that I'm sitting in a parking lot beside Dee Barton and Roxanne Swain with a pair of binoculars that we will use to spy on Natalie Green as she tries to flirt with my ex-boyfriend.

Seriously?

It's been the weirdest summer.

We couldn't drive the Trooper to the driving range—it's not exactly subtle—and my car is still in the shop, but my neighbor, Mrs. Mason, was more than willing to loan us her Subaru, since I sold her panel curtain sets on craigslist for thirty-five dollars each. Dee straightens the humongous sunglasses I loaned her and asks, "So, what's Natalie doing now?"

I adjust the binoculars and focus on Natalie, which is hard to do considering we're parked on the far side of the packed lot. "Okay, she's in the pro shop waiting in line. And, girls, it looks like she's talking to herself again."

Poor Natalie. She's probably repeating the same *I am Superflirt, hear me roar* mantra that she nervously muttered during the drive here. But even if Natalie is a wreck on the inside, she's fabulous on the outside. After convincing her to trust me—after all, I have been cutting my mother's hair since age seven—I chopped off four inches, giving her a sweet, pixyish bob that's proportionate to her petite frame. I also did her makeup and put her in a pair of sleek white shorts and a drapy pink top that is both hot and athletic at the same time.

Okay, not to brag or anything, but yeah, I'm good.

And it was fun! So, maybe I should . . . I don't know, take some cosmetology classes at the vocational school that's right behind Riverside High. I've never thought about it before. Well, no, I *have* thought of it, but the people in my crowd make fun of Vo-Tech students. Especially Torrance, who thinks girls in cosmetology only cut hair because they're too stupid for anything else, even though she's the one who spends a hundred fifty dollars on highlights every six weeks. And after today, there's a good chance I'll never be welcome with my crowd again.

Do I even want to be?

"What about Blaine, can you see him?" Roxanne asks, scooting up in the backseat so she can get a glimpse of herself in the rearview window and fluff her freshly cut hair. After much persuasion, I gave her a makeover, too, by covering that awful red with a semi-permanent brunette wash and making her skin glow with bronzer, light mascara, and gloss.

So yeah, I'm calling my guidance counselor on Monday.

But today is all about Operation Blaine. "He's still with his instructor," I say, watching him through the binoculars. "Who is wearing the most hideous yellow striped pants ever. Yuck, does playing golf require a lack of good taste?"

"I hate golf," Dee says.

Got that right. I sweep the binoculars back to the pro shop, where a father and two little boys are walking out. "Okay, Natalie is at the front of the line now. Hey, the guy behind the counter is kind of cute in a shaggy way. He's getting her a bucket of balls."

"Let me see," Dee says, taking the binoculars. "Oh, he is cute! With that hair, he kind of looks like Orlando Bloom in *Pirates of the Caribbean.* There is something so deliciously sexy about movie stars with long, dirty hair, but I'm more into the high-and-tight look, like Channing Tatum. Did you see him in—"

Dee stops when she notices Roxanne staring at her.

"What?"

"Hmm, Jake looks like Channing Tatum," Roxanne teases while reaching for the binoculars. She holds them to her eyes. "And Natalie's leaving the shop. She's walking to the driving range now. Has she ever swung a club, Dee?"

"Only the putt-putt kind," she says. "And Jake does *not* look like Channing Tatum."

If they are talking about the Jake Bollinger who danced with Dee at the campground, then she must be in serious denial mode because yes, he does. But instead of calling her on it, I take a sip of my cherry Slurpee—I am *so* not in the mood for diet soda—and squint at where Natalie is setting up four stalls down from Blaine. "What's happening now, does he see her?"

Roxanne nods, the binoculars bobbing up and down as she says, "Oh, yeah, he notices her. So does his instructor, the perv. Wait . . . Orlando Bloom just walked out of the pro shop—he's taking something to Natalie . . . She must have forgotten her change . . . And now he's talking to her. Oh, man, is this going to screw up our plan?"

I shake my head. "No, it will help. Blaine will be more intrigued if there's competition involved."

Sure enough, once Orlando leaves and Blaine's lesson is done, Roxanne reports how he pulls off his gloves and then hauls his expensive golf bag to the stall next to Natalie's. He leans against the dividing partition, watching as she drives a ball one hundred fifty yards. Huh. Not too shabby.

"Okay, he's giving her some pointers," Roxanne says. "You should be proud of her, Dee, she just did a kick-butt imaginary lint pick! But oops—she flipped her hair and got it stuck to her lipstick . . . and she dropped her club . . . and she knocked over her golf balls."

Come on, Natalie, keep it together!

Roxanne shifts in her seat. "Okay, it's all good. They're laughing. But man, why didn't we think to get the Cutsons' spy gear? We could be listening in."

Dee turns to face us, curling her legs underneath her as she says, "Oh, that's easy. He'll probably talk about his stellar golfing accomplishments before moving on to the stimulating subject of his favorite movies, including, but not limited to, anything starring Chuck Norris, Jason Statham, and—of course—Clint Eastwood."

Now it's my turn to shift toward her. "Ugh, do you know how many times he's forced me to watch *Heartbreak Ridge*?"

"Oh my gosh, I know!" Dee slaps her knee. "I mean, it's a

good movie and all, but I *hate* the scene where the soldiers go to that college campus where all the students are being held hostage in a classroom by terrorists except for—"

"Except for that one busty blonde," I continue. "Who is for *some reason* taking a *shower* only to—oopsie—drop her towel when a soldier bursts in the bathroom giving the quintessential boob shot. Really? Showering during a terrorist attack? But Blaine never saw the fallacy of that scene."

"Duh, of course he didn't," Dee says, wagging her finger. "Not him."

Roxanne lowers the binoculars and pulls at the strap with a worried look on her face. "Okay, I hate to ask, but why did you both date him if he's so horrible?"

Dee's amusement fades to grief. She turns to the window, running her finger along the Subaru's door handle before saying, "Well, I was pretty messed up after my father died, I guess, and for a while . . . Blaine filled that empty void, you know?"

Yes, I do know.

I have that very same void. But Dee's father died? I didn't know that—or maybe I did hear about it but didn't care enough to pay attention. It makes me think of all my father's recent phone calls that I've been ignoring, and the letter he sent me. Maybe I should read it. Give him a chance to apologize. And, for the first time, I'm realizing something else.

Just how much Dee and I have in common.

"Wait! Blaine's leaving," Roxanne says, leaning so far forward that she is nearly in my seat. "That can't be good news, can it?"

But it is good news. Because while Blaine is loading his golf clubs in his Mercedes, Natalie calls Dee's cell and reports that he didn't recognize her when she introduced herself as *Priscilla*, of all names, and that she did, indeed, secure an invitation to his house to watch—wait for it, wait for it—*Heartbreak Ridge.*

Oh, and Orlando slipped her his number.

I can't avoid it any longer, even though just thinking about Rex Reynolds makes my chest ache.

Mom's in the kitchen when I get back, fixing an early dinner of cheater chili—canned kidney, black, and pinto beans, and diced tomatoes sautéed in onions and topped with sour cream. On the table, fresh wildflowers are arranged in the ceramic vase, the one I now know Rex sent her. The other girls and I are supposed to be leaving for Blaine's soon, but if tonight is the night for resolutions, then maybe I should start with her.

"Hey, Mom, you got a second?"

She stirs the chili and says, "Sure, something on your mind?"

Oh, boy, you have no idea.

"Yeah . . . I know it was Rex who sent you those flowers."

This announcement causes Mom to flinch, dropping the spatula and sending bits of onion and beans all over the floor. She grabs a tea towel and starts to clean up the mess with quick, spastic movements. "How did you—Oh, Dee, I'm sorry, let me explain—"

"Mom, stop, it's okay." I kneel to help her. "I'm not upset nor would I have any right to be. I just want you to be happy, just like Dad would have. So whenever you want to talk about it, I'm here."

Mom freezes, her fingers poised over a wayward kidney bean as though she expects me to protest—or *wants* me to protest. She abandons the bean and slumps down on the floor, leaning against the stove. I sit beside her as she says, "Dee, I thought I was ready to date. And Rex really is a nice man, but . . ." Mom sniffs, red blotches dotting her cheeks. "It was so easy with your dad. I never had to think, you know? I could be myself around him. I could . . . *fart* and he wouldn't care, but with Rex . . . How can you go back to casual dating after you've spent half of your life as a devoted wife? It's like going backward, and maybe . . . maybe I just don't have the energy to start over, sweetie."

"No, Mom." I lean into her and loop my arm around her bent knee. "It's going *forward*, not backward. And honestly, you never farted in front of Dad at the beginning, did you? At least I hope you didn't."

A slow smile spreads on her face. "No, of course not, but who am I kidding, what would Rex want with a stressed-out widow with a multimillion-dollar lawsuit against her? No. Forget it. I wouldn't know how to act on a date, anyway."

"*What?* First off, Mom, the case is *not* going to trial if I have anything to do with it. And second, you have me as your own personal coach! My first bit of advice," I say, pointing to her chili, "is to stay away from the beans if you'd rather not have gas."

❧

Before we leave, the Cutsons, wearing magician's capes and curly mustaches drawn above their upper lips, run up to the Subaru that Sabrina borrowed. Lyle doesn't skip a beat when he sees Natalie and me crouching on the rear floorboard so Mom and Ivy won't catch us with Sabrina and realize we haven't already left for a sale at Kohl's. Lyle simply hands me all of his spy gear through the open window: binoculars, mini-recorders, goggles— what for, I have no idea—and a notepad. "You sure you don't need us to come along?" he asks, staring down at me with eyes round like brown acorns.

"Yeah, what if you need backup?" Tanner says, resting his chin on the window ledge and glancing at Sabrina and Roxanne in the front seat.

I take in their eager, dirty faces. The little creeps only want to be included, so it wouldn't hurt to give them their own assignment. "Hmm, I'll tell you what, boys. My grandmother, Madeline, has been acting very suspicious. Why don't you spy on her and report back to me later, okay?"

"Okay!" the twins yell before running off.

As Sabrina starts the car, the significance of being with Roxanne and *Sabrina Owens*—the girl I've hated for so long— hits me. And we had *fun* today, despite everything, but what will happen when school starts again? Will everyone but Natalie and me go back to being enemies? I hope the answer will be no.

So far, so good.

We drop Natalie and my bike that was stowed in the trunk off at Riverside Estates' entrance before parking behind the

Swains' dumpster. As Natalie rides to Blaine's, Roxanne stays in the car while Sabrina and I creep to a curb near Larson's house that is shielded from view by a row of unruly barberry shrubs. We sit, pretending to talk on our cells so any snooping neighbors will see us as normal teenagers—not two girls about to commit a misdemeanor. Or is breaking and entering a felony?

"Are you sure Blaine won't recognize your neighbor's car?" I whisper.

"Relax. He wouldn't, so stay focused. Okay, Natalie is at the front stoop, she's ringing the doorbell."

We hear Blaine answer with a slick "Well, hello, there!" I peek around the bush and see Natalie pretending to admire Larson's elaborate hickory door before stepping inside.

Be cool, Nat, be cool.

Minutes pass in slow agony as we wait for her cue.

Then, finally, my phone vibrates once. I nudge Sabrina. "Okay, Natalie has Blaine out of sight in the kitchen."

We half creep/half casually walk to the front steps and stop at the door long enough for Sabrina to ask, "Do you think he set the alarm?"

"No, he never did whenever I visited. You?"

"No, but if it goes off, we bolt. Got it?"

Sabrina grabs the doorknob. She takes a deep breath and cracks the door open. We wait for the alarm. Nothing, thank God, so we tiptoe into the foyer, clinging SWAT-team style to the wall. Sabrina pulls a flashlight from her pocket and opens the basement door as we hear Natalie laughing at a lame joke of Blaine's. As we sneak down the steps, memories flood my thoughts—all the movies I let him pick, the food I let him choose, all the times he tried to pressure me into doing something I wasn't ready to do.

Yeah, I really was a Miss Almond Pudding.

No. Get a grip, Dee.

Sabrina goes straight to Blaine's desk and hands me the flashlight. I try to slow my breathing as she starts to open the drawers, one by one. "Keep the light steady, okay?" Sabrina whispers, while flipping through a pile of wrinkled papers and old essays. "Come on, come on, where's that report card?"

At the top of the stairs, the basement door creaks open. Blaine's voice echoes down the steps. "So, Priscilla, you want to see the downstairs?"

Oh my Lord. They aren't supposed to come down here. Natalie is supposed to get him outside somehow. Every hair on my body rises in panic. Sabrina jumps, slamming her thigh against the drawer and biting her lip to keep from calling out.

"Absolutely," Natalie purrs, even though—hello—we'd be totally busted. "But didn't you say you had an *amazing* view of the river from the deck? I'd love to see that first."

You go, Nat, whip out the Superflirt.

I let out my breath when the door closes. Sabrina attacks another drawer with extra frenzy until she finds what she came for. "Aha! Here it is, his old report card. It's from a school in Philadelphia."

I yank at her shirt. "Okay, then let's hurry!"

We creep back upstairs. Our plan was to use the report card to find out what part of Pennsylvania they came from, and then snoop in Larson's office for some kind of evidence that he's up to no good. But after we slip inside the room, I lean against the closed door as Sabrina dashes to his clutter-free desk. "This feels wrong," I say. "We shouldn't be in here."

Sabrina stops digging through a drawer long enough to say, "Dee, we would never be in here had he not decided to mess with our mothers, so start searching."

Good point.

But snooping through his file cabinet freaks me out, especially when a horn blast comes from outside. I run to the window that faces the Swains' driveway. "Oh, man, Roxanne is waving for some reason. Should we leave?"

"No, just keep looking!" Sabrina whispers, opening another drawer and finding a green vinyl bag, the same kind Mom uses for bank deposits. She unzips it and pulls out a deposit slip with several checks attached with a paper clip.

There's more honking as Sabrina reads one of the checks. She gasps. "Dee . . . it's for ten thousand dollars from Kathleen Myers, the woman you saw Larson with!"

Ten thousand dollars?

Sabrina hands me the check. "Quick—the copier. Turn it on."

I run over to the copier, but before I can flip the switch, I hear what sounds like the garage door opening.

No. It can't be Larson.

Moments later we hear the mudroom door open. Footsteps echo in the foyer, footsteps that are too heavy to be Blaine's. It *is* Larson, *that's* why Roxanne honked! "Hide!" I hiss, grabbing Sabrina's arm and pulling her behind the leather sofa.

The door swings open.

Someone walks in.

Don't panic, oh, for the love of God, don't panic.

The desk chair squeaks. My lungs ache from holding my breath as Larson picks up the phone and dials. "Henry! It's Larson, calling to let you know I'll be mailing the interest payment for the second mortgage on Monday. And thanks for being patient, Henry, I can assure you there will be no more late payments. I have everything under control."

Yeah, that's what he thinks.

Larson hangs up and taps his desk a few times, his chair squeaking again as he stands and walks back out of the room. When he closes the door behind him, I swat Sabrina in the rear. "I thought you said he was on a business trip and wouldn't be back until tomorrow night!"

"Well, golly gee, he must have lied, imagine that!" Sabrina whispers back, kneeling to unlock the window. "Come on, let's get out of here."

No. The check in my hand. We can't leave without a copy for proof. "Dee, let's go!" Sabrina pleads when I creep to the copier and place it on the glass. *Please be a quiet one!* Thankfully, the copier doesn't rumble and groan like ours does, but a red light comes on, saying the machine needs to warm up.

Come on, come on!

The light finally turns green. I hit the button, grabbing the copy as soon as it comes out. "Okay, now we can go," I tell Sabrina.

But it's too late. The footsteps return.

There's nowhere to hide except for beside the file cabinet. I press my back to the wall, my heart pounding like an out of control jack hammer. The copier! The copier is still on, with the check inside. *Crap, I'm going to be arrested after all.* Breaking and entering? Violating a restraining order? How many years is that going to get me?

The doorknob turns.

The door inches open.

Larson steps in, but just as if it's God Himself coming to our rescue, someone pounds on the front door. I can hear Larson curse underneath his breath before he leaves to open it with a surprised "Roxanne, is everything okay?"

Roxanne!

"Mr. Walker, thank goodness!" she says, sounding both desperate and dumb. "One of the toilets in our new house is leaking and water's getting all over the hardwoods!"

No way.

She's playing the helpless card!

"Now, now, don't panic, Roxanne," Larson says in a condescending tone. "There's a shutoff valve right at the base. All you have to do is—"

"You mean *inside* the toilet?" Roxanne timidly asks.

"No, it's at the base, by the floor," Larson chides.

Seriously, does he think she's that stupid? No time to analyze. "Let's go!" Sabrina whispers as she eases the window open. I grab the check, returning it to the bank bag and turning off the copier before running to the window and climbing out. We both land right in an evergreen shrub.

"Ouch!"

"Shh! Be quiet!"

We sprint across the lawn like a rabid dog is nipping at our heels, not stopping until we reach our rendezvous point at the development's entrance. My lungs ache as we flop down by a hydrangea bush. Sabrina lies on the grass, her face beet red and her chest still heaving when Roxanne drives up in the Subaru and Natalie joins us on my bike. Nat lets it fall to the ground and slumps down beside us. "I—I—pretended to get a text from my mom, saying I had to come home, after I heard Roxanne talking to Larson," she wheezes. "Did you find anything?"

"Oh, yes, you bet your sweet tush we did," I tell her.

After filling Natalie in on all the juicy details, Sabrina turns to me. "Dee . . . I'm sorry."

"About what? You were fantastic back there."

She shakes her head. "No, about the letter. It drove me crazy, the way Blaine always talked about you. I wanted to humiliate you so maybe—he'd talk about me, instead. And," she says to Natalie, "I'm sorry for taking that picture of you. I was a total . . ."

"Jerk?" Natalie provides.

"Yeah, a giant jerk." She tells Natalie to get out her cell, and thrusts most of her index finger straight up her nose. "So go ahead, take your best shot. I deserve it."

After our evening of misdemeanors, Natalie and Sabrina head for home, but Roxanne bravely volunteers to help me show Ivy our discovery. I'm hoping Ivy won't scream as much over *how* we found the check if someone is with me. Yeah, right, *wishful thinking*. Before we can make it to Ivy's RV Victoria Swain appears.

"Roxanne, there you are!" She smiles and holds up a large pamphlet. "I've been dying to show you what came in the mail today."

Roxanne mumbles an annoyed "not again" under her breath.

"Mom, I'm not interested in seeing any product brochures or samples for the new house right now, okay?" But when she notices an auto mechanic posing on the pamphlet's front page, she stops. "Oh, is . . . is that for Lincoln Tech?"

"It sure is! Did you know there's a branch right here in Columbia and—" Mrs. Swain stops, twisting an earring, realizing that, of course, Roxanne already knows this. She gives me a polite glance that is laced with guilt and says, "I, uh, also have an application, Roxanne, that maybe we could fill out together. And maybe you can tell me about that first female NASCAR pit chief, what was her name, Cindy Woodsy?"

It seems as though a silent truce is formed between them, one of acceptance and hope.

Roxanne takes the pamphlet. "Woosley, Mom. Cindy Woosley."

Huh. Well done, Mrs. Swain, well done.

They leave together—which would have been delightfully touching had it not been for the fact that I now have to face Ivy on my own. Oh, well, time to put on my big girl panties and get it over with. But as I pass the playground, the Cutsons jump off the monkey bars, their foreheads slick with sweat and their capes now torn.

"Miss Dee, we did what you asked!"

"Did what?" I ask them.

"Duh! Spy on that Madeline woman," Tanner says. "We don't fool around with secret missions. Should we report to you now or later?"

Right, my secret "mission" for them. "Sure, what's the scoop, fellows?"

Lyle leans forward, darting his eyes left and right to make sure there are no other spies hiding in the pine trees. "Well, she spent an awfully long time arguing on the phone with some Arthur guy. He your granddaddy? She kept yellin' and saying it weren't right for him to talk to their lawyer while she was gone."

"Yeah," Tanner says. "And don't tell my momma I said a dirty word, but she also said to him, 'Piss on your papers.' So we think—"

"So we think your granddaddy got a new puppy named Lawyer who he's trying to potty train!" Lyle finishes triumphantly.

Just hearing the word "lawyer" makes me shudder. And pissing on papers? That doesn't make any sense. But the Cutsons look so proud of themselves that I lean forward to kiss their grubby cheeks. "Good job, guys. I knew I could count on—"

Wait. Lawyer? Papers? And the fact that she's been here for so long without a good reason? I think I know why.

Madeline is a Miss Almond Pudding, too.

"Young lady, I was just about to turn in early for the evening," Madeline barks from her open cabin door, dressed in pajamas, dirty tissues littering the floor behind her. "Is there some kind of emergency, Dee?"

I shift my weight, hearing laughter and the sound of metal hitting metal coming from the horseshoe pits. Should I ask to be invited in? No, from the way she's gripping the doorknob, I know what her answer will be. So instead, I hold up the white box I was hiding behind my back and say, "No, I just wanted to bring you something."

She reads the box, her brow furrowed. "Skinny Cows? You felt it was necessary to bring me junk food?"

I nod. "Yeah, they come in handy . . . when you're upset or when you need to really talk about something."

Madeline stiffens, fidgeting with her pajama collar with one hand and clutching her stomach with the other, making it look like she's both pushing and pulling herself at the same time. "I have no idea what you're talking about, Dee. I'm not upset, nor is there anything that needs to be discussed, so if you don't mind—"

There is no way to get to it other than the direct route.

"Is my grandfather asking you for a divorce?"

She steps back, her aloof mask refusing to budge. "Young lady, I don't know what you're—"

"Is that why you're here? Why didn't you tell us?"

Her face pales, making me realize that I am right. Madeline sucks in her cheeks and stands tall. "Well, Dee, I suppose that's . . . What I mean to say is . . ."

She releases the death grip on her collar and tries to compose herself by smoothing out the wrinkles. She then walks to a rocking chair on the porch, sitting daintily as though she's dressed in heels instead of sloppy pajamas. "What I meant to say is that yes, Arthur and I are separated. But I felt no reason to bring up the topic because I have the situation completely in hand."

Uh, no. She doesn't.

I sit beside her, saying nothing, just feeling the sweet dampness of July night air and listening to the chirping crickets.

Madeline gazes out over the trout pond, her mouth held in a grim line. After her neighbor at the cabin next door hangs wet beach towels on the railing and a round of choruses comes from the horseshoe pit over someone's ringer, she takes a quick breath. "Yes, there's nothing to discuss and there's no reason for any dramatics, because I'm okay. I'm perfectly okay."

"Oh." I say softly. "I just—"

"After all," she interrupts, her back rigid and ankles crossed like an etiquette school graduate. "A woman of my capabilities surely can handle life on her own . . . even though starting over isn't what I expected after forty-five years of marriage."

She clasps her hands.

"And the fact that Arthur now wants to live without me is of no consequence . . . even though you would *think* that a life-long spouse who you *thought* was the one person who loved you would *at least* offer some kind of a warning that your world was about to be flushed down the toilet."

Her lower lip starts to quiver. "And it doesn't matter that Arthur wants to keep the RV, the only home I've known for so long. But securing new living arrangements will not be an issue. I can live . . . I can—"

She turns away, hiding the tears now streaming down her face, tears that I suspect she's been hiding for a very long, long time. I tear open the box of Skinny Cows and hand her one. But before she can take that first bite, a voice comes from the path below.

My mother's.

"You can live here."

27 ∾ Sabrina

Mom, we really need to talk."

On Sunday evening, my mother leans close to the vanity mirror, pressing loose powder on her face, her hair up in curlers. The smells of meatloaf, mashed potatoes, and rhubarb pie come from the sparkling-clean kitchen; Mom has spent the entire day scrubbing, cooking, and baking. She glances at me, the beige powder coating her bare lashes giving her a blank, creepy look. "Sorry, sugar, like I told you before, I don't have time to talk. Larson is going to be here in less than an hour, and I haven't even started to put my eyes on yet! And heaven's sake alive, I forgot to make the salad."

"But that's who I need to talk to you about. Larson."

I pull up an ottoman and sit, a copy of the check and the photo of Larson with Kathleen feeling hot and dangerous in my hand. Mom sweeps a makeup brush over her entire face, sending dusts of extra powder onto her shoulder. Without thinking, I wipe it away.

Mom seems startled by my touch. "Oh. Um, thank you, Sabrina. But really . . . I can't talk right now."

"Mom, please."

She bolts from her chair, knocking over her perfume bottles. She quickly walks to her closet and begins to rummage through her clothes. "Whatever you have to say, sweetie, will simply have to wait. Larson will be here for dinner soon, and afterward, we need to plan our trip to Vegas."

I bite my lip before asking, "And whose credit card will it all go on?"

Mom hesitates.

"Well, Sabrina, mine, of course." She digs deeper in her closet, hiding her face from me. "Business at Larson's inn has been slow, and since we're about to be married, it doesn't seem like such a big whoop-de-do, now, does it?"

I stand and unfold the copy of the check. Mom steps out of the closet with a bright yellow cardigan in her hands. When she sees what I'm holding up, she freezes, clutching the sweater to her chest. "Sabrina, what is this?"

For a second, I consider balling the copy into a tight wad and throwing it away. What if we're wrong? What if Larson is legit? But no, we're right, I *know* we're right, so I say nothing as she snatches the paper and reads what is written on the check.

She raises a hand to her mouth.

"Mom . . . Larson uses women for money," I whisper.

I wait for it to sink in, but she drops the paper and stalks to her full-length mirror instead, yanking the cardigan on and buttoning the front. "No. You're wrong, Sabrina. I'm sure Larson has a perfectly good explanation and I should have known you would do this—try to ruin the one good thing I have going on in my life, just like you always want to go running back to your father, even though he cheated on me."

"Mom, this check is from the woman in the photo, a rich widow whose husband died only last winter. This just might prove that the only reason he's marrying you is because—"

Because of the money you could win . . . not because he loves you.

I can't bring myself to say those words.

"No." Mom sits at her vanity with a thud. She strokes bronzer on her cheeks and then grabs her eye shadow, rubbing her brush hard so that bits of shadow fall on the table. "Just get out of here and go back to your father. That's what you want, right? That's what *everybody* wants, for me to be out of their lives. You. Your father. Jane Barton. Larson wants me, Sabrina. Do you understand? He wants *me!*"

Tears fall down her face, smearing her makeup.

She's right.

At first, I did want to be with my father, even though he clearly prefers his new life with Belinda and Angela to me.

Why do we always want the people who don't want us?

"I'm sorry, Mom, for never realizing how much Dad's affair hurt you. I was just so mad about the way you reacted by dragging him through court. And I'm sorry for making you feel so alone, Mom," I continue, placing the photo of Larson with the other woman on the vanity. "But if you marry Larson, things will only get worse. The Bartons could lose their home, and Larson will break your heart. Let's end this, Mom. Drop the lawsuit and then see if Larson wants to stay."

She clutches her makeup brush and releases a shaky breath.

"But what if he doesn't stay? What will I be left with? Friends? I don't have any. Career? No one will hire me, and Chuck has already found a replacement. You're going to college soon and I'll be all alone, just like that psychic said I would be. What then?"

I shake my head. "Mom, you won't be alone. I promise."

Mom picks up her mascara. "Well, I already feel alone, Sabrina. So no, I don't believe anything you have to say about Larson. I *can't*."

She stares in the mirror, running a finger along the harsh wrinkles lining her mouth and forehead that came from her lifelong struggle to find some kind of stability, someone she could put her faith in. It should've been me—I should have been that someone—but because I wasn't there for her, she turned to Larson instead.

As I walk to my room, I realize there's nothing to do other than activate the alternate line of attack that me and the other girls thought up on the drive back from Larson's.

I dial Dee's number. "No go. It's time for Plan B."

She giggles on the other end. "I like Plan B!"

28 ～ Dee

Time for Plan B," I announce to the women gathered in the store. And Jake, of course, who offered to cover for us while we're gone.

"I like Plan B," Ivy says. She grabs her briefcase, looking powerful, sophisticated, and oh so anti–Miss Almond Pudding in her silk wrap dress.

Of course, she did NOT look the same last night after I confessed to her all of my recent illegal activities, including, but not limited to, violating restraining orders, breaking and entering, and spying. She was furious, fuming, and downright peeved. But after briefly yelling at me—for three minutes, twenty-one seconds—Ivy calmed down long enough to realize that our discoveries could help with the lawsuit.

And, hopefully, make it go away.

"Where's your mother, Dee?" Ivy asks, before glancing at her watch. "Lord, how long does it take her to pack?"

It's almost unbelievable that Mom will be driving my grandmother all the way to Florida tomorrow so they can haul back her belongings—and to offer moral support when Madeline signs the divorce papers, the ones she told my grandfather to piss on. It's also unbelievable that Madeline, the woman who once terrified us, is going to live here. Permanently.

But hey, I'm starting to think we can handle anything.

When Ivy sees Mom walking down the path from our cabin, she tosses Roxanne her keys. "Good. Jane's here, so you go fire up the Beemer and escort our guest out."

Roxanne gazes at the keys as though they hold special meaning and then hands them back to Ivy. "Well . . . it might be better if fewer people are there, so Mom and I are kind of going shopping instead."

What? She's missing this to go *shopping?*

Victoria Swain stops munching on her Skinny Cow. "Yes, I'm so excited—Roxanne and I have tickets for a NASCAR race at the Pocono Raceway in August, but I don't have a thing to wear! What you're doing sounds so exciting, though, like in the movie *Thelma and Louise*. Except you're all clean and showered. And you're not going to shoot anybody." She pauses before asking Ivy, "No one's going to be shot, are they?"

Natalie picks up her backpack, which is holding two laptops. "I wouldn't count on it."

As Ivy ushers all the ladies outside, I linger behind, making a show of adjusting my flip-flop—which really didn't need adjusting. For some reason, I think of how Roxanne said Jake looks like Channing Tatum, and yeah—okay—maybe he does resemble him a little. Especially when he smiles. Which he's doing. Right now. At me.

"Uh, pretty crazy stuff going on, huh?" I ask.

A clump of hair falls adorably over his forehead. "Yeah, pretty crazy."

"Yep, pretty crazy," I repeat. *Honestly, Dee? Is that all you can say? Okay, try again—coherently this time.* "Look, thanks for all your help lately. You've been . . . awesome."

Usually Jake would give some kind of smart-alecky response. But instead, his face grows serious. He leans forward, like he's going to tell me something. What, that he likes me? Or . . . that he's dating someone else? Either way, I can't deal with it right now. So when Ivy blares her horn outside, I run out the door before he can say anything.

"Larson! I'm so hap—" Mona says, after yanking open the door with animated excitement. But her joy fades when she sees Ivy, Mom, and me standing on the mat. "W-what the—you can't be here! What's going on?"

Sabrina steps up behind her. "It's okay, Mom, they're just here to talk. Please, give them a couple minutes. For me."

The oven timer rings.

Mona runs her hands down her apron before dashing to the kitchen and pulling on a pair of oven mitts. "Well, I would love to chat, but Larson will be here soon and I need to set the table and mix up the salad dressing, and—"

"Mom, please," Sabrina begs. "You have to listen to them!"

"And," Mona continues, "I forgot to take the rolls out of the freezer and I bet you didn't grind the coffee like I asked, Sabrina, did you?"

Mom goes to her side. She gently shuts the oven door. "Mona, I owe you an apology for the way I judged you and didn't give you another chance. I'm truly sorry."

Mona stands silent, nervously biting her lip before saying, "Well, thank you, Jane. And I do accept your apology, but right now, I want to make the salad dressing."

Sabrina takes off her mother's oven mitts and leads her to a bar stool on the other side of the counter. "Mom, please sit down, Miss Ivy needs to show you something."

Mona's lip starts to quiver, but she doesn't sit. "Sabrina. *I need . . . to make . . . salad dressing.* Larson loves fresh salad dressing."

"Larson loves a lot of things, like using women for money," Ivy says, before placing on the counter a newspaper article from five years ago that she found online this morning. The photo shows Larson and a woman named Hilary Saunders standing in front of their new Irish restaurant in Philadelphia. Then she lays out another article—one that shows how the same Hilary Saunders had to file for bankruptcy a year later around the same time Larson moved to Maryland.

Mona scans both articles, and then goes to her pantry to pull down olive oil, balsamic vinegar, and dark mustard. "Right, well . . . I'm sure Larson has a very good explanation. And about the silly check Sabrina showed me from that Kathleen woman—she was probably just paying him back for something, that's all."

Ivy peers at the closed front door as though she dreads what she is about to do next. But in a burst of determination, she opens it and says, "Mona, meet Kathleen Myers, who has quite an explanation for you."

The next time the doorbell rings, the table is set with dinnerware, fresh flowers, salad, and . . . salad dressing. Warm rolls are lovingly wrapped in a cloth napkin and a bottle of wine sits waiting, with a corkscrew beside it. Mona opens the door, the late July heat wafting over the threshold, bringing with it a very dashing Larson Walker. "Darling! I was beginning to worry about you! Always late, always late, my special man, aren't you?"

Larson kisses her cheek and then tweaks her nose. "Yes, but I assumed you would call when dinner was almost ready, so you can't blame me, can you?"

Mona smacks her forehead with a girlish giggle. "Oh, silly me! What was I thinking, expecting you to arrive at seven when you told me you'd be here by seven. Point taken! Now let me pour you some wine. I have some exciting news for you."

Chair legs scrape as Larson sits, accepting the drink Mona serves with a flourish. "What kind of news, about the lawsuit?"

"Yes, *fabulous* news about the lawsuit," Mona says, clapping her hands in excitement. "Oh, golly, where to start? Okay, Jane Barton? Well, she's offered me a permanent job because, *apparently*, DJ Drake is moving to Denver. Did you know that? I certainly didn't know that."

Larson almost drops his wineglass, staring at Mona in disbelief.

"Isn't that wonderful, honey?" Mona asks.

Larson takes an awkward sip and shifts in his seat. "Well, yes, wonderful, but won't that be a bit uncomfortable with you suing her?"

Mona lets out a casual *pfff.* "Oh, right. That. I told my lawyers to drop the whole lawsuit thingy."

Wine almost flies from Larson's mouth. He starts to choke, his face turning bloodred as he spews, "You . . . dropped . . . the . . . lawsuit . . . *thingy?*"

"Oh, honey, are you okay?" Mona asks, mopping his face with a cloth napkin, even though he keeps trying to dodge her. Mona then presses a hand to her chest. "Darling, are you mad at me? I thought you'd be happy because now we can just go to Vegas and get married without all those pesky meetings to worry about."

Larson stands, his chair almost crashing into Mona's china cabinet. "Of course I'm mad, you stupid—I mean . . . you had no right to drop the lawsuit without talking to me first!"

Mona leans back in her chair and picks at an imaginary piece of food trapped in her teeth. "Oh, yeah. Maybe I should have. Sorry, love."

"Sorry, love? *Sorry, love?*" Larson sputters. "Well, you need to call the lawyers back and tell them you've changed your mind. Now!"

"Can't." Mona pours herself some wine and takes a delicate sip. "It's too late to change it, so stop fussing! Let's enjoy dinner and then talk about Vegas. I do hope they play a movie on the flight out."

"Screw the movie," Larson yells, the veins now starting to bulge on the sides of his neck. "Screw getting married! How can I marry you if I can't trust you?"

Mona sighs and then puts her hands on the table, slowly pushing herself up. "Well, see, I was afraid you were going to say that, Larson. But it's funny how you say the word 'trust.' See, I trusted you. And you know who else trusted you?"

"Who?" Larson snarls.

"That woman right there."

Larson turns when we walk out of the guest room, where we've been watching the scene thanks to Natalie's duel laptops and webcams. His confidence fades to horror when he sees Kathleen, the woman whose loneliness and desolation after her husband's death caused her to believe Larson's lies. The woman who would do anything to keep him with her—even if it meant becoming an "investor" in his restaurant.

She stops in front of him. "Well, hello, Larson. I came to get my check back."

The Superflirt Chronicles
. . . blogs from a teenage flirtologist

Saturday, July 24

THE TRUTH SHALL SET YOU FREE
MOOD: Complete
MUSIC: "Learning to Fly," Kate Earl

The time has come for me to tell you—all my readers—the truth:

I am not the real Superflirt.

I'm Miss N, the one who used to be too shy to even pull off a decent hair toss. I've been pretending to be Superflirt because it made me feel powerful. Needed. Liked. Maybe even loved. But because of this blog, I set certain things in motion that could have led to disastrous results, and for that, I'm sorry. I'm also sorry for deceiving you. But am I sorry for starting this Web site?

No.

This blog has made me stronger and no longer willing to hide from the person I want to be. (For example, instead of waiting for a certain Orlando Bloom look-alike to ask me out, *I* asked *him*.) It's helped the real Superflirt to embrace her true self, and even though she's sworn to never flirt again, maybe there's a chance she will with a certain go-kart racer—if she knows what's good for her. It's also helped one girl to stop fighting hard to stay on the outside and it's helped another girl to stop fighting hard to stay on the inside.

And come on—let's all give it up for our girl Meghan, who just had her sixth date with a handsome pharmacist who just might be the prescription she's been searching for.

So, with your forgiveness, I want to keep The Superflirt Chronicles alive. It will be a place where ladies of all ages can hang out, ask questions, maybe even learn something every now and then. With that, I'd like to propose a new set of rules:

Superflirt's Nine Rules of Living

RULE #1: Don't dump your friends for a fellow. Except, of course, if your friends are a bunch of belittling, deprecating twits who judge, sabotage your happiness, encourage self-doubt, or any combination of the above. If so, then get new friends.

RULE #2: You are NEVER too old to flirt.

RULE #3: Avoid the Mr. Booty-Baggers.

RULE #4: Daughters—appreciate your mother's wisdom. Mothers—let us teach you how it feels to be young again.

RULE #5: Never underestimate the power of Skinny Cow Fudge Bars . . .

RULE #6: . . . But also remember that life is too short for light.

RULE #7: Never allow yourself to be a Miss Almond Pudding, ladies. In other words—don't allow yourself to be forced into something you do *not* want to do.

RULE #8: Life's full of storms, so when one hits you in the face, keep your hands on the wheel and keep driving.

RULE #9: Don't dance with a guy just to make your ex jealous, don't jump to conclusions, don't forget to pay your insurance bill, and for God's sake, always, *always* hold on to the handrail while walking down steps.

With total love and sisterhood,

The Superflirts

Welcome to the Barton Family Campground's
CHRISTMAS IN JULY WEEKEND!

Friday, July 23:	7 pm	Jingle Bell Rockin' with Butch and the Boys
	8 pm	Tonight's movie: MUPPET CHRISTMAS CAROL
Saturday, July 24:	10 am	Kids' Crafts: Felt stockings
	3 pm	Ho-Ho Horseshoe Tournament
	5 pm	Holiday Hayride
	6 pm	Announcement of the best-decorated site!
	7 pm	Caroling with Mona's Low-Key Karaoke and a possible visit from you-know-who!
	8 pm	Tonight's movie: IT'S A WONDERFUL LIFE
	10 pm	S'mores & cocoa by the community fire
Sunday, July 25:	9 am	Nondenominational church service

After spending a hot yuletide day decorating stockings, over-seeing a highly competitive ho-ho horseshoe battle, hauling kids in the packed hay wagon, and announcing that Mrs. Swain won for best-decorated site (thanks to the reindeer she put on top of their motor home), I am more than ready to slip into a most delightful, most decadent poolside nap.

Natalie and her blog, however, have other plans.

So does Roxanne, who wakes me by saying, "No, I would edit the first rule," before passing the laptop back to Natalie. She adjusts her brand-new swimsuit—the first one she's worn all summer—and says, "It's too wordy."

Natalie picks up my cherry snowball and helps herself to a bite. "But wordy makes it sound more dramatic. I'm going for *drama.*"

Sabrina bends her knees to keep from getting wet when a herd of kids jump into the deep end after diving sticks. "Oh, please, hasn't there been enough drama for one summer?"

"Amen to that," I say, as a guest with twinkling Santa lights tied to his golf cart drives past. "And, Natalie, why did you say that about Jake? Honestly. For the rest of the summer, until school starts, I'm going to be absolutely guy-free!"

"Ugh, school, must you mention that word?" Sabrina cringes and drops her sunglasses down her nose. "You three do realize the consequences of us arriving together on the first day, don't you? Everyone from my old crowd with an A-level rating now hates me. Especially Torrance, over what's happening to Blaine, boo-hoo-hoo."

What's happening to Blaine is the worst thing he ever could imagine—he had to get a job and is now working at the driving range instead of taking lessons. And there's a FOR SALE sign posted in front of Larson's fancy house, now that his female financial backers have caught wind of his schemes. But I truly believe that Blaine didn't know about Larson's cons. And it's hard not to worry about him, despite everything. Is he going to have the same future as Larson, never knowing what love really means?

Who knows, maybe a job will be the best thing for him.

At least, I like to hope so.

"And come to think of it," Sabrina adds, "anyone with a C rating or less pretty much hates me, too."

"What does that leave us?" Natalie asks. "With B cups?"

When a little girl surfaces with more diving sticks than the boys, I grin and stretch my arms out wide. "We're going to be icons!"

"And don't forget, Sabrina, we're Vo-Tech gals now." Roxanne rubs at an oil stain on her thumb. She's Jake's official pit crew now, except for next weekend when she's going to that

NASCAR race with her mother, something Victoria is very excited about, judging from her new Jeff Gordon T-shirt.

Her father isn't going, but that's a battle for a different day.

And speaking of Jake. I'm about to ask Sabrina if she'll give me free haircuts now that she's signed up for cosmetology courses, but when I notice a certain someone approaching the pool, I take my hair out of its ponytail and tousle it at the roots.

Sabrina laughs and wiggles her big toe at me. "Pardon me, Miss Absolutely Guy-Free, but why are you fluffing your hair? Does it have something to do with him?"

She motions to Jake, who is striding through the gate with the chlorine kit, his biceps flexing. I force myself to turn away. "No, duh, I was getting a ponytail headache."

"Hmm-mm," Roxanne teases. "And why are you putting on lip gloss?"

I throw the gloss back into my tote and scowl at them. "My lips are dry, okay? Do you want me to be chapped *and* have a headache?"

Jake kneels by the shallow end, opening the kit and looking up in time to see Natalie, Roxanne, and Sabrina give him exaggerated girlie waves. "Heyyyy, Jake," they call out.

Honestly!

I put on my sunglasses and lean back again amid all of their amused giggles. But after Jake finishes the test and heads back to the lodge, Sabrina sits up at attention, as though her hotness radar just went on high alert. "Seriously, that guy is so cute!"

My stomach plummets, almost right out of my bikini bottoms. She isn't talking about Jake, is she? Oh, man, I do not want to go down that road again. But Sabrina isn't looking at

Jake. Instead, she's watching a guy stepping out of a Ford 350 truck with a Ryland camper behind it. A guy who is wearing a thin white wife-beater.

Beater Boy.

"Sabrina, honey, no. Really, no!"

Mom is standing by the open store window, nervously biting her nails as she watches the entrance where a large inflatable snowman and a row of elves welcome our guests to Christmas in July. She fingers the hem of the cute new dress I helped her pick out and asks, "Dee, are you sure this outfit isn't too young?"

"You look beautiful, Mom," I say, pulling her hand away before she kills her manicure and noticing how bare her ring finger looks without her wedding band. Eventually, though, the white stripe of untanned skin will fill in with new memories.

"But it's been so long! Do men still open doors or do women open their own now?" Mom asks, as a boy wearing green Grinch gloves chases his sister around the packed store. "And why on earth did I make plans on one of our busiest weekends?"

"Relax, Jane, everything is under control," Madeline says, breezing past us with an armful of returned golf clubs, wearing a hunter green apron that she embroidered with BARTON FAMILY CAMPGROUND in bright yellow. She made one for each of us, and she's even trying to convince Mom that employees should wear full uniforms.

Yeah, we still have some territorial issues to iron out.

"And as a woman," Madeline continues, while hanging the clubs in meticulous order, "you certainly should expect a man to open the door for you."

Okay, live in the 1800s much? But to my surprise, Madeline adds, "Not because we are weak, but because we are worthy of being treated with dignity and respect."

Oh. Nice.

Mom jumps when a vehicle pulls into the driveway. "Is that him?"

No. It's a yellow Trooper. Mona parks and steps out, wearing a bright red skirt that ends at her knee instead of mid-thigh and a pretty golden shirt with green trim. She adjusts her furry Santa hat and garland boa. This outfit is totally different from the conservative getup she wore at the lawyer's office—and totally better. Totally *Mona*.

Mom opens the door and welcomes her. "Hey, you ready for tonight?"

Mona awkwardly crosses the threshold, as though she is still unsure about taking over DJ Drake's duties. But when she notices Mom's outfit and haircut, she whistles. "Hubba, hubba, you look like the cat's meow! You got a hot date or something?"

"Well," Mom says, touching her hair, "I do . . . with Rex Reynolds."

"My, my, he's just darling!" Mona lets out a joyous whoop, but then a guilty blush fills her face. She steps to the jewelry display, fingering an earring as she says, "You know, Jane, Rex talked to me . . . at the Swains' house. He, uh, asked me to drop the lawsuit. Lord, I'm sorry I didn't listen, and I'm sorry for what I put you through. He also offered my old job back, if I needed it, so—" Mona turns back to Mom with a smile. "So you just might have found yourself a really nice guy."

Yeah. Maybe she did.

"As for me, I'm taking a break from dating. You know, to have some special Sabrina time before she goes on vacation with her father. Turns out they have some patching up to do as well," Mona says, before taking a small pair of scissors from her purse and using it to clip a loose thread on Mom's sleeve. "Now. Don't forget your breath mints and mad money, sugar, and for the love of everything holy, please tell me all the juicy details, okay?"

Later, after Rex walks Mom to his car, I watch as he opens the door for her like a true gentleman. It's so odd and unnatural, watching my mother being driven off by a man other than my father. And yet—it's so mature at the same time.

And it's good to hear her laugh.

I walk out onto the porch and lean my head against a column. Nearly every campsite is festooned with lights that sparkle and dance among the trees, and the lodge is picturesque with draping garlands covering the railing and twinkling icicles hanging from the gutter. Footsteps come from the other side of the porch. Jake's footsteps. "Hey," he says.

"Hey."

Jake faces the pavilion, where karaoke has started and Natalie, who's wearing the sparkly pink mouse ears I bought for her upcoming Disney vacation, is butchering a nasty version of "Jingle Bells" with Sabrina, much to Roxanne and Danny's delight—who, by the way, are sitting close together. Very close. "I have about an hour until it's time to suit up as Santa. You want to go hang out with them for a while?"

Yes, but there's something else I want to do first. I want to see the campground—my campground—where I will spend my life, first helping my mother, and later when she turns the business over to me.

"Jake, do you want to go for a walk?"

After all, it is my favorite time of day. And this is my favorite weekend theme, when we get yuletide joys *without* the cold. Together, we stroll past the playground with its squeaking seesaws and sweaty children. A few men are still fishing, and at the Cutsons' site Lyle and Tanner frown at the dinner their mother served. They ping their peas off their plates when her back is turned, and then shoot me evil little smiles.

I give them a wink.

When Ivy sees Jake and me together, her lips curl up with satisfaction before she goes back to her paperwork. She's now volunteering her legal services at a Baltimore shelter for abused women, and she decided to stay in Maryland year round. Ivy is also helping us work out the details for a yearly bluegrass festival. They've been wildly successful at a Gettysburg campground, bringing in more revenue in one weekend than three whole regular months. And it's something Chuck Lambert does *not* have.

At the river, we sit at the end of the pier, my toes dipped into the chilly water. Lightning bugs flash in the darkening woods and water slaps against the columns with a hypnotic lull. As smells of barbeque on the grill drift over us, I peek at Jake's strong profile and then slowly inch my hand along the wooden plank until it brushes against his. Jake takes off his battered cowboy hat. "Pardon me, Dee Barton, but are you *flirting*? I thought you were retired."

I drop my chin and gaze at him through a thick fringe of lashes. "Well, powers such as mine *would* be a terrible shame to waste, you know, so what's the harm of reserving them for one person only?"

Jake leans forward, reaching behind me to put his hat on my head. He gives me that cocky half grin of his and then asks me the very same question he did at the beginning of summer. "You *really* don't expect me to fall for your bullcrap, do ya, Dee?"

"Actually, yes. Yes, I do, Jake."

He leans forward and softly kisses me.

Gotcha.

Acknowledgments

Many, *many* thanks to the following people who have blessed my life:

To Karen Grove, Eric Luper, Andrea Rice, and Carole Shifman, for bravely reading the earliest versions of my book. How you survived that mess, I'll never know!

To my wonderful Starry Night Writers: Larissa Graham, Susan Mannix, Lona Queen, Jeri Smith-Ready, Tricia Schwaab, and Lois Szymanski for your laughter and encouragement. A special thanks, also, to Jeri and Susan for your great critiques; to Starry Night Bakery, for the coffee; to Paul Zimmerman, for his legal expertise; and to Al Barnes, for helping me with the world of kart racing.

To my dear friends Pam Smallcomb and James Proimos, for your friendship, your inspiration, and your ability to keep me from jumping off a cliff when I think too much. Thank you!

To my phenomenal agent, Rosemary Stimola, for your continued faith and all your lovely XO, Ro Stimo's. I'm so grateful to have you in my life! Thanks also to Naomi Milliner, for the matchmaking; to Lisa Graff, for giving me that wonderful glimmer of hope; and to copy editor Karen Ninnis, copy chief

Karla Reganold, designer Roberta Pressel, and all the folks at Farrar Straus Giroux for bringing *Just Flirt* to life.

To my amazing editor, Beth Potter—wow—thank you for your belief in my story, and for helping me take it to a whole new level. It's been a pleasure, and I mean that with total love and sisterhood!

To my father, Alfred Barnes, for being such a fantastic dad; my brother Al Barnes—best kart racer *ever*—and Jenny, Al, and Evan, for being awesome; my stepfather, Al Roberson, for reading another "chick" book, ha ha; and my mother, Betty Barnes— the only person I'll ever show my rough drafts to—for her unwavering support.

Thanks most of all to my dear husband, Bob, for always holding my hand when I need it the most, and to my boys, Broc and Cooper, for bringing me so much joy and happiness. I love, love, LOVE you guys!